the
Marked

the Marked

LILITH SAINTCROW

The Marked Copyright ©2016 by Lilith Saintcrow
ALL RIGHTS RESERVED.

Cover Art © 2016 by Skyla Dawn Cameron

First Edition October 2016

eBook ISBN: 978-0-9899753-5-3
Paperback ISBN: 978-0-9899753-6-0

www.lilithsaintcrow.com

All rights reserved under the International and Pan-American Copyright Conventions. No part of this book may be reproduced or transmitted in any form or by any means, electronic or mechanical including photocopying, recording, or by any information storage and retrieval system, without permission in writing from the author.

This book is a work of fiction. Names, characters, places and incidents are either the product of the author's imagination or are used fictitiously, and any resemblance to any actual persons, living or dead, events, or locales is entirely coincidental.

Acknowledgments

THANKS ARE DUE to Mel Sanders, who encouraged me as usual, and to Miriam Kriss, who cheered me for the finish line. A very large portion of thanks go to Skyla Dawn Cameron, for services above and beyond the call of editing. You three are a Trinity of Holy Terror, and I adore you.

Significant thanks are also due to my Indiegogo backers. Thank you for believing in me, and in this book. Super-special thanks goes to Ann Aguirre, who I'd always want in my corner.

Last, but never least, thank you, my Readers. Let me continue to show my gratitude in the way we both like best—by telling you a story. Come in, shut the door so it's more private. Sit where you please, close to the fire if you like. Let's begin on a winding road...

Chapter One

BURGERDOODLE

THE SITUATION CALLED for desperate measures. "Jesus *wept*," Jude said, but softly, her knuckles white on the steering wheel as she braked. A thread of dark hair fell into her face, and she blew it away, impatiently. Their ancient brown and white van slowed even further, windshield wipers struggling to cope with the downpour. "I know it's scary. But we'll be at Auntie Aggie's soon, and dinner tonight is burgerdoodle."

"Burgerdoodle!" Simon crowed and clapped his hands, his eyes all but dancing with glee.

Essie, however, was a little more skeptical. "Really?" Her daughter's face screwed up in the same *I-don't-believe-this* expression she'd worn when first born, and Jude had to tear her gaze away from the rearview and concentrate on Bath End Road. "But you *hate* burgerdoodle!"

I will do just about anything to get out of cooking tonight. "Well, I did have some liver and onions I was planning on." Jude managed to keep her tone level as another flash of lightning cracked the sky.

The roll of thunder was eight seconds behind instead of twelve, and that was worrisome. The trees, almost fully leafed-out at the end of spring, thrashed wildly under a lashing wind. There hadn't been anything on the radio about a storm, but then again, it was the season for quick weather changes. "But if you two are good while I talk to Auntie Aggie, and don't try to break the balustrade, I *might* be persuaded to stop at the Shack and get you cheeseburgers. With French fries."

"And mayo and a choclik shake? *Pleeeeeeeeeeeeze?*" Simon was now wholeheartedly in "negotiation mode", and Jude reflected that she was setting a bad precedent.

Well, if she hadn't already screwed both kids up for life by divorcing that no-good sonofabitch, fast food this once wasn't going to do it. "Maybe, Simon. We'll see." Of course, she thought as she slowed down even further to negotiate a tricky curve, the wind suddenly shoving at the van like a living thing, she shouldn't have married him in the first place.

But that would have meant no Essie, and no Simon, and that was one thing the lately-Jude Edmonds, née and once again Altfall, couldn't even bring herself to wish. Even if she was exhausted. She couldn't even worry about the money she would spend on burgers and shakes, either, and *that* was a disturbing sign. The van would smell like grease for a week.

Aggie would want to go along, and she'd want to pay for the food, too. Jude's stomach closed like a fist at the thought.

Essie, true to form, was not calmed by the prospect of mayo *or* a shake. "What are *you* gonna have?"

"Liver and onions at home." Jude grinned at their chorus of pointed *uggggh* sounds, squinting, and decided not to risk turning the defroster fan up another notch. Sometimes it blew out if you turned it to "high." And the windshield wipers were old, but still working, and that was good because the rain was in full-on Noah and the Flood mode—

Another bolt of lightning, sizzling-white. This time the thunder was immediate, and Essie let out a tiny scream lost in its immensity. Jude blinked, clearing the sudden blindness. God was taking pictures or striking sinners, as Granny Lefdotter would've said.

"Relax." Jude's hands tightened again on the wheel's thin cushioning as the van shimmied. The rain was coming down in curtains, and she was not going to get to the old house in anything under a half-hour. It hadn't been more than damp at the apartment, a fine drizzle more like enthusiastic mist than anything else. She'd chosen to cut through Bath End because it was so pretty, with the trees making their green tunnel nearly complete since summer was around the corner. Besides, she needed to brace her nerves, because Aggie would give her the Look again, and she would suggest—*again*—that Jude and the kids come and live in the old house. *I rattle around here like a pea in a pod, Jujube. Come on.*

It would ease the financial strain, that was for damn sure, especially since the layoff notice had come through just that morning, on tissue-thin pink paper. She'd thought pink slips were just in the movies, but apparently not.

Dave knew where her parents' house was. Jude was granted full custody, and Dave had just sat there, staring at her from the other side of his stolid, gray-haired lawyer. Jude, her left third finger bare except for a divot, had not been comforted. She knew that look.

"Relax," she repeated. She hadn't even changed out of her work clothes, and her skirt was a little too big, so it was bunching in weird ways the longer she drove. She should have changed into jeans, but that would have required going back to the apartment. "It's only thunder. Any lightning will hit the trees on top of the ridges, not us."

"Are you sure?" Essie was no doubt clutching at herself, her fingers digging in. She didn't have Simon's sunny optimism. Of course, she was a full two years older, and she took that very seriously. Esther was *born* taking things seriously. Kind of like Jude herself, while Simon had all Aggie's let-it-ride.

It was funny to see genetics play out. Downright hilarious, really.

"Yes, I'm very sure. It's what lightning does— it goes for the highest point." Jude squinted, hunching to look through the glass the defroster was managing to keep clear. The wipers were on high and the windshield was still wavering under a sheet of ripples.

Fuck this. Bath End took a long curve just ahead, with the creek at the bottom of a sheer but short drop on the left and the bulk of Cameron Hill rising just as steep on the right. There was a wide flat graveled area between the shoulder and the Hill, and she could pull over there and wait for the storm to subside.

"Mom?" Simon, plaintive now. "I hafta go potty."

Oh, for the love of—

That was as far as she got. The curve opened up in front of her, lightning smashed down, and a moving shadow in the road alerted her just in time.

"SHIT!" She hit the brakes *hard*, the van rocked, and Essie's more full-throated scream was drowned in a crescendo of thunder that poured through the van on a wall of vibration. Tires locked, skidding on the wet road, and Simon screamed too. The accident played out in slow motion inside her head—metal buckling, the van tipping, glass shattering—until the van halted with a jerk neatly in the right lane and sat obediently running, wipers swishing back and forth ineffectually against the monsoon.

Rain drummed hungrily on the van's roof. The man just *stood* there, a smeared shape through the blurring on the windshield, and hot acid fear crawled up Jude's throat.

"You said a bad word," Simon whispered, sounding more awestruck than anything else.

"I know I did." She swallowed, hard. *Is it him? Please God, don't let it be him.* "I was surprised."

"What's going on?" Essie sounded near hysterical. If Jude showed any sign of cracking up now, she'd start crying and heaving. She remembered things Simon was too young to. Loud noises, Dave's fist banging through drywall, tears leaking down her mother's face.

"She's gonna puke," Simon volunteered, helpfully.

"There's something in the road." Jude's particular Mommy Voice came out, just like always. Authoritative, firm, clear through the persistent thunder and the rain's drumming. Maybe labor flipped a switch in your brain and made it not only possible but mandatory to use the I-am-in-charge-and-it-will-be-fine tone. "Essie. Calm down. Do your deep breathing." *Please do not let it be him.*

If it was…the thought of pressing on the accelerator floated through her head, was shoved hastily away. Vehicular homicide, however appealing, would leave her children afloat. Especially if it was only *attempted*, not actual.

Jude shoved that thought away, too.

"I think she's gonna puke, Mommy," Simon persisted.

"I am *not*." Essie was calm enough to object, at least. That was a good sign. Progress had been made.

All sorts of it, since she'd left Dave. "Just keep doing your breathing. There's something in the road, I'm going to wait for a second." The whistling was Jude's own breath, coming high and hard. Her pulse throbbed in her wrists and throat, and the fine hairs all over her body were standing up. The guy in the road was too tall to be Dave, and there was no way he could have known she was going to Aggie's today…but still. Fear did funny things to you.

He stood right in her lane, arms slightly spread as if daring the van to come for him. Jude frankly stared, trying to see through the water pouring down the windshield.

"What's in the road? Is it a deer?" Simon bounced in his seat. The van rocked slightly, and thunder muttered. "A wolf, mebbe? Oooh, is it a coyote?" His class was doing a section on animals this week. Everything was a wolf to him, and Jude had told him coyotes were more likely.

She peered out the windshield. The man's back must have been to her, because he began to turn to face the van. Still with his arms spread, and there was something on his other side. Some indistinct shape, black in the eerie gray-yellow stormlight.

It was wrong. And the little spatters and crackles of light around him were wrong too. A screaming gust of wind rocked the van, and Jude let out a soft unconscious sound, trying to make the blurred images through the windshield turn into a comprehensible picture.

Thunder boomed. The rain slacked a little, enough for the glass to clear a bit. The radio, turned down low and forgotten since they'd hit the storm at the beginning of Bath End Road, gave a squawk and started to fizz. She reached for the volume knob, as if in a dream.

"Ooooh! Is it a coyote?" Essie bounced too, forgetting her momentary terror. Between the two of them, they could probably destroy the shocks in the van if she let them. Not that there were many shocks left, the van was older than dirt. Older than Jude, at least, and she felt ancient most days.

"Hush now." Jude inhaled sharply, deciding. Whatever the man was doing was none of her business. It was a hell of a storm, and she had two kids in the car to protect. Her headlights were on, and she had to chance that nobody would be coming around the other, sharper end of the curve. If the guy was hurt or something, he'd be trying to flag her down, wouldn't he? Instead he was just standing there, and the darkness behind him moving.

Stalking.

Her arms tensed to turn the wheel. Her foot slipped off the brake.

The world turned over as bolt after bolt of lightning touched down. The last thing she heard was Essie's scream as the van lifted, hurricane winds funneling down the road hugging Cameron Hill and the bulk of Gray Mountain on the other side of the creek. Air squeezed into one howling blast managed not to uproot every tree in its path, almost as if it chose not to. Everything turned greasy-white as pure force walloped through the van, glass shattering.

Jude Altfall did not even have time to scream.

Chapter Two

HOTEL PATCH

HE BARELY MANAGED to get the motorcycle into the parking garage, and if there were any cameras he'd look drunk or stoned. Wouldn't the tabloids just love that.

The storm vented its fury overhead, but its animating force was spent. It was just a regular spring bluster now, barely making its thunder-grumbles heard through concrete and rebar. He might even have enjoyed watching it fade from a high window, with a finger or two of good Scotch to hand.

Instead, there was *this*. It had been a long, long time since he'd hurt so badly. He limped toward the elevator and tore at the soaked, charred remains of one of his favorite hunting shirts. The power he'd acquired so cunningly was taking its revenge, and he had nothing to show for it; his entire right side seized with a gigantic cramp.

He fell, perilously close to clipping his head on one of the chipped concrete posts that kept idiots from driving into the elevator. He was shirtless and smeared with mud, but none of that mattered if he could just get into the room without anyone seeing. Maybe he shouldn't have gone after this one, but it had just been so *tempting*. He would fly out tomorrow first-class, and there was no reason for anyone to connect this shambling, shivering mess in a cash-pay fleabag motel with his other self. If he hadn't been hyperventilating and dragging his nerveless left leg, he might have felt a skincrawling irritation at having to come back here, instead of just using newfound, luxurious power to clean up, and vanishing to appear at the more appropriate hotel downtown where the rest of his luggage waited.

The cheap, anemic metal key wouldn't work the first time, and he fought for consciousness, teetering on the edge of blacking out. His left hand hung slack and useless, and when the key finally turned he barely had the presence of mind to kick-slam the door shut behind him. Once that was done, he fell headlong onto short, harsh nylon carpet, smearing mud in a long slugtrail as he writhed, trying to get his right hand to the other side of his body.

His fingers skated ineffectually along his ribs. For a few seconds, as the pain came in great gripping waves, he couldn't find the edge of the borrowed patch.

He'd left the cheap, bolted-down bedside lamp on, and its bulb dimmed slightly as the pain intensified. This one did funny things with electricity, but now it was all used up. He'd wanted to acquire another with the same flavor, to perhaps replace this depleted scrap, but something had *happened* and he couldn't think, there were sharp vicious teeth in his muscles, chewing down as the power refused the body it had been temporarily grafted to.

The flesh-edge curled, shriveling, under his fingertips, and he peeled the sheet of taffy-stretching skin away from his side. It fought, just as it had fought to stay attached to the freak it had originally been granted to, but he was stronger, and the madly writhing lines on his own raw, cracked skin underneath could finally breathe enough to repel its guest.

Stinging his wet fingers, the square of skin with its dark, zigzag pattern sought to cling to his skin and inflict as much damage as it could. The darker ones were more vicious, he often thought. Finally, collapsed on the greasy carpet, he could breathe again. The cramps slowly lessened, and in a little while he would get up and stagger to the shower. Even tepid water would do to sluice the gluey mud from him, and he had a change of clothes in the bag under the bed with two twenties—if anyone ever cleaned under the bed here, they might have found it, but the money was less than a raindrop. They were welcome to it.

The clinging, stretching thing on his fingers began to liquify. Now he had a hole in his collection, too. What had *happened*?

It didn't matter right now. He lapsed into a doze, every once in a while wincing as his right side cramped slowly and released, lines of something too dark to be ink moving up and down his ribs like fingers on a xylophone. When it finished, when he could take a shower, he would walk out of here and begin the process of finding out.

Chapter Three

PERFECT CENTER

HER CELL BUZZED, rattling against the only clean patch of workroom counter. She was going to have to scrape everything down soon.

Aggie Altfall exhaled softly, her fingers shaping the lump as the wheel purred. This was a good one, she could just tell. Her foot eased up on the pedal, slowing the wheel *just* enough, and her hand cupped, diving for the perfect center.

She leaned into her work, golden hair pulled carelessly back and her eyes half-closed. The whole rest of the afternoon into evening stretched in front of her. She could throw a few pots, maybe smoke a bowl and stack some greenware in the kiln, and maybe call Jude in a little bit. Her sister would be home from work and bone-tired, but at least Aggie could hear her, and talk to the kids.

Now *that* would be nice. She hadn't seen the little monsters in a while; hearing their delighted shrieks and the funny things they said from one minute to the next really did fill something inside of her. Just like something would eventually fill what she was shaping.

The workroom—built onto the back of the old house, its window full of gray stormglow and the good mineral smell of clay filling it to the brim—echoed with the wheel's sonorous whispering hum. Her phone buzzed again, but Aggie was in the zone. She began coaxing the sides of the clay up, slowing the wheel only to dip her fingers in the slip-water and going right back to shaping a lovely restrained curve. Maybe it would turn out to be a pitcher; this lump was bigger than the ones she used for cups. She could attach a handle, and then it would only be a matter of choosing the glaze. She had some new samples, and maybe—

A distant rumble intruded on her half-trance. Sounded like thunder. Spring storms. The weather report hadn't said anything, but that wasn't unusual.

It would be nice to sit upstairs in her bedroom with a glass of wine and watch the lightshow. That would be even nicer than a bowl, though it might give her a headache if the change in barometric pressure was big enough. Decisions, decisions.

Afterward, she would curse herself for not checking her phone immediately. For not *knowing*. It wasn't until she had used the wire to take the pitcher off the wheel and cleaned up that she found three voicemails, each one from a different emergency service. The first one, squawking through the speakerphone setting while she scraped the wheel, nailed her in place, the bencher falling from her nerveless fingers and her mouth opening a little in shock. She looked like a woman who had just had a hell of a good idea, clay smeared on her pretty cheek and her hazel eyes wide, before the expression turned to horror and she ran for her phone, snatching it up and shaking it as if that would make the news somehow less awful.

She turned and blundered for the workroom door, banging her hip against a butcher-block table, as the westering sun struggled from behind a pall of inksmudge clouds and filled the backyard with gold. The wheel slowed majestically and stopped.

The storm was over.

Chapter Four

CLOSING IN

THE NUMBER WAS one he recognized, which could only mean trouble. Preston Marlock grimaced, leaned back in his busted-down office chair, and hit the *talk* button. "Lawson. Always a pleasure."

"Hello to you too," Lawson rasped. He'd been a detective for more than twenty years, and you could *hear* it in each word. Linoleum, greasy food, antacids, and the bottle of Chivas he kept in the drawer.

Or maybe Press was just catching the overflow. The damn premonition at the base of his neck just wouldn't stop itching, but he told himself this could be one of the false alarms. Sometimes he had a rash of calls, not a one of them anything he was looking for, and the real one would pop up on the cell six hours later. "You've got something for me, you bastard."

"Who's a bright boy?" The alcoholic fuck laughed. "Almost like you're puh-sychic."

You don't know the half of it, little man. "Almost." As usual, it could have been a joke. They never knew, these helpful little elves, that it was the closest to telling the truth he'd ever get with them. "Or I could just have Caller ID."

Lawson coughed slightly. He'd probably taken up smoking again. Hard habit to break. "Well, listen up. Eric Sturmen, mean anything to you?"

Sturmhalten. God. He glanced at the map, unfocusing his eyes until a small pinging throb showed up, a dot of darkness. If he had to fly out there…*Christ. Not him.* Erik was one of the good guys. Well, no, not precisely.

But he was a friend. If Marlock could be said to have one, that was. "Cause of death?"

"Well now, that's where it gets interesting." Click and an inhale. Yeah, Lawson was definitely smoking again. "Lonely road, thunderstorm going on, and here's your buddy Sturmen. Can't find a goddamn car, but he can't have walked out there. Then a civilian happens along—"

"Civilian?" *Eric doesn't drive. It makes him nervous.* His stomach had turned into a mess of snakes, dammit. It never got any easier.

"Mom in a minivan, two kids. She tried to stop and help him, looked like. Damndest thing." Lawson exhaled, hard. Probably twin streams of carcinogenic smoke out his nostrils, like the world's roundest, pinkest, hairiest dragon.

"What?" *Come again?*

"Hit by lightning."

The swimming feeling of missing something made his knees feel weird. Thank God he was sitting down. "The civilians?"

There was a shifting sound, and if Preston concentrated, he could *see* what the other man was doing. Maybe grinding out the smoke he'd just lit. Lawson wasn't the forgetful type, but he didn't like uncertainty. It was part of what made him a good detective, and also probably responsible for his ulcers. "And Sturmen. *Damndest* thing. Had to make ID from dentals."

That takes time. God *damn* it. How far was he behind now? "How long ago?"

"'Bout a week. He's on the list, but listen, Marlock, you sure he's one of yours? He ain't got no tattoos."

Impossible. "You checked the body?" He glanced at the open laptop on his desk, not seeing its glowing screen. What had he been working on? He couldn't remember, now. It didn't matter.

"Course I did." Lawson's tone plainly said *you asshole, I know my job*. "Checked all three."

"Three?" *Wait a second.* Preston's eyes narrowed, and the blood had drained from his face. He even *felt* pale.

"Sturmen's face was done to a crisp, his hands too. Rest of him was just fulla weird tree-lines. Doc said it was lightning-marks, and hundred percent normal. Lichtenstein or Lichberg marks, or something. The kids had 'em too."

"Which kid?"

"It's a helluva thing. Mom in a van, two kids, stopping on that road, then they all get blasted to

Kingdom Come. One of the kids was in ICU, they thought…well, anyway, the mom, she survived. Freak accident." Lawson cleared his throat, and there was another soft snicking sound of a lighter, another inhale. Lawson always swore he'd quit, especially after the diagnosis. Looked like he was chaining them now, though. "She's in the hospital."

Pulling the tar-black lumps from Lawson's lungs had cost Preston a lot of energy, but it had paid off. And wasn't that another reason to hate himself, Marlock decided, that he hadn't just done it because he could? He pinched the bridge of his nose, hard. "Let me just get this straight. The mother survived? Without a scratch?"

"Well, she's prolly got whiplash, and the lightning might have cooked an internal organ or two, but they say she's stable."

"Does she have markings?" He'd almost said, *is she Marked*? Lawson wouldn't understand. "Any tattoos?"

"Shit if I know, Marlock. You owe me hard cash, by the way."

Had a potential come along, right when his quarry was doing deadly, dirty work? It beggared belief. Press rose from the fake-leather chair, his heart pounding so hard he thought he might faint. This could be it.

He swallowed, hard, brought himself back to reasonable pessimism. He'd thought so before, and it hadn't panned out. Maybe they'd missed a chunk taken from Sturmhalten's corpse, and the minivan had just run over his dead body as lightning struck.

Yeah, right.

There had never been a survivor near the site before. At the very least he'd have to question a grieving mother. Big fun.

Lawson didn't like pauses, either. Not with money on the line. "You hear me? This one's two-fifty, I had to sweet-talk the autopsy photos. They get funny with kid cases."

"Thank you, Detective. You'll see your money tomorrow."

"It's *retired* detective, and I will?"

"Yes." Marlock's teeth bared. It wasn't a smile, and it did nothing for his bony face. "I'll be bringing it personally."

That stunned the asshole into silence, and in any case, Press thumbed the phone off. He turned in a full circle, the office—crammed with paper, windowless, a map of the US on a bulletin board with colored pins clustered around certain cities, the file cabinets groaning under the weight of ephemera, paper, photos, speculation, attempts to find the pattern—held so much that might be useful if he could just get fucking close enough. Each case he knew by heart. Each case he'd made the same promise, over and over again.

I promise I won't stop. I'll find him. I'll get him for you.

"God," he whispered. "You son of a bitch. I'm closing in on you."

Chapter Five

HURT BAD

"Essie?" Her own voice, slow and slurred as if she was drunk. Jude hadn't had so much as a beer since the pee-on-a-stick test had told her she was carrying cargo, though. Dave's face had been wide-open, melting with tenderness, when she showed him. He'd treated her like she was made of spun glass during her first pregnancy.

Thinking that a baby would solve the problems had been stupid. Of course Dave had wanted a boy. But Essie was so precious, so tiny, her little fingernails and her big solemn eyes. *We can try again*, Dave had said. And when Simon was born, all was gentle again.

For a few months, at least.

"Syyyyy?" A heavy low moan, her tongue too big for her mouth. What was *wrong* with her?

"Jujube." A familiar voice. "It's okay, I'm here. I'm here."

"Aggie?" She blinked, trying to focus. The world was a haze. Something was wrong.

"It's okay." Aggie sounded like she had a cold. She never had the sniffles anymore, though. *Immune system of cast iron*, Dad had joked, *once she hit eighteen.* "I'm here."

"Sy. Essie." Her mouth wouldn't work right. Something bothered her.

"You just relax," Aggie whispered. "I'm taking care of everything."

Wait. The road. The car. "Liver…and onions…."

"What's she saying?" A stranger's voice. Older woman's, crisp and professional. "Did you tell her?"

"She's just…" Aggie sounded helpless now. She was a reddish blur, the other voice was a faint blue stain. "Don't, don't do that, she doesn't need it—"

"Honey, you might not think so, but she needs all the rest she can get." Sound of hand patting cloth. "Doc'll take her off the good stuff soon, and…well. Just let her rest now."

"Jujube." The warmth was a hand stroking her forehead. Aggie's cold had gotten worse. When she was a kid, she'd been snot-nosed all the time, and Jude had fetched tissues and tea, sometimes rolling her eyes at the dramatics. "She just added something to your IV. It'll make everything better."

What? You're the sick one. The one winter she thought Aggie had 'galloping consumption' because she read it in a book, and made Aggie wear Granpa Lorne's dinner jacket because she figured it was close to a peignoir, which sounded classy and French enough to ward off consumption. How

Mom had laughed when Jude finally explained, after a tussle with a recalcitrant Aggie who didn't want to wear the damn jacket anymore because it smelled like cigars and old man pee—

You. A stabbing searchlight through the fog, a hard hurtful voice. **Where are you? You stole it, I want it *back*!**

Aggie sniffled, as if she was twelve again. Softly, she began to sing. "Hush a bye…don't you cry, go to sleep, my little baby…When you wake, you shall have all the pretty little horses…"

It's the lullaby. Confusion swamped Jude. *Someone must be hurt. Hurt bad.*

Chemical sleep grabbed her in its bony fingers. She fought, but it was no use. She descended a long staircase, and the dream swallowed her whole.

Chapter Six

HANDS

MACHINES BEEPING AND *squeaking, shapes under thin blankets. Each one sent up a colorless ripple like heat over a summer road, and Jude tried to shut her eyes. The pole she dragged along was attached to her hand by a needle, and its wheels made funny squeaking sounds. Nobody saw her; she drifted through the halls in an envelope of mist, stopping when a head turned or a gaze threatened to swivel her way.*

Even with her eyes closed, she could see the heat-ripples rising. Heart disease, *said one, in a swirl of complicated shapes like Chinese ideograms.* Beating, *said another.* Cancer, *whispered yet another.* Car accident, *one piped up, a forlorn little voice. The symbols shaped themselves, then dissolved like rain running down a windowpane as soon as she grasped their meaning. It was like seeing a National Geographic special about bodies—layers of muscle peeled back, different organs exposed and color-coded when she glanced at the shapes instead of just above them. Fuzzy voices came from far away, and Jude squinted. It was getting brighter in here.*

Her hands began to ache as she halted before a screened-off enclosure. Behind it, something glowed a low burnt sienna, a painful color. Hurt and fading, bones shattered and lungs almost collapsed—

Jude pushed the curtain aside, and let out a long, painful, sobbing breath.

A small shape lay on the bed, a tiny figure lost in tubes and industrial-laundry sheets. A screen showed her heartbeat, but Jude didn't need to look at it—she could see the chunk of muscle, the size of a child's fist, struggling. It was leaking, and the brain was swelling against its hard bony pan, and a fractured rib had pierced the left lung.

Bile whipped Jude's throat. Her palms and fingers crunch-screamed with pain and she moved forward, tearing the needle from the back of her hand with a hiss. It itched, and a dot of bright blood appeared, but she didn't care. Her legs shook, and she pushed close to the bed.

Esther. My little girl. *Her lips shaped the words.* Mommy's here, honey. Mommy's here.

Her hands reached down. They were so hot she was afraid she would burn the tiny body on the bed; they peeled the blanket and sheet back. There were sounds outside the bubble of silence she was trapped in, running feet.

Quickly now. The pitiful little legs, the left one in a cast all the way to the hip—Jude clasped the right one, her fingers clamping home with sudden hot strength, and a roaring filled her.

It's okay. Mommy's here. Mommy's here.

A sense of something wrong brushed through her head, and she looked down.

It wasn't Essie at all. It was a redheaded child a few years Essie's senior, but Jude's hands didn't listen. They closed, clawlike, and a black hole swallowed her.

Chapter Seven

POOR BASTARD

I HATE DOMESTIC flights. Marlock pressed his handkerchief to his nose. The envelope of cash had been placed safely in Lawson's big, beefy, chapped hands, and the former detective had led him down the stairs and into what might have been a very nice foyer in the twenties, but was now the grimy antechamber to a special slice of administrative and medical hell.

Lawson's shoulders swayed under his sports jacket; his tread was heavy and a bit pigeon-toed. "Hey, Ross."

A thin dark-haired kid blinked myopically behind a pane of bulletproof glass. The opening for documents at the bottom, slightly discolored, held a single lonely blue Bic pen. "Hey, Burt. What's up?"

"Got a fellow here who mighta known one of the stiffs." Lawson's small dark eyes were avid, and not necessarily kind.

"Thought you were retired." The kid's blinking looked like a nervous tic, or maybe something neurological. He didn't look nearly old enough to be working nights in a morgue. Really, though, everyone had started to look too young for everything. One of the hazards of living too long with a Mark.

Lawson's sigh was a masterpiece of weary resignation, while he scratched the side of his thick neck. "I get tired of golf and sitting on the crapper. Buzz us through."

"You gonna sign in?" Ross's blinking intensified. He wore a rumpled lab coat, but no nametag. A Merck's Manual lay open just to his right, its onionskin pages riffling a bit as a stray breeze touched them. Maybe the kid was doing some studying.

An inelegant snort made Lawson's lip wrinkle. "Why, when you're sitting there with nothing to do? You can thank me later."

"Does your plus-one have ID?" Not just a kid, but a play-by-the-rules type. *Fun.*

"Don't bust my chops, kid."

"Fine, fine." The kid shook his head. A small nest of whiteheads on his left cheek showed where probably rested against his hand during the long hours of the night watch. When they receded and he finished growing, he might be handsome, except his eyes were a little too close together. And he was faded, too.

Like all the unMarked. Civilians never looked as real as those carrying the not-ink.

Press followed Lawson, as he'd followed so many other helpful elves into the caves where they stored the dead. Refrigeration hummed; Lawson turned hard left and they ended up in one of the bays, its back wall full of blank metal cabinet doors. He glanced back at Marlock, who kept the starched handkerchief tight, just in case.

Sometimes they sensed him. His skin darkened a shade or two, his control slipping a fraction. The lights in here were harsh, but he could pull on them if he had to. Empty meat in the steel lockers, waiting for a spark to fill it.

Any spark at all.

"So, that list of yours." Lawson reached for a cabinet door, sank back on his heels to pull the barlock. "What I can't figure out is—"

"Do you really want to know?" *Because if you do, I'll show you. And drop you off at the nearest asylum.*

Or, you know, we're already at a morgue.

Lawson shook his bullet head. "I have enough fucking trouble with your other little tricks. Never mind."

"Wise man." He couldn't help but sound grimly amused.

The frame clicked, bearing the body out by degrees with a rusty sound. Marlock squinted, and it took only a few seconds for him to determine two things.

The first was easy. "That's Eric."

"So you knew him." Lawson's detective ears, large and well-molded, all but perked.

We generally know each other, on the dark side of the fence. But damned if he would explain to this inquisitive asshole. "Sort of."

"Why am I not surprised?" Lawson muttered.

What little uncharred skin remained on the body was mapped with delicate treelike traceries. They reminded Press of Sturmhalten's Mark, and a brief moment of vertigo seized him. The second thing he realized hit after the weightlessness, a thunder-roll after the initial strike. Marlock's heart leapt into his throat.

No Mark. And none of the signs. He's not ruptured like the others were.

In other words, the body before him might as well have been a civilian's. Press swallowed his excitement and a reminder of the wheatgrass smoothie he'd forced himself to drink at the airport. You couldn't get anything approaching a decent meal on a domestic flight, dammit. Not that wheatgrass counted as a fucking meal either, but it was better than nothing and didn't seize up his innards like anything solid would after a flight and a visit to the dead. "No next of kin." *Except for her.* "What about the body?"

"His boyfriend's taking care of that." Lawson kept the entire sentence impressively neutral.

Boyfriend? Oh, Cat. It was an ignominious end for an old soldier, naked on a steel tray. But Eric had done the almost-impossible, and, in the process, given Press an opening.

Marlock coughed. The heaviness in his throat wouldn't retreat. "And the survivor? The woman?"

"I called Sutter General this morning. They released her." Lawson hunched inside that violently plaid sports jacket. There was a stain on the knee of his chinos. Despite his retirement, his waist was still trim. It wasn't all golf for him. You could take the detective out of the force, but you couldn't take the...well, you couldn't stop what was worn into them over years and years of seeing the worst over and over again.

So the woman was released. *Interesting.* "And the kid?"

"Which one?" Half angry, half tender, Lawson slid the body back into its sterile cave.

"The survivor?" Hadn't the detective told him one of them had made it? He couldn't remember, and that was a bad sign.

"No survivor. One dead at the scene, the other coded in the ICU. They've both already been signed for."

It was like pulling teeth. But that meant the woman...It *had* to mean she was a potential. "By whom?"

"*Whom.* Listen to you, Mr. Grammar. Mom had a sister with power of attorney."

A grieving mother with family. Well, there were harder interrogations, and he wasn't in this to make friends. "Hell of a thing."

"Yeah, well. I guess." Lawson's chin poked forward, stubbornly. Instead of wingtips or trainers, he wore canvas slip-on deck shoes. Retirement might have been good for him, but relaxing made a man unprepared.

Marlock exhaled, not quite a sigh. It warmed the handkerchief pressed over his mouth, and he dropped his hand. Hard to breathe through the thing, even if it was dangerous to open up here. He could muffle himself again if he had to, and they wouldn't be here much longer. "I'll need what you have on them, then."

"You want my left fucking kidney too? Christ."

"Well, I *am* hungry. I just got off a flight." As soon as the words were out, Press regretted them. His voice bounced off the tiled floor, and the drain in the middle sent up a thin tendril of steam. He stepped hurriedly back, and his back was running with tingles now. Dead bodies would try to draw on his Mark, twitching as false life pulled and poked on their tissues. And in turn, he would pull from the nearest energy sources—Lawson, the lights, maybe even the kid in the foyer.

His Mark was waking up. A brightly lit room and a bunch of corpses, of course it would pick *now* to get restive. He clapped the square of folded cloth over his mouth *and* nose. *If the mother's a potential, and Eric threw his Mark…a potential, then. And a boon.*

Lawson grumbled, but the moment passed and the cabinet door clanged shut. He led Press up the stairs again, and on the way out, the kid behind the bulletproof glass chirped a cheery falsetto "Good night, boys!"

"Fuck you," Lawson snapped by way of reply.

Press forced his shoulders down. Once he was out of the building he could breathe without side effects. The nervous itching would go away, and he wouldn't be at risk of one or more of the corpses beginning to twitch.

The Mark only shows what's inside, they all said. At least the bastard he was chasing hadn't been able to take Eric's. A potential with a boon, Christ Almighty.

Now the Skinner would be coming for the woman. Probably already was.

Press pulled the handkerchief away, took a gulp of rain-laden, balmy late-spring night flavored with exhaust and the flat mineral smell of the polluted river running through the town, and tried to squash the strange feeling in his chest. It felt, he thought, as Lawson stopped to drag a battered pack of Camels from his jacket's inner pocket, like hope.

Chapter Eight

CRUSTS OFF

SAME BRICK-RED double door, left half bolted shut and the right cheerfully creaking as it opened. Same high foyer with parquet floor and the stairs marching neatly alongside the intricately carved balustrade, same rattle-tinkling as the small chandelier welcomed each new visitor. *Rich girl*, Dave had sneered at her more than once, not understanding—or maybe not caring—that the estate paid its own property taxes and a small monthly sum for upkeep and that was about it. The trust fund only disbursed in small amounts. The Altfall family had learned a conservative lesson or two; real control of the money had to wait until Jude was forty.

Sign it over to me.

Her own voice, breathy-nervous, thinking that he just didn't understand. *I can't, Dave. It's not legally possible*— Her body had understood, though, her heart hammering and her palms wet.

And Dave's eyes going terribly blank. *Bitch. Rich bitch.*

Jude's hands hung, empty and lifeless, at her sides. She looked at the foyer as if seeing it for the first time.

Aggie, dropping her keys back in her fringed purse, waited for her to get all the way in before sliding past, back through the door. "I'm going to go get the suitcases. So, apparently it was a records mix-up. You should have seen the doctor's face when the second set of X-rays came back, and the kid piped up *can you take this thing off my leg?*" Aggie swiped at her blonde bob—her bangs had grown out, but she still irritably brushed at them every once in a while. Habits were hard to break. "Kass said she'd never seen anything like it."

"Hospitals," Jude agreed, wanly. Black-haired Kassandra Appel, now a nurse, had gone to school with them both, and she'd been in the room when the detective sat down and said *Miz Edmonds, there's something—*

It's Altfall, Jude had snapped, *and I want my children, please.*

That had been the signal for Kass to excuse herself, and the first intimation of doom had landed on Jude with a sickening internal thump. The words—pale, useless, stupid words, crowding her, piercing the protective static filling her ears, her head, her throat...

Now she was home. Except *home* was the apartment, with Simon and Essie's familiar clatter, chatter, and constant questions. Jude swallowed, hard. "Let me help you carry something. Anything."

"Oh, no you don't. Go on into the kitchen, I have a craving for one of your famous grilled-cheese sandwiches." Aggie bounced up on her toes, and for a moment her fair oval face was just like Simon's, except for her paler eyebrows.

Miz Altfall— The detective's face under the hospital room's soulless, flickering fluorescents, Aggie's stricken expression, and suddenly, hopelessly Jude had known what he was about to say.

"All right." She put her head down, took a reluctant step farther into the foyer. The chandelier stilled, and the whole house was silent.

"I got sourdough. And Havarti." Aggie's brow creased nervously. "I…I hope that's all right."

"Of course." Jude glanced down, habitually, at where Simon should be, with his innocent smile and tousled cornsilk hair. Checking to make sure her duckling was safely within reach.

There was nothing. Just the parquet, and the same padded fist striking her in the guts again. Maybe the sun had come out, because it was too bright, which never happened in here unless it was the dead of winter and all the trees had lost their leaves. Blinking steadily, she set her jaw again. Her teeth ached. So did her neck. They'd given her prescriptions for the pain.

Don't wait to take them, Kassandra had said, with all the earnestness of a professional helper. *You're going to need them, to manage the discomfort.*

Discomfort. What a word. There was no pill for any of this. She kept glancing at where they should be, Simon on one side, Essie on the other. Kept listening for their footsteps, for the sense of breathing *presence* you learned quickly to pay attention to when you brought a little bundle home from the hospital. When they started sleeping through the night you sometimes woke up, in a panic, and tiptoed into their rooms just to hear that soft, beautiful sea-roll of lungs working smoothly.

Poor Aggie. She was doing the nervous-talking thing. "We might as well use it, or I can call out for Chinese, or—"

Jude had to shift a wad of something dry and bitter in her throat. "I'll make sandwiches. Peanut butter." Maybe it came out sounding odd, because Aggie's brightness faltered for a moment. Jude tried not to glance down again at her right side, where Essie should have been, tugging at her hand to get her mother to hurry up because Auntie Aggie's kitchen was a wonderland of special foods they didn't get at home. "Do you still take yours with the crusts off?"

"Well, not since I was six." A small smile touched Aggie's face, tiptoeing onto her mouth like a thief. "But I wouldn't say no."

"Good." Jude tried a smile, too. Her cheeks ached, and her teeth didn't want to stop grinding against each other.

I…I did the paperwork. Her sister's lip trembling as Jude sat on the hospital bed. *With that power of attorney and all…I knew you wouldn't want them there.*

She loved her sister, and Aggie had done the right thing. It wasn't Aggie's fault that Jude had been in a doctor-prescribed haze while two tiny little lifeless bodies were handled and processed by people who didn't know how Simon got cold at night, that Essie's favorite juice was Cherry Berry, that they loved apples as much as their mother did, that when Simon had nursed she had sometimes been possessed of the fierce desire to pull both of her children back into her own body, where she could be *sure* they were safe.

If she hadn't chosen Bath End, none of this would have happened. Jude put her head back down and set off for the kitchen. *Sure. Get everyone something to eat.* Her brain refused to work properly, no matter how many times she reminded herself what she was doing. It was easier if she just focused on the next footstep, and the one after that. She barely saw the stainless-steel refrigerator, the butcher-block island, the familiar white and black kitchen linoleum, the new granite countertops and the roomy double sink with the high-arched faucet Aggie had endlessly debated and saved up for before finally contracting.

She found everything right where it should have been, peanut butter and fig jam and the Wonder Bread that the kids only got in daycare or at Aunt Aggie's. At home it was wheat bread, because that was healthier. The Jude of outside, the one who pushed her hands around and kept her stupid body breathing, was a sliver. A bookmark in the physical world.

The rest of her had turned sideways inside her skin, numbly rocking back and forth. At the hospital, a handful of brochures on grieving had culminated with a nervous psych resident asking her questions. The outside Jude accepted this, dazed by sudden disaster, numb with grief, and her bossy blonde sister had all the proper paperwork. Before Aggie had dropped out of law school to follow her art, she'd learned a thing or two. Lucky to have her, lucky to be alive.

If she concentrated on the sandwiches, maybe she could...

The thought stopped. She caught herself staring at the sink, the jar of almond butter in her trembling hand.

What comes next? The bread. Put the peanut butter on the bread, Jude. But it was *almond* butter, and she decided it didn't make a difference. She found the juice boxes right where they always were, Cherry Berry for Ess and apple for Simon. They sat at the breakfast bar, two lonely soldiers, right in front of the two stools the kids had graduated to instead of highchairs.

Jude's hands turned to stone. The knife clattered on the granite countertop, and she stared at the bay window over the sink. The apple trees were in full bloom, marching in neat rows at the far end of the slightly ragged garden. White clouds, and sunlight glittering on drops of moisture caught on leaf-tip and flower-edge. Her mother had loved the trees, and her father had good-naturedly cursed their small, hard fruit when it came time to mow the orchard grass.

"Yes." She heard the Mommy Voice come out of her again, soft and very reasonable, clear and untroubled. "It's going to be fine."

She shut her eyes, but that was no good, because the image of a lighthouse returned. Its searchlight, bright white and pitiless, sliced towards her, and something in its predatory sweep jolted her eyelids back open.

Oh, God. Everything inside Jude fought to turn back to front-facing, the tears a scorch-lump in her throat and her fingers cold as ice. After a few deep breaths, her strength won out. Just barely, but enough so she could make the two sandwiches. She even found baby carrots in the fridge—Ag's attempt at eating healthy, probably. There was some two-percent milk that hadn't gone bad.

There were sounds from the foyer, and Jude cut the sandwiches into quarters, filling each plate. The two stools sat silent. They didn't argue over who had more carrots. They didn't swap juice boxes for sips. Jude leaned against the counter, tried to close her eyes again despite the sense that if she did, the searchlight would fasten on her.

It didn't work. She stared at the plates, willing the spaces behind them to be less empty.

When Aggie banged into the kitchen, filling it up with her healthy young vibrant self, she set her purse down with a thump. "Oh, man, we're going to have a lot of fun living together. It'll be just like college. You know…" The words trailed off. "Oh." She sounded hurt. "Oh, Jude. Judy-bee."

"College," Jude said weakly. *Crap. She asked for grilled cheese, didn't she.* "I'm sorry. I...I don't know what..."

"It's okay." Aggie's arms folded around her. Her sister smelled of oranges, cedar, and the clay she worked, a familiar, earthy scent. "I like carrots. You can have the apple juice."

Jude took a deep breath. Her eyes swelled, prickled hotly, but she didn't cry. Why couldn't she cry? *I'm not hungry.* But Aggie was trying so hard, Jude couldn't say no.

Aggie settled her on a stool, took the other one. Jude stared at the sandwiches—neatly made, but she'd forgotten to put the fig jam on. They were dry almond butter and bread, turning to gluey paste when she sipped at the apple juice.

"Just like college," Aggie said again, quietly. "You should take a pill, Jude. Whiplash takes a while to show up, and it's nasty."

"Okay," Jude agreed, softly. She made no move to look for the bag of prescriptions, though, and thin spring sunlight poured through the bay window.

Chapter Nine

FINALLY ALONE

IT WASN'T UNTIL later, when Aggie retreated to her own bedroom—probably with a sigh of relief, she'd been talking so long and hard about everything other than the elephant in the room all damn afternoon—that Jude could finally stand in the middle of the kitchen and close her eyes as dusk filled the kitchen window with purple. For a brief moment she saw the searchlight again, a vicious white glare, but she pushed it away with a stomach-clenching effort. Instead, she saw…nothing.

Blackness. Blank.

Her heart thrummed. *I am, I am,* it said. Her lungs kept working, pushing air in, pushing air out. She was in remarkable shape, the doctor said. Lightning was just a matter of luck, it looked like the engine block had deflected it just enough. The bolt had probably traveled through the metal of the van's sides, and the fire…

The detective, freshly shaven but with a ketchup stain on his lapel, had said the same thing.

There was nothing you could have done, Ms. Altfall. Guy in the road was damn lucky not to get run over, but…yeah. Nothing you could have done.

Lies. She could have taken the front way to her parents'—now her sister's—house. She could have pulled over when the storm got too bad.

She could have died, instead of her solemn little girl and her funny little boy. Her little Ess-Wess, her first baby, with her tuft of dark hair and her sweet smile. Her little Sy-bye, the baby they had expected to come out blue and floppy because of the fetal distress monitor. Instead, he was rosy and perfect, and in the fog of pain Jude had clasped him to her chest while Dave said *a boy, a boy…*

Maybe every man secretly wanted a son. Jude, full of weary surprise at having done something right as far as Dave was concerned, had held the tiny bundle to her chest. The clarity of exhaustion made her stare at her then-husband's face with a kind of dumb wonder, and the thought that the little bundle she held might turn out just like his father had collected in her brain like bad gas in a mineshaft. Later, Aggie had brought Essie, her sister scrupulously polite to Dave, who ignored both of them. He had his son.

That was probably the first crack in the careful wall she'd built to convince everyone, including herself, that her marriage was actually functional. Eventually she'd lunged for freedom, not just for herself but for her children, too.

Now look what you've done, Jude. Look straight at it.

Jude sank, slowly, every bone and joint creaking in protest. Aggie must have changed the lights in here. It was too bright, the dark behind her eyelids turning crimson. Her knees touched hardwood older than her parents and she bent over, her forehead coming to rest against the cabinet that was actually a flour-drawer; Gramma Lefdotter had dipped into it with a pitcher or teacup to make her bread. The house was full of them, transparent ghosts of family members walking or laughing or weeping. The tapping of her mother's fingertips on the old oak table, her father whistling as he repaired the floor in the living room, Aggie coughing in her upstairs bedroom, Simon and Essie squalling or sleeping, laughing, running through the upstairs halls and her own voice calling *Aggie Marie, your lunch is ready!* The first few nights after she'd left Dave, her bruised face throbbing in the middle of the night, Essie's restless sleep, Sy's shivering even under the blankets...

Jude slid all the way down, curling around the empty whistling hole in her belly. The sideways part of her turned back, and she sobbed as she had learned to do when Dave got angry—muffled, because if she made any noise the kids might wake up or it might inflame him further. A soft cricket-like moan rose and fell as she fought for breath and silence both. Snot bubbled on her nose, her cheeks turning hot and wet-raw. She clutched herself, and all the ghosts in the house gathered to stare down at her with pitiless-shining eyes.

Esther, she keened. *Simon. I'm sorry, babies, I am so sorry, I am so sorry, so sorry...*

Alone and undrugged at last, Jude Altfall could weep.

Finally, cheeks and nose chapped and crusted, she lay in a deathly doze, staring at the strip of boarding under the cabinets. The floor was cold, and she floated in and out of a doze until the thought of her sister finding her and worrying made her rise stiffly, wincing, the sobs coming at longer and longer intervals. They were quiet now, she could hold her breath when one struck, making only a muffled shudder-whisper like a soft wind over a wet wheatfield.

She groped her way to the stairs, each one familiar-friendly in the dark, and went up silently, avoiding all the squeaks she remembered from childhood. The clothes Aggie had brought to the hospital for her now smelled like disinfectant and pain, and Jude's skin crawled.

The shower was loud, from the curtain-rings rattling on the metal hoop to the thrumming of the pipes delivering hot water, and once in its warm embrace the earthquake heaves came again. Her left hip hurt, throbbing—maybe she'd lain on it the wrong way down in the kitchen—and the rest of her ached too.

Everything hurt. Even the hot water on her skin, *too* hot, as if she could blanch the pain out. She stayed in as long as she could, and when the water shut off there was nothing but a faint sniffing when she inhaled too quickly to show she'd been crying. She'd forgotten to put a towel on the small white-painted cabinet next to the bathtub, and the instant her bare wet feet hit the cool tiles she began to shiver, reaching for the rack that held scratchy company towels instead of the comfortable ones. She'd change them out tomorrow.

Good God. How could something so inconsequential even *occur* to her, when the entire world had stopped spinning? There were people in the neighboring houses eating dinner, watching television, doing whatever it was people did when the sun went down. The only person the earth had stopped for was her, and she was sliding off because it still spun for everyone else. How could she still be breathing? *How?*

The mirror over the tall pedestal sink wasn't steamed, because she'd left the bathroom door wide open. Jude swung the white-painted wooden door closed, but didn't latch it. She halted, staring at the mirror.

Red-nosed, red-eyed, her hair lank seaweed and her ribs standing out, the stretch marks on her breasts familiar—you couldn't nurse two babies and expect to remain perky, really—and a shadow on her left hip. At first she thought it was a bruise, but it was oddly shaped. It looked like one of those tribal tattoos popular with kids just out of high school these days. Vaguely star-shaped…no, she decided, it was like a sun, a perfect circle flushed a deep violet surrounded by a thin strip of pale unmarked skin. Then the rays spread, curved daggers, the whole thing only as big as her palm.

When did that happen? She tried to remember if anything was in her pocket that day. No, she'd been wearing her pink work skirt. They'd given her purse back, waterlogged and reeking of smoke, but none of her clothes had survived. *The van's a total loss,*

Aggie said. *You should see it, the front's all smashed in, it's all charred. It's a miracle.*

Jude's damp fingertips hovered above the bruise, the scratchy blue good-company towel hanging from her right hand and her hair dripping down her back. She might have stood there for a long time, staring vacantly, if there hadn't been a soft knock at the bathroom door.

It was Aggie. "Jude?" Soft, tentative. "Jude, honey?"

She sounds like Mom. Jude wrapped herself in the towel, and realized she hadn't brought in any pajamas, or any fresh clothes at all. The small white pebble-tiles were cold against her feet, and when she opened the door a crack, her sister's expression held all the worry in the world.

"I'm fine," Jude whispered. "I just wanted a shower."

Aggie examined her for a long moment. Her usually sleek hair stood up in all directions, and her patchwork kimono was full of holes showing the thermals underneath.

Don't look so hurt. Jude bit her lip, hard, to discourage the words from spilling out. *Leave me alone. You can't fix this.*

It wouldn't stop Aggie from trying, though. It never did. Her little sister believed sheer bullheaded stubbornness and relentless optimism could fix *anything*.

"Okay." A trace of red lipstain lingered on Aggie's mouth. Her shoulders were tense, and her slippers were on the wrong feet. "Just checking."

"I'm not going to do anything drastic." It sounded like a lie. Her hair had turned cold, resting against her shoulders. She'd been blonde as a child, but when she hit puberty it had darkened. Aggie's had stayed golden, and teenage Jude had almost-despised her for it in the way only a sister could. Of course, Aggie had almost-despised Jude for her curls in return. "I promise."

That sounded like a lie, too. How could anyone promise anything? The entire world was a gigantic mistake, and Jude had added to it bigtime.

"Okay." Aggie still hesitated. "I love you."

"I love you too." Jude closed the door, slowly, and rested her damp forehead against it while she listened to Aggie shuffle away down the hall.

Chapter Ten

HUNGRY MARK

MORNING RAIN GAVE way to bright spring sunshine, everything dripping and green. Marlock arrived at the graveyard early, and spent a while looking the whole place over. The water was good—it insulated his Mark from the dead lying underground. Fresh bodies were the worst, he could feel the pull from them as soon as he got within twenty feet. Here, though, the embalming chemicals and a good layer of wet earth made it less dangerous. The newer graves throbbed a little, but not bad. He found a dry spot with good cover, and settled himself to wait.

So much of this was waiting. For the premonition, for his quarry to make a wrong move, for the next goddamn death. How many cemeteries and graveyards had he stood in by now? How many memorial services had he lurked at the back of, an anonymous, forgettable man, his Mark prickling all up his back and around his ribs, tasting the misery in the air? A little bit of pressure on the environment and he slid right through like a thin knife through the ribs, leaving no trace. Every goddamn time he forced himself to watch as the victim was shoveled in and cried over. He'd heard all the same platitudes in all the same speeches, and each time the dull rage sat in the bottom of his ribs.

This one didn't go the way he thought it would, though it wasn't the first time he'd witnessed a very small coffin slid from the back of a hearse. This time there were two of them, meant for holes side by side. He shifted from foot to foot, watching the knot of mourners. Mostly women, a couple married pairs, which was kind of thought-provoking. They stood on one side of the grave, curved protectively around two slim females with the same general shape to their shoulders and hips. On the other side of the gaping earth-wounds, a dull-red bruise that was a very angry man simmered, glaring across at everyone else. A gray-haired crow was the priest, obviously a friend of the family's by the way he bent a beneficent gaze on the two chief female mourners. The caskets were lowered, slowly, respectfully.

Altfall, he reminded himself. *One divorced, one never married.* He hadn't been able to pull ID files just yet to get an eyeball.

It didn't look like he'd need it.

The blonde was pretty enough, her skirt above the knee and her calves nice and lean under what had to be silk stockings. There was some good meat on her, and she clasped her hands white-knuckle tight when the brunette stepped between the graves with two small bunches of bright yellow and orange. Looked like sunflowers. A cheerful choice for a funeral. Probably some sentimental significance.

It was the brunette Marlock squinted at. That had to be her, Judith Altfall, married name Edmonds, but she'd gotten rid of that according to the accident paperwork.

The mother. He leaned forward on his toes, and his Mark wasn't prickling. It was downright *throbbing*.

A potential with a boon. They were rare, but not impossible. She gave off a glow—a clarity normals wouldn't be able to see. They'd feel it plenty, though. She'd already done her first major work, by the look of it, and Marlock thought it was pretty likely it had occurred in the hospital somehow. The numb shock of the first responders on the scene came through on the accident report; power and thunderclap had both hit the brown and white van, crunching the front as if it had run smack into an abutment. Everything inside caught fire, the mother mostly shielded by the back of her seat. A cop car cruising along the road to check if the creek along one side for signs of flooding had found the wreckage and pulled the mother out before the flames could swallow Judith Altfall. Who was remarkably uninjured.

The damndest thing, Lawson would say. Didn't make it any less true.

Sturmhalten's last act, transferring his Mark—maybe to save civilians, maybe not, though the old man certainly had something approaching a moral code that might cover that—had given with one hand and taken away with the other. As per usual. Never a silver lining without a cloud, when you survived a near-death experience and woke up plugged into an invisible line forcing power out through your entire body.

Judith the brunette dropped sunflowers in one hole, then in another, and the guy across the grave said something. Whatever it was didn't sound nice, and a movement went through the black-clad mourners. The priest shook his head, his book open, and a few syllables reached Marlock in his dry hidey-hole under a massive cedar that was probably feeding on some of the graves around it. Sounded like the good Father was trying to keep the peace.

Now what do you think is going on here, Preston? He *extended* a little bit, invisible feelers delicately waving. Couldn't afford brushing against her in this state, she was raw enough to scorch him. Besides, it would be a helluva shock if his Mark began pulling on the two little bodies in their coffins and made them bang on the lids to get out. There was a time in his life when that would have been amusing, in a bleak way, but he'd grown out of it.

Or so he hoped.

The clarity around Judith Altfall radiated deep, translucent warmth. His skin tingled pleasantly, probably darkening a little to draw all that energy in. The boon would act as if she'd already ascended for the first time, and if she'd done a work, she was firmly on the daylight side of the fence. Wherever her Mark was, it was probably a beaut, and if the Skinner guessed, she'd be his next target. She'd be a laughably easy one, too.

Women generally were.

The asshole on the other side of the grave was most likely the ex-husband. There was a bit of pudge on him, but he looked like he'd done some sport in his youth. Probably football, with all that aggression. Some of the court records were sealed because minors were involved, but you could tell a lot from the way a case moved through the legal canals. The blonde sister—Agnes, though Marlock would bet money she had another name she liked better—looked about ready to go over the grave *at* the ex, her weight on her toes and her eyes narrowing. One or two of the husbands or boyfriends on the Altfall's side puffed up a little, but none of them stepped forward. Afraid of making a scene, or cautious of tangling with a broad-shouldered man whose entire body shouted *violence*?

The ex leaned a little more, as if he would be happy to hurl himself across the graves too. His mouth moved, but brunette Judith, too thin as if she'd been under stress for a while, didn't even glance at him.

Oh, I'll bet that burns. She's not paying attention to you, jackass. Marlock's hands knotted up into fists; he shook them out with a long slow exhale. Judith Altfall was glaze-eyed with grief, and her aura sent out a low but extremely powerful burst of emotion that rippled through the entire graveyard.

Raw, aching loss. Wine-dark grief, a hot diesel kick of guilt, a burning thread of rage buried so deeply she probably didn't even know she felt it.

Marlock's shoulder hit the tree trunk. He was surprised the headstones didn't tilt. Good *God*. A strong cocktail, and someone had to show her how to control whatever her Mark would end up doing.

I'm no teacher. But she needs something. Erik wouldn't have taken on a daysider. Who else is local? He filed the problem away for later and kept watching, his hands tensing and releasing as the Asshole Ex said one last thing, a low venomous hissing under each word. David Eugene Edmonds, the court paperwork had called him. Marlock would bet every dime he had that the asshole wasn't paying the mandated child support.

That did make the brunette look up. Marlock's focus brought her face into sharp relief, and it was a surprise. Getting his vision to telescope was a good trick, and one he was now a little…grateful for? Was that it?

She was pretty. Too thin, those cheekbones startling and model-high. Hazel eyes, threads of green and gold in the irises, an aristocratic nose. It was the mouth, though. Soft and lush, drawn thin with pain now, but it was the kind of mouth that would make a man fall over himself to bring a smile to. Those eyes, too, deep quiet wells that could light up in a moment if you did something funny or thoughtful.

In short, a goddamn catch. He could just imagine her, young and in love with the dark-haired ex who had probably been a broad-shouldered jock. A real prize, maybe even a cheerleader, and he'd been sweet enough to get her to marry him. Then, Marlock suspected, the gloves had come off.

She'd left him, and leaving a man like that was a chancy proposition at best.

What are you thinking, Press? It wasn't his problem. His problem was watching her until the Skinner showed himself.

There was no reason he couldn't do a good deed or two during the vigil, though. Right? Sturmhalten would approve. That something-almost-moral about him had always rubbed Marlock the wrong way, as only a friend could.

That was the other problem. He didn't have many friends. Well, to be precise, now he didn't have *any*.

The brunette said something. Marlock's ears didn't telescope nearly as well as his eyes, but his lipreading was fair enough. He watched that mouth shape soft syllables, and if he hadn't been concentrating so hard, he might have cracked a rueful, half-admiring smile.

"*Go to hell,*" she said, probably very quietly. She stepped back around one of the graves, brushing in front of the priest and instinctively putting herself in front of the blonde and the fellow mourners. Her black shoes were off-brand waitress hooves, thick-soled and battered; her dress was polyester, too big for her, and cheap as chintz. But there was Mama Bear in every line of her, and any sane person would know not to get in her way.

The humidity had gotten into her hair, and she probably hated the curls, but a man would want to bury his hands in it. The silken mop just begged for it. Her chin lifted, and the corner of Marlock's mouth, losing the battle, tilted up in a sardonic smile.

Yeah, she was gorgeous, and she had just lit a fuse under her ex. Marlock could feel the man thinking about how to get his hands on a gun, if he hadn't already.

David Eugene turned and stamped away, ignoring the priest's arrested movement as if to call him back. The bruise of resentment and fury darkened around him, and Marlock realized what made him even more dangerous.

There was no hint of grief in the big dark-haired man's cloud of emotion. Just anger, and possessiveness. He felt, as far as Marlock could tell, *cheated*.

Oh yeah. Definitely time to do a good deed.

Besides, his Mark was hungry. Two birds with one stone.

A few moments later, the mournful, witnessing cedar stood alone in the graveyard.

Chapter Eleven

HAVING A MOMENT

"THE BASTARD," AGGIE fumed, dropping into the driver's seat and glaring out the windshield as if she saw Dave in front of the car. "The motherfu—"

"Language." Jude rested her aching shoulder against the doorway, wishing she could put her forehead on the cool windowglass. "Please." As if the kids were in the car.

God. She couldn't even turn sideways right now, because the image of that stabbing white searchlight kept intruding whenever she did, filling her with unsteady terror. There was no numb solace, no haven to be found.

Her sister kept going. "Why did he even bother to show up? Jesus."

Because he just had to tell me he would make me pay for this. "Maybe he misses the kids, too." Amazingly, she sounded steady, and the blurring in her eyes probably wasn't visible. Her sister's door closed with a heavy, secure sound. She shouldn't have lost her temper, she should *not* have told him to go to hell. That was like dropping a match into gasoline.

Her sister's cream-colored Volvo wasn't new, but it was more comfortable than the van. It still had taken a few moments of deep breathing and feeling incredibly ridiculous before Jude could make herself get in on the passenger side, and right now she congratulated herself on her hands not shaking as she buckled herself in.

Aggie's knuckles were white, and her chin was set in that particularly mulish way it got when she saw something she thought was an injustice. Essie had inherited *that*, somehow—the fury at something unfair, no matter how inevitable. Cool air blew through the car's vents, and the silence was thick as a brick wall. Her sister inhaled, exhaled sharply, and did a few more. Deep breathing was an article of faith for a crystal-healing yoga instructor.

People actually pay for that? Jude had tried not to sound amazed, and oh, how Aggie had laughed. She even had a degree in kinesiology, achieved well after she'd left law school. Mom would have had a fit. Altfall girls were to marry well and achieve much, and the words *doctor* or *lawyer* were said with increasing weight as they approached college age. Woo-woo was not Serious Enough to ease their mother's mind.

It didn't matter, not since that rainy night and a sharp bend in the road. Maybe the family had a car curse now.

"Are you okay?" The parking brake released; Aggie put her arm over Jude's seat and dropped the car into reverse with a quick, habitual motion.

Bile crept high in Jude's throat. She had to swallow several times. "Yeah." She shut her eyes, not wanting to see Aggie's expression. The dark behind her eyelids wasn't comforting, either, because she kept expecting to see that stupid searchlight. Maybe it was from the lightning, or headlights from the cop car, even though she didn't remember being pulled out of the van? "I pretty much expected him there."

"I know." Aggie hit the brake, maybe a little too hard, and the jolt made Jude's stomach turn over.

Oh God. She should have said something, changed the subject, maybe. But she couldn't think of anything that wasn't even more wildly inappropriate.

The car began to creep out of Saint Paul the Redeemer's ancient, weedy parking lot. Father Dannon was a good man, he hadn't even given Jude any grief about the divorce. *God loves you, child,* he said. *This is hard to bear, I know it is. God loves you, and will keep your children warm and safe with him.*

At least there was that. He'd *baptized* them, for God's sake. Both of them.

"He's such an asshole." Aggie was likely searching for a stronger term, and she'd probably find it, too.

Jude wanted to rub at her eyes, couldn't because her fingers had locked together. Tighter and tighter, until she thought she could probably hear the bones in her hand creaking. "Please."

"It's true." Soft but mutinous.

What could Jude say? You weren't supposed to badmouth the other parent, they were *really* clear on that in the obligatory so-you're-getting-divorced-and-you-have-kids classes she'd had to take—the ones Dave hadn't bothered to show up for. It was a moot point now, but the habit of refereeing her own thoughts on the matter was strong.

On the other hand, what sort of complete asshole would go to his child's funeral and say things like that?

Are you happy, Jude? Was this what you wanted? His lip lifting, the sneer that was one of his faces she dreaded most. *Are you fucking happy?*

"Jude." Aggie, very businesslike now. "I have movers going by the apartment. They'll box….everything and put it in storage."

Oh, God. "There's not much to box." Jude's lips were numb. "Clothes." At least Aggie had brought most of hers to the house. "And the…the toys." *Nothing in the kitchen, we had three plates and two bowls.* Every spare dollar went to the divorce lawyer, even though Dave was supposed to be footing those bills. It was in the judgment, but Jude could have told the office of Vinston and Stroud they wouldn't see a dime from *him*. Even if they had lowered their fee since old Mr. Stroud had known Dad.

At least the kids had never gone hungry, and they hadn't had to change schools.

Panic rose behind the bile. The car accelerated, she kept her eyes firmly shut. "I forgot. The school, what about the—"

At least that got Aggie off the subject of Dave. "Chillax, they know what's happening. I had a nice chat with Principal Saffron. No moss grows on *that* woman, let me tell you. She checked my ID twice, *and* the power of attorney. It's a good thing you listed me as emergency contact, too."

"Has…" She wanted to ask if Dave had shown up there, but that was probably a bad idea. Mercifully, now that Jude could just sit for a moment, everything inside her turned sideways again and the searchlight didn't show up. She could pretend Ess and Sy were simply napping in the backseat and Aggie was driving them home. "God, Aggie. What would I do without you?"

"Oh, you'd deal, but it wouldn't be pretty." Aggie laughed, a lovely ringing sound that had a forced edge to it. She was still trying too hard, treating Jude like a china figurine. *I'm fine,* Jude wanted to say. *I can handle this. I've handled everything else, I am the big sister, I am perfectly fine.*

Except she wasn't. Her eyes had begun to leak, Jude breathed through her mouth as the salt water ran down her cheeks. The car stopped, probably at the light on Harbour Street, and Aggie leaned over, fishing in the glove box. An anemic travel-box of tissues landed in Jude's lap.

Oh, Aggie. Even when she could turn sideways inside her skin, it didn't help to keep everything down. It had worked during some of the really bad nights when Dave got angry, and it had also worked during the divorce, when she never knew what direction the next attack would come from. Just putting her head down and turning that secret internal screw a bit, so that she was only partly inside her body and could look around calmly at things that really didn't affect *her*.

As a coping mechanism, it was great. Until it stopped working, and until that damn searchlight showed up next to the breathless crackling sound of someone else's rage.

"It'll be all right, Jude." Aggie hit the turn signal, the car jolted forward, and Jude knew, miserably, that she wouldn't be able to stop crying even when they got home. Aggie didn't need Jude going to pieces now. She had to be strong, be stable, for her little sister.

The problem was, Jude didn't have any strength or stability left.

Chapter Twelve

ABOUT YOUR WIFE

DRIVING BACK TO the small, empty tract house pissed Dave Edmonds off. It always smelled stale and unused in there. Even the drapes were dusty, and without a cunt to scrub the floors, they got grimy. He'd bought the goddamn crackerbox for the ungrateful bitch, and she wanted child support now too. Eight months after they'd moved in, *pow!* She took off, and that blonde bitch of a sister had probably talked her into the divorce.

Are you fucking happy, Jude?

His lawyer was useless, sitting in his cushy office with slight distaste smeared all over his well-oiled, close-shaven weaselface. *The State will garnish your wages if you don't pay, Dave. She didn't even ask for the minimum, the judge awarded it anyway.* Already his hours had been cut, because of that little incident with the cunt in HR. If Jude garnished his hard-earned money, he'd lose the mortgage. Would *that* make her happy?

She used to be so *cute*, too, with those big eyes and that long hair. Acting all weak and helpless, but cunning. Insisting on condoms, like she didn't know that a single prick with a needle made them worthless. She hadn't even gotten ugly during the pregnancies like most women do. Just rounder, softer, and no trouble at all.

Now she'd killed his son. *His* son. David Eugene Edmonds's son. A kid who would be a star quarterback instead of a running back like his daddy, one day. And he wouldn't have let the kid get shacked with a lying mealymouth cunt and fuck up his chances of college and superstardom. He'd even told Jude as much, and she'd simply looked at him with those big dark eyes. Like he was an insect buzzing around a rich girl, one that wasn't worth the trouble of shooing away.

The blue Camaro roared as he put it through its paces, daring a cop, any cop to pull him over. *I was at my son's funeral today, Officer.* With a quaver in his voice and just the merest suggestion of manly tears. That would get him off the hook. At least the bitch couldn't take the car. Could she?

Are you fucking satisfied, rich girl?

Except she wasn't. She'd just looked at him, that same disdainful rich-girl expression.

Dave hit the brakes and smoked through the turn onto 138th. It was too cold for that dried-up biddy Mrs. Cantwell to be out on her porch with her disapproving glare. Everybody in the neighborhood was at work except the wives, the ones that looked away when Dave walked past. Even when he'd let Jude go out with the stroller, holding her arm and grinning like he was a goddamn idiot, the wives had greeted Jude but looked away from *him*. Scared of a real man, or she'd been lying behind his back, laying her plans already.

The Camaro slowed, and he drove sedately down Trotter Avenue because a cop lived on *that* corner. The houses, small two-story crackerboxes built in the fifties, pursed their lips and glared at him. His was the only lawn on the block that hadn't been neatly clipped and winterized, last year's leaves from the spindly tree in the front yard clotting the small round space where Jude had put red flowers once.

Without asking him.

He'd taught her to ask before she went messing around with *his* house. Then she had to go and call the fucking cops. On her own husband. On the star of the Cloverdale Chargers, the guy who had once run a seventy-yarder for a Homecoming game. Nobody minded their own fucking business anymore.

The garage door opened regretfully. His sanctuary was neat and well-swept, the tools on the pegboard each in their proper places, the racks for his *other* tools shining silver-mellow. He had them all, especially his pride and joy. Oh, the big rolling toolchest was fine and red and gleaming, but there was the pneumatic drill, the press…oh, one day he'd get the bitch's head under it and *zoop* it would be all over. Or the air compressor. You could do a lot of things with a compressor.

The Camaro barely fit, but he wouldn't leave it in the *driveway*, for God's sake.

He sat for a few moments, then cut the engine, rubbing at his eyes. His shoes were probably ruined from wet grass. It was like the world conspired with that goddamn rich bitchgirl he'd married, just to burn him. He finally hit the button on the opener clipped to the visor; habit brought him out of the car quickly, and he didn't notice the shadow sliding under the descending garage door.

His first intimation of something wrong was a small sighing sound, a breath against his nape, and iron fingers closed over his shoulder. The doorknob rattled in his hand, and his left side exploded with pain. At first he thought it was a heart attack, and he let out a tiny mewling sound, his boots slipping on the crudely built wooden step he'd put right in front of the door. It wobbled when you stepped on it, and a brief memory of setting it up and seeing it wasn't perfect slid through his head, along with the short gasp torn out of Jude as he pushed her from the doorway ten minutes later. She'd been bringing him a *beer*, for God's sake, when he didn't want one, and the step had wobbled, wobbled. *Can't fucking do anything right,* Dave's father had snarled inside his head, and Jude had hit the concrete floor with a surprisingly soft sound.

His daughter had started crying from the kitchen, and he'd wrapped his hand in Jude's curling hair. *I will bash your brains out if you don't shut that kid up, for Chrissake.* The way she'd looked at him, those big eyes full of tears, and that had set him off again because behind the swelling water, there was that rich-girl disdain.

The pain vanished, all at once, but the fingers clamping his shoulder remained, viselike, holding him up.

"Hello, Mr. Edmonds," a man said, pleasantly. His breath, edged with mint toothpaste, touched Dave's cheek. "Let's talk about your wife."

Chapter Thirteen

INFERENCE

THE PLACE WAS a sty, and it smelled like an abandoned warehouse. It was a far cry from the garage, but Marlock would have bet solid cash the man sitting rigid on the hassock in front of him didn't know how to use three-quarters of the shiny-new tools out there. Including, and probably especially, that candyass sky-blue late-model Camaro. All show and no muscle, and the tires were bald, too.

He leaned back, taking a good look at the guy. The leather recliner was the most comfortable stick of furniture in the house, and he thought the missus probably hadn't done any of the decorating. Certainly most of the dishes in the kitchen, with its black and white linoleum, were shattered, probably while hubby was on a violent bender.

Although really, the Pabst cans scattered around told a story of their own. Who wouldn't get angry, drinking *that* piss?

Marlock stretched his legs, tapping his thin cheek with one finger. His Mark prickled and rang with pleasant heat. There was a lot of turgid black rage and deep inadequacy in this guy. The best kind of fuel. It was tempting to think of tapping in and taking it all in one gulp.

Settle down there, Press. Questions first.

He eased off a little, and Dave's breath lost its wheezing edge. He stared like a kid in a nightmare, his eyes—washed-out blue, the pupils shrinking and growing as stress chemicals poured into his bloodstream—refusing to blink. Soon the orbs would begin to dry out. Marlock had once held a guy like that until he talked, unable to bear the feeling of the stroma and sclera desiccating, the cornea collapsing.

It had only taken about three and a half minutes. Marlock didn't think this guy had that kind of fiber in him, and you always had to leave yourself a little room for escalation. "So. Tell me about your wife." His finger didn't stop its steady tapping, his lean face turning blank and focused. "Cheerleader, huh?"

"Nah, that was her bitch sister." The subject's voice was flat, squeezed unwillingly out, just like from a corpse. "Jude was the library girl. Rich girl in a big house."

Interesting. He had an afternoon of public record searching ahead of him, but he wanted more than just the dry recital of facts, no matter how much you could infer through them. "What about her parents?"

"Car crash. She came home from college and we got married. I was good to her." A whining, wheedling tone won through. "I got a good job, but she ruined that."

"How?"

A shudder ran all the way through the big-shouldered guy. Definitely going to fat, an aggressive little gut sitting on his middle and his hair thinning on top. Even Lawson was in better shape than this. At least the Mark had saved Marlock from the ravages of age.

It had also shown him enough of humanity that he'd lost his taste for small-scale aggression. There were thousands of guys like this all over the world, petty tyrants in their little houses. No idea of a wider world, and no desire to seek one.

The subject had probably been attractive enough in high school. Now, his face was just blurred with the wattles you got from too much cheap beer. He began to babble. "McMartin wanted happy families. She showed up with the bruises on her face, the lying little cunt, and the bitch in HR—"

Marlock's finger stopped tapping. Man, this guy was *stellar*. He watched as Dave turned purple, tissues starving for oxygen. When he let little Davy breathe again, the whooping, terrible, harsh sounds were gratifying.

"Mister..." The asshole's chin wobbled. "Mister, are you the Devil?"

Close enough. "If I was, David Eugene, what do you think I'm doing here?"

"I'll give it to you," the man whined. "Anything."

Jesus Christ. He hadn't even put up any real resistance. What a prize. "What do you think I want from you?"

"Um, my, uh…my, uh…" Those washed-out blue eyes now blinked rapidly as the subject searched for the right words.

Speed it up. "Your soul? Now there's a thought. All I want is what you know about Judith." *She doesn't look like a Judy.*

"Jude." A prissy little correction. Even half-strangled and held riveted to a footstool, the guy was annoying.

"Hey Jude," he murmured. It suited her. *Talk about a sad song. There's no making this better.* She was pretty enough, and it looked like she'd had a helluva sad song up to now. It was about to get even worse, now that she had a Mark. And what if the Skinner didn't catch wind of a survivor? If he could be certain the Skinner had taken the bait…

Shit. The practical route was, of course, to let the killer know.

"You're fucking her." Dear hubby said it like it had just occurred to him, trying to writhe against Marlock's invisible grip. "You son of a bitch. You're fucking my wife."

Why would I be asking you for information, then? And she'd *married* this guy. What the everloving fuck for? Marlock decided now was the time to find out. "You got a divorce, remember?"

The body on the hassock struggled with surprising strength and his Mark rang with delight, waking up a little more. Such delicious rage, and so easy to turn into deep, smoking, wine-red pain. Marlock uncurled from the chair, and the man's struggles intensified. Despite them, his physical frame didn't move one bit. Marlock's hold was steady—it would take more than one balding ex-football player to break those chains.

"You know, pal, I was just gonna talk to you." *That's a lie, Press. You know better.* "But I don't think I can stand to lose any more brain cells."

So it's time to take what I need, and implant a few things.

A sharp hot smell of urine rose, a normal response from a body pushed past fear and straight into terror. Marlock smiled, his eyes—so dark you couldn't tell pupil from iris until you were very close—lighting up, and for a moment he looked nearly handsome. Almost, in fact, *happy*.

This was going to be fun.

Chapter Fourteen

Being Tidy

THE WINDOW WAS vast and very clear, a solid sheet of glass. It framed the city across the bay nicely, especially as dusk descended and the lights began to glitter. So many little stars, and the secrets pulsing underneath them revealed to only a few. Did any of the others feel lonely? Perhaps the collector was doing them a mercy, taking away what made them different. Relieving them of the burden of uniqueness.

Sometimes on long nights, when the hunger grew sharp but he did not have a particular square of patterned hide set aside or a retrieval to plan or anticipate, he would think of all the souls he had liberated from fleshly prison, all the burdens he had lovingly collected, and something inside him would expand with warmth. In those moments he almost cared for the grotesques he set free; he saw himself tall and robed in white, a hurtful radiance about his brow and voices singing a grateful chorus as he sat enthroned.

THE MARKED

Other times he regarded himself as an exterminator, using the filthy insects' own weapons against them in a never-ending war. More brutal, but perhaps, more truthful. He was very aware that he was considered a handsome man. A good catch. A *playboy*. The word "wunderkind" had even been used once or twice, next to pictures in the newspapers. There were approved photos on websites, too, most of his good side, shot from slightly below. The image had to be flawless, and the marking on his ribs helped make sure the damn paparazzi didn't get much. He didn't like having to make himself invisible, but it was better than giving the vultures something unflattering to feast upon.

Tonight, his chin touched his chest, an untouched glass with two fingers of good bourbon sat on the small, very expensive table to his right, and he boiled with fury, blinking slightly bloodshot blue eyes.

A small sound, halfway between a cough and a shuffle, told him that though he had dismissed his secretary, the latter had not left. Which could only mean one thing.

He exhaled, irritation rasping up his windpipe. Mr. Bell was valuable. Attractive in a bland, well-groomed way, athletic without being overly stacked, dark-haired and self-effacing. Despite all that, his employer didn't want to be disturbed, dammit. Unless it was good news. Which Bell would know.

When the collector could speak without the irritation showing, he did not shift in the chair. His well-polished wingtips were a little uncomfortable, but he wouldn't take them off just yet. "Yes, Mr. Bell?"

"There's news, sir." Quiet, modulated—he had the perfect butler's voice, really. A suggestion of well-bred enunciation, but not enough to be snide.

"Is it good news?"

"It could be, sir. The mother survived."

The collector's lip curled. He let it; when he spoke, it was a single word. "And?"

"One of the children in the intensive care unit had some good luck. There was a mix-up with X-rays at the hospital." A delicate pause. "Either that, or the child was miraculously healed of several broken bones and internal injuries."

Miraculous. What a wonderful word. "I see."

Mr. Bell made no reply. Unlike most, his waiting was not full of small noises meant to attract attention. The collector could almost *see* his employee, dark hair slicked back and his suit of good quality and well-tailored but not showy, his cufflinks plain and his own calfskin shoes buffed to a moderate gloss.

Now the lights across the bay looked like tiny twinkling elf-eyes, each laughing at him. A survivor. Miracles.

It was probably too much to hope for, that this one would take the Storm Dragon's place in his collection. Still, he was in the habit of being tidy. All his brooding had only returned the maddening image of the stump of a dead lighthouse on a rocky shore. He didn't like being balked, but was unwilling to expend one of his collected beauties on what could be a dead end.

"Find out everything you can," he said, finally.

Mr. Bell's satisfaction was just as quiet as the rest of him. "Yes, sir."

Chapter Fifteen

COPING

THE SCHOOL THERAPIST, Vanessa Carr, was a small, round almost-brunette several years Jude's junior, her dishwater hair pixie-cut and livened with a streak of pink that reminded Jude of middle school experiments with bleach and Kool-Aid. Her office was full of pint-sized furniture, and Jude already knew her from assemblies and classroom events. It was good to have a familiar face for Essie, someone who knew about the divorce.

Cresston Elementary was a good school, and sometimes Jude suspected the principal had been through a bad divorce herself. It would explain a lot. Of course, Jude was hardly the only parent who had suffered a nasty custody battle. They were common as cupcakes at a bake sale. The principal's zero-tolerance policy on spouses who were not legally supposed to get near the school was stringent, and she'd refused to release Ess and Sy to Dave that one sunny day before summer vacation. Had even called the police, because she had the custody order on file, and when they arrived, it had been the principal who had spelled out that her ex-husband was looking at attempted-kidnapping charges, which the district would pursue *in loco parentis* if Jude wouldn't. Magically, that calmed the situation down and Dave had agreed to leave the school quietly.

To date, he hadn't returned.

Principal Saffron did not look like a bulldog crossed with an avenging angel, but she certainly *behaved* like one. Likewise, Ms. Carr the therapist was able to turn a group of sobbing or scrapping little savages into a quiet circle of rapt listeners with a few short words. When Simon had "accidents" at school, it was Ms. Carr who came to the nurse's office to help him into dry pants and bag the wet ones, and each time she called Jude with a sober "just to let you know" tone that nevertheless held a great deal of compassion.

He'd gone for a whole three months without a single accident, but the therapist still had a small stack of his Fruit of the Looms and his tiny, off-brand jeans, left here at the beginning of the school year and still smelling faintly of Jude's preferred brand of fabric softener. The paper bag holding them was on Ms. Carr's desk, but Carr was sitting cross-legged on the floor.

Jude froze in the doorway, looking at the collection of half-size furniture.

A little girl with dark, curly hair craned to peer over her shoulder, and for a moment it was Essie, and a great swell of relief began under Jude's diaphragm, pushing up like it was going to dislodge the breakfast she hadn't eaten and her heart in the bargain. Jude's throat turned to dry, slick glass. Her bruised hip ached, as if a muscle had torn or the contusion was particularly deep. The weird bruise—the more she looked at it, the more it looked like a tattoo, a stylized tribal sun—wasn't getting any lighter.

Carr pulled at her cheerful orange hand-knitted cardigan. "Oh, hello. Amber, you remember Ms. Altfall. Excuse me a moment."

"Oh, hi, Essie's-mom." A cast glared white on the little girl's arm. "I broke my arm bike riding." Multicolored scribbles showed all over the cast, large looping scrawls and tiny careful scratchings.

"Oh." Jude's hip gave a short plucking twinge to match the one in her chest. "I'm sorry to hear that." Jude managed to sound firm instead of breathless. *I can do this. It's just picking things up. I can do it.*

Fortunately, Carr was a master of redirection. "Amber came to visit me for lunch. We were just finishing up."

"Will we play with the wheel next time?" Amber's voice wasn't as sweet as Essie's. Esther and Simon had both come home talking excitedly about the Wheel of Feelings, each child given a chance to move the wheel so the pointer came to rest on one of their feelings. It was supposed to help the confusion of a contentious divorce become more navigable for kids, and Jude was pretty pathetically grateful there were professionals involved who knew how to do it.

God knew her own attempts to steer had been practically hopeless.

Carr's grin was as close to deep childlike joy as an adult could manage. "We can, sure. I think everyone's out on the playground, now."

The halls were abuzz with small people, most of them remembering to walk instead of run. Lithe blonde Principal Saffron was in C hall, greeting children by name as they filed past on their way outside, and she smiled down at the girl holding Carr's plump hand. "Amber! Very nice to see you today. How does your arm feel?" An encouraging smile lit her Valkyrie face, the two braids crisscrossed over her head adding to the picture of a Teutonic maiden who took no shit from *anyone*.

"Better, ma'am." The little girl's eyes were owlish. Being named by Miz Saffron was always an Event. The awe the children held her in was matched only by their respect for Mrs. Eldridge the librarian.

"Hello," Jude mouthed, and the flash of pity on Saffron's face was eclipsed by a smile at another third-grader who had something, apparently, Very Important to tell the principal. Amber fast-walked away, scratching absentmindedly at the cast. Jude's own arm twinged in sympathy, and she breathed out, a long slow soft exhale meant to dispel nervousness. Amber vanished at the end of the hall, and a familiar door loomed on Jude's right. Ms. Carr was at her elbow, pulling at her cardigan's hem again.

Esther's teacher was at her desk, neatening a stack of paper with her broad, brown, capable hands. She glanced up, and her surprise was not as awful as the image of Essie on the projector screen. A school picture, Ess in her bright red coat and with the two red ribbons Aggie had carefully tied in her hair that day. The small tables were all empty, including the one that had Ess's nameplate under a layer of clear packing tape, the sunflowers Jude had drawn on it glaring yellow.

"Hi! Oh…" Miss Josston reached for her computer, and Jude guessed what she was looking for. "We were sharing, before lunch. Sorry."

"It's fine," Jude said. "Really. It's…it's fine."

"How are you holding up?" Josston found the buttons she wanted, and Essie's face vanished. A sharp, precise pain went through Jude's chest, and she groped internally for the switch that would turn her sideways so she could get through this. It didn't matter if the damn searchlight was there, she needed somewhere, anywhere, to escape to.

"Fine," Jude mumbled. Aggie had taken care of calling the school while she was in the hospital, yes. This was organized. Not routine, but there were rules for the situation. Right? "You know. Coping." She'd practiced saying it in front of the mirror. *Don't look at me.*

The therapist kept talking. "When you feel up to it, Annie Lieber wondered if you'd want to talk to…to Simon's class. They're doing a memorial wall for him." Was it nervousness, lurking below Ms. Carr's calm? A therapist would know the rules for this kind of thing, right? What else were they *for*? "They'll have it up for the rest of the school year. We were thinking about doing the same, if you didn't mind."

"I don't at all. Of course." *Don't you dare cry.* The burning in her eyes wasn't tears. "It was a freak accident." Repeating the same words, over and over, like a charm. "Lightning, on Old Bath Road." In other words, *I wasn't irresponsible. It was an accident. Right? Please tell me I'm right.*

It sounded thinner and thinner each time she was forced to say it.

Miss Josston, probably Essie's favorite person next to her mother and Auntie Aggie, pulled her sweater sleeves down. Her hair was in several small braids with yellow beads at the end. "I couldn't believe it when Annie called me."

Annie. Annie Lieber. Simon's teacher, a birdlike gray-haired woman with the sharp face of a fox, and gentle wrinkled hands. She'd understood about Simon's occasional acting out, just like Josston had about Essie's.

"We're all so sorry." Miss Carr touched her elbow, and Jude realized her hands were fists. She tried to arrange her face in a neutral expression. How the fuck were you *supposed* to look when your babies had...

Had *died?*

Oh, God. God, please. God was a monster who probably didn't exist. The lump in her throat would not go down, no matter how many times she swallowed. "Thank you. I'm just here to pick up...the things."

"Yes." Another paper bag. Esther's spare coat. Her schoolwork, forever unfinished now.

"May I give you a hug? It's just so…we can't believe it." Miss Josston was slim as an ebony statue, but there was a softness around her middle that hadn't been there a month ago. Something rippled in Jude's memory, but she pushed it firmly away.

She let the woman hug her, even patted her on the back. "Essie loved you." The words didn't hurt, mostly because everything had gone blessedly numb again. Jude's face was frozen, she hoped the expression wasn't a grimace. Hoped Miss Josston wouldn't think it was *her*.

"Oh, honey." The softest of female tones, like her divorce lawyer patting her on the shoulder after the final hearing. Josston's thin gold bangles chimed against each other, sweetly. "I can't even imagine."

No. You can't. "I…I should go." Playground time would be over soon, and all of a sudden, the thought being in the halls when the second and third graders came back through in their neat lines was a ball of dread inside her skull.

"Of course…If I come across anything else, I'll call. If you need anything, anything at all, please just let me know. If you ever want to come in and talk to the kids, or anything, we'd be glad to have you." Josston held Jude's arm, manifestly unwilling to let her go. It was compassion, and Jude was grateful for it, even as she wanted to scrabble-scratch away. Run. Escape.

God, please, get me through this. "Thank you."

Out in the hall again, she could hear the distant clatter of the lunchroom—the fourth and fifth graders would just be filing in now. The walk back to Carr's office was much shorter without a crowd in the way, and Mrs. Carr handed her the paper bag full of Simon's clothes. Jude accepted it silently, and stood with both bags in her arms, looking awkwardly at the carpet. It had a pattern of trains and streets on it; Simon would have loved to get down there with a toy car or two and pretend...

Her eyes were burning. *Don't you dare cry. Say something polite.* "Thank you. I should go."

"I...Ms. Altfall..." A long pause. Was she about to tell Jude not to cry, that things would be all right? Hustle her off to the front door? "Jude, we have resources for...times like this."

What, you mean God? The church? Jude nodded, numbly. Sunday was coming up, and she dreaded the event. Aggie didn't go to Mass anymore. Deciding whether or not Jude should go herself suddenly seemed a giant, insoluble problem, rivaled only by the problem of getting the fuck out of here as soon as possible. "I should go."

"Here." Three small pamphlets in Carr's plump little paws. She really was a very nice person.

Grief and Grieving. Parental Support Options. Family Therapy. They were glossy, nice paper. Good God, there were actual *pamphlets*? Who wrote them? Who thought that was a good idea? Jude turned blindly, set off for the door. "Thank you so much." *Is that the right thing to say?* It wasn't like losing Mom and Dad, Aggie's call in the middle of the night and Jude's immediate swinging into big-sister action.

This was far, far worse. When you were old enough, you understood on some level your parents might not be eternal. But not...not your children. Not your *babies*.

"Their classmates will grieve, it's natural." Carr had to trot to keep up with Jude's strides. "Often, though, nobody thinks about how the parent is dealing. I don't want to intrude, I just..."

Jude searched for something to say, an expression to paste on the thin, horrified mask her face was likely to be. "It's...it's really kind of you. Really kind. Thank you."

"Don't hesitate to reach out—"

"I know," Jude managed. "If I...I'll call."

"All right." Carr looked dissatisfied, and Jude caught a flicker of motion out in her peripheral vision. It was Principal Saffron, leaning on the office counter and talking to the receptionists— Sandy Maltby and Sharon Axline, both tall, cheerful, and perma-bouffant. They probably kept AquaNet in business. Any moment the principal would see her, and all of a sudden Jude could not stand the thought.

"Thank you," she repeated, desperately, and all but bolted for the front doors.

It wasn't over, though. It took a good five minutes, shivering in the buttery spring sunshine, before she could make herself unlock Aggie's Volvo and sit in the driver's seat. She'd insisted on driving to the school by herself. *Get back up on the horse,* she'd said firmly. *That's best.* Never mind she couldn't force herself to take the freeway, never mind that she crept along at exactly the speed limit, never mind that she clutched the steering wheel like a drowning woman the entire time and had sweated through her bra. The waistband of her jeans was soaked.

Out on the playground, tucked behind the school's brownstone bulk, a little girl with dark curls swung her cast, laughing. It didn't hurt anymore, it just itched, and in a month a doctor would be puzzled at the lack of muscle atrophy and no sign of the healed break on follow-up X-rays.

Jude would never know. She only knew it was too bright out here, something glaring through the windshield. Her eyes stung, watered. Jude put her head down, burying her face in the bag holding Simon's clothing, smelling paper and fabric softener, the other bag crinkling underneath it. The tears wouldn't come, just filled up her throat and twisted inside her chest.

She hyperventilated, waiting for the panic to pass.

Chapter Fifteen

A WOMAN'S KEENING

ALL OF DAVE Edmonds's blathering about a rich girl made sense when Marlock found the Altfall house. Public records had shone a little light on the whole thing—there was an estate and a trust, and the Altfalls had a long history in this part of the country. Some branches of the family had gone downhill.

Jude's had not. Maybe it was a thin strand of *potential* running in them, although Marks did not often follow family lines. It was more likely luck, or good parenting. Probably the former.

The place obviously been a farmhouse once, but a well-to-do one. The lots in the Laurel Hill section were nicely sized, even though the city had grown around them. Big and white, half stone half timber, with apple trees at the bottom of its backyard, the Altfall house slumbered cozily on an oak-lined street with wide sidewalks and the reek of old-fashioned money and graciousness in the air. Paul and Beryl Altfall had died in a car accident on a rainy March night; a picture of their funeral had made the papers. Daddy Paul was an investor and stockbroker, mother Beryl was on several charity committees and probably what they used to call a "society matron." Old money, kept in conservative investments and hedged with various legal defenses, probably made things easier *and* harder on the Altfall sisters. Dave was still incensed Jude hadn't wanted to sign over her trust fund to her loving husband. It was more likely she hadn't been able to, no matter how little Davy menaced her. After digging a little through Paul Altfall's business dealings, Marlock had come to the conclusion that no grass grew on that old man; he'd taken providing for his family very seriously.

Even after his demise.

A sweet spring rain was just moving in as Marlock crouched at the bottom of the yard, eyeing the gap in the fence he'd squeezed through. Too narrow for an adult human male, but stepping into the blur helped with that. And he had a full charge from little Davy's paroxysms of rage and fear. There was never any shortage of fuel hanging around, but few things were as enjoyable as serving a petty tyrant a taste of the darker side of Marlock's cursed gifts. He enjoyed dishing out the pain, where warranted.

Enjoyed it maybe a little too much.

Above the gently sloping gardens, a glassed-in porch stood to the left and a large bay window to the right. Looked like a kitchen, if the glimpse of cupboards behind and the arch of a faucet was any indication. The window was crowded with greenery, low box hedges underneath and houseplants inside. For a moment Marlock thought they had high-output floodlights in there, before he realized the light wasn't really coming from a fixture. It was that same clarity he'd seen at the graveyard.

Looked like Jude, *hey Jude*, was home.

He moved forward slowly, up a pathway made of bricks probably older than the house itself and slippery with moss. In the summer this was probably a fairyland—looked like the blonde sister liked gardening. She had a degree in some froufrou yoga thing and a business selling various pottery items to boutiques in the gentrified sections of town. It was the sort of hobby-turned-job someone without kids or basic financial uncertainty could build into a going proposition. He'd bet the sister had lots of moxie. An abundance of it. According to Dave, she'd been a cheerleader, and a highly desirable one too. Edmonds had probably figured he didn't have a chance with *her*, and moved in on quiet, brunette Jude instead.

Marlock was fairly certain he wouldn't be seen—the days were lengthening, but dusk had gathered in every corner and unless they turned some outside floodlamps on, he was relatively safe. Besides, that clarity was…tempting.

Dark head bent, her slender shoulders under a blue wool sweater with a wide ballet neckline, Jude Altfall was bent on scrubbing something in a sink. Dinner dishes? A pan or pot? She was really going at it, bobbing back and forth a bit to get her whole body involved, and Marlock's eyes narrowed, his forehead crinkling. Something he couldn't quite put his finger on…

Then he figured it out. She was crying, probably silently, her cheeks reddening and the tip of her nose pinkening. From behind it would just look like she was really into her dishwashing.

His Mark began to tingle again, pleasant and warm like a hot bath. Marlock took another step, brushing past last year's sunflowers, probably left out to give the birds something to eat during the winter. An invisible border trembled as his boot-toes slid over it, and he halted.

She didn't appear to notice. It was a hell of a lot of energy hanging around her. Jesus. She had all the force of Erik's gift, and all her own potential.

"Hey Jude," he whispered, without realizing his lips were moving. "Don't be so down." *Well, she's got a right to be down, you jackass.* Her grief was a dark wave, towering over the house, probably soaking into the floorboards and ceilings.

The worst thing about his Mark was that it didn't matter where the pain came from. It was all *food*. Her sorrow was as much of a banquet as little Davy's baffled, entitled rage. Ever since he'd triggered in the prison yard, bleeding out through the gap in his ribs made by a filthy shank, it had been that way. You found your level in life, and his was with the bottom-feeders.

Or maybe it hadn't been the triggering itself, but the first Act he'd performed. Healing in one vertiginous moment and tearing the life from his attacker with invisible force the next landed him firmly on the dark side of the moon. Made no difference, really.

Hang on. He pitched forward a little. The delicious warmth slid up his shin, caressed his knee. His Mark gulped it, greedily, as if he hadn't glutted himself a few hours before. *Where do you put it all?* Erik had wondered aloud, once, back during the war.

Who cares? Marlock had answered. *Give me the fucking eyes.* Motioning sharply for the field glasses, so he could peek out into a wilderness of mud, barb wire, and stiffening bodies.

He'd warned Sturmhalten about the Skinner again about a month ago, and the man had laughed. *I can take care of myself, Herr Leutnant.* How could the killer lure out such an old fox?

Marlock focused on the present, watching a civilian's face through the window, alert for any sign that she noticed the draining from his Mark.

She kept crying, scrubbing away at the sink. Whatever she was cleaning was going to be worn to a wafer, soon. Steam rose—the water was running. Probably boiling, too, unless they had a water heater capable of setting itself below scalding.

Jude Altfall didn't *notice* him. Whatever she was emitting, he could grab, but she didn't turn pale or sway on the verge of passing out. Maybe the pain of loss was too big for her to notice anything he did. Marlock, frozen, watched the blonde sister's face rise over Jude's shoulder. The blonde lunged, slapping the faucet handle down, and grabbed Jude's hands. They were bright red, clutching a wad of steel wool, and there was a faint tinge of rusty crimson on the snarled metal strands. Agnes—Christ, how she'd probably hated that name all through high school—pulled her sister forward, stroking her dark, curling hair, her jaw set and her eyes sparkling-bright with tears. A complex stew of pain, concealed anger, guilt, and other deep emotions pushed out, at normal strength. The blonde didn't even have potential; she was a weak glitter next to her sister's burning lucidity.

They swayed together, a dusk-framed picture of agonizing grief. Marlock's eyes narrowed. It was dark enough they couldn't see him, and getting physically darker by the minute, but still. No use in making the job any harder on himself.

He extended a tiny tendril towards the window. Brushed against all the hot, bubbling emotion from blonde, pretty Agnes.

Who stiffened, her eyes widening. Even normals could feel Marlock's touch. They wouldn't know what it was, but they could get the cold sense of something *not right*.

Jude Altfall *still* made no sign. Maybe she was just hurting so much more pain didn't matter. She hunched her shoulders, and Preston Marlock could almost hear the low noise she was making. An ancient sound, a woman's keening, muffled because the world was a merciless pit that ate everything.

If he had anything resembling a conscience left, it might have pinched a bit. He could probably dangle her as bait for the Skinner, drop a few choice words somewhere he suspected the killer might be listening. The only thing stopping him was the fact the bastard was a smart sonofabitch, and could afford to outwait any watch Marlock might set on this little piece of new-Marked flesh. He could even strike elsewhere, if he suspected someone had caught onto him. Marlock had a few helpful elves in most major cities, but he had no institutional backup. The agency had marked him MIA, or even KIA, and he liked it that way. More latitude, especially since the agency had signed off on catching the bastard.

He stepped back, carefully, watching as the wariness drained from Agnes's expression. She rocked her sister, that tiny soothing movement women were so good at. Her mouth moved, probably making comforting noises. What did it feel like, to be held like that?

One of those questions he'd never get the answer to. If the Mark hadn't taken it away from him, his life before its awakening certainly had.

He stepped back again. *Turn around. Get out through the fence and recon for tomorrow. Things have to be just right.*

It was small comfort that Dave had already planned what he thought was his vengeance. All Marlock had to do was tail Jude, and things would work out perfectly. He might even be able to teach her a thing or two before the Skinner showed up.

If, if, if. Almost as much of a motherfucker as the word *should*.

He stayed there, staring, while Agnes drew her sister out of sight. The crying was probably good for both of them. Get all the bad chemicals out of the bloodstream, exhaust Jude into sleeping. There were dark circles under her eyes. Was she getting any rest?

Marlock shook away the question. When they vanished from the kitchen window, he eased back down the slope, turning every few steps to glance back at the house. Its few lights were rich and golden, somehow warm.

He hoped she *would* get some sleep. She was going to need it.

Chapter Seventeen

THAT ADMISSION

"ORGANICS ARE EXPENSIVE," Jude said for the fiftieth time, restraining the urge to bite her lower lip. "Aggie, come on."

"Jesus, Jude. We're *fine*, we have enough. Quit worrying."

"I should go back to the apartment." Jude's hands clutched each other, and she peered at the Laurel Hill Market through the rain-spotted windshield. It was a wet spring, but the nights were getting softer. Even the sycamores had leafed out, and the plum branches were full of pink fleece. The blossoms all over the apples at the bottom of the garden were fading, replaced by green. Last night another spring storm had come over the city, and Jude lay awake listening to distant thunder, her entire body alternately icy and volcano-hot under Granma Lefdotter's sunrise quilt.

A normal part of the grieving cycle, the pamphlets said. Nightmares and insomnia were common. Jude's fingers creaked, she clenched them so tightly. *The stages of grief may not occur in order; or you may experience two at the same time…*

It wasn't the sort of thing you could mark on a day planner. There was no scheduling for this. A hot swell of guilt would rise whenever she thought there *ought* to be, because a mother shouldn't ever get over something like this. Wishing the pain would ease up was a coward's move. How could you claim to love your babies if the pain ever stopped?

Jude's temples throbbed. So did her hands. The fine lattice of cuts on her fingertips and knuckles stung, and she'd been lucky not to scald herself into blisters. Maybe the water heater wasn't working as well as it used to.

"You're staying with me." Aggie's chin jutted again. She looked like Mom when she did that, right down to the two rapid blinks of irritation and the decided little nod at the end of the statement. "It's safer, and cheaper, and you don't have a car now."

"Yeah." *Really, though, I* am *a coward.* Being sneakingly grateful someone else could arrange for movers so you didn't have to go back and see your son's toys scattered over a cheap-ass studio apartment was one indication of a severe lack of bravery, all right. There really wasn't much to pack—she'd left so much behind in the tract house on Ash Lane. *I don't want the house*, she'd said, over and over again, because she knew Dave had the keys. Coming back after she'd filed the papers and had the temporary injunction had been one of her worse mistakes.

Not really. That one was okay compared to this.

This morning she'd even grabbed three bowls from the cupboard for the cereal, instead of just one for Aggie, who thankfully hadn't noticed.

Aggie pulled into a parking spot under a thinly greened birch, its long fringes fluttering a bit as she cut the engine. Jude let out a long breath she hadn't been aware of holding. Getting behind the wheel was unpleasant, and Aggie had seen her white and shaking yesterday after…after the elementary school.

"You're agreeing with me an awful lot." Aggie dropped her clutch of keys in a large canvas purse, little strips of multicolored fabric tied to the strap holders swinging when she walked.

"Hard not to," Jude mumbled. She had one of Aggie's old bags now, the sunshine-yellow messenger bag Aggie had sewn funny patches onto—Lichtenstein comic panels, a vintage Star Wars patch, a couple of flags from different countries.

"I'm going to remind you of that admission every few minutes from now on." Ag glanced at her hair in the rearview, an instinctive, habitual motion, and popped her door lock. Jude's breath hitched briefly, but she forced herself to unlock her own door.

The parking lot was a smooth black mirror, recently repaved. This part of town had always been what they called 'gentrified', and Aggie's Volvo sat comfortably among other sedate but expensive cars. Dave had never understood—

Don't think about him. She followed Aggie, concentrating on avoiding the infrequent puddles, shoulders hunched as her sister kept up a running commentary.

"I think some tomatoes, and if they have good strawberries—you like strawberry shortcake, right? Oh, and some fudge ice cream—"

"Too early in the season." Jude's heart lodged in her throat. "Too cold for ice cream, too."

"Oh." She sounded crestfallen. Essie preferred popsicles. It was Simon who loved chocolate ice cream.

Jude glanced guiltily, at her left side, where Simon should have been if she let him walk. No, he should have been holding her hand, in mittens and a knit cap, his big bright eyes taking in the entire world and greeting it with a cherubic grin. Her sunny little boy. Esther should have been on her other side, looking at signs and puzzling out their sounds. She loved new words.

She almost ran into Aggie, who was weighing the question of what size cart to grab. "We need milk, right?"

"I think so." Jude didn't have the faintest idea. She was too busy trying to swallow the rock lodged at the very back of her tongue, the one tasting of bitter iron. No, she realized.

That copper tang…it tasted like *blood*.

The world grayed out, came back in a rush of rainy color, black parking lot, red metal shopping carts, and a rack of organic herb and flower starts set to one side of the automatic door. "*Get Growing For Spring!*" its sign blared at her, and she remembered her children in the backyard at Ash Lane, Essie's fascination and Sy's *ewwwww* face as they found worms. It was always Essie digging up the bugs, hoping to squick her brother out.

Aggie was looking at her strangely. "Jude?"

"Sorry." She shook her head. "I just..." *I keep seeing them.*

"Did you want to wait in the car?"

"God, no. Let's go." To prove she was all right, she grabbed for a cart, her purse slipping off her shoulder. She hitched it back up, and Aggie grabbed at the other end of the cart, pulling it for the doors.

"You push," her sister said. "I wonder if they have asparagus? I could braise it."

"It makes your pee smell funny," Jude muttered, wishing she could glance over her shoulder. Something felt...weird.

"It's actually very *healthful*." Aggie tugged the cart through the door, Jude had no time to look back, not unless she wanted the push-bar yanked from her grip.

"Dammit, Aggie." She didn't say it very loudly. It was kind of a relief not to have to think, to just follow in her sister's wake. There was something bothering her, though.

Had she looked back, she might have been more than *bothered*, because a tall man wearing sunglasses and a tan jacket had unfolded from a low-slung sky-blue Camaro parked at the far edge of the lot.

And Jude Altfall would know that car.

Chapter Eighteen

FIXED HIM GOOD

HIS SKULL WAS full of bees. He barely remembered his name, with them buzzing and crawling and poking behind his face. They whispered, too, under the buzzing. Something he had to do.

Tell me about the sister, Davy boy.

He was vaguely aware of the parking lot. It was familiar—he'd waited here plenty of times, trying to catch the blonde bitch so he could follow her. Once or twice during the divorce she'd met his cunt of a wife in a public park or coffee shop. Sometimes he would watch them, and occasionally they would laugh at him, his cunt wife with her hand cupped before her mouth as if to catch it, the bitch sister throwing her glossy head back and letting loose with a cackle or two. They never seemed to get tired of meeting to plan how they were going to fuck with him next.

You've followed her? Naughty little Davy. The mocking voice in his head, the bees turning furious, roaring and dragging their stingers along the inside of his braincase.

He must have seen them. Either of them. Where was the other man, the lean guy with the hard face and the eyes that turned black from lid to lid? He was the Devil, and he'd told Dave to do something.

Why were they always after him? Didn't they get tired of fucking with the guy who could go seventy yards to win a game? Everything had gone wrong when he married the cunt. But she'd been so pretty, so polished, and easier to get than the blonde bitch cheerleader. She was supposed to hand the money over from that big house on Laurel Hill, because Dave Edmonds *deserved* it. The money would have fixed everything.

He paced through the wet parking lot, back and forth at a slow amble, carrying his buzzing head gingerly on its stem of a neck. Kept an eye on the two doors. They'd have to come out, sooner or later. When they did he could do what he needed to.

Most of the shoppers were women. Some of them pushed fancy strollers, or carried snot-nosed brats, mostly in slings on their chests. Those were all the rage with rich bitches this year, maybe. His cunt wife hadn't even gotten ugly during pregnancy, she'd looked like a magazine illustration. He'd almost been ready to forgive her about everything when his son came. The boy that would run touchdowns and then get interviewed and say *it was all because of my dad*. His daughter wasn't bad, either. Just a solemn little afterthought with her wide dark accusing eyes, like her mother's. *You make that kid stop looking at me like that, or I'm going to talk to her.*

His son. Who would have thought a rich cunt's vag could squeeze out a man?

Do what I tell you, Davy, and everything will be all right.

Dave Edmonds had his hands in his jacket pockets, as if he was cold. Heavy, dangerous metal filled the right-hand one; he'd chosen this coat because it had enough space. Hammer, muzzle, chamber, *Saturday Night Special* they called it. The guy at the shop had barely blinked when Dave spread the cash on the counter.

The thought of money made him think of the mailbox at the end of the driveway, a white-painted arch full of bills and "reminders." He'd had a job once, a good one, even after the cunt had shown up at the office with a bruised face and McMartin had gotten that pinched, sly, suspicious look. He'd gotten another job, to keep the rich girl happy, but then there was the bitch in HR getting all pissy when he'd just made a joke or two about how they should go out for coffee. A divorced man had the right, and did she think she was so special, with her office and her forms and her curly long hair just like Jude's? Fuck, he'd just been giving her a *chance*. She probably hadn't been laid since the last presidential administration.

Now his son, Dave Edmonds's son who was supposed to be a quarterback, was dead and Dave's head was full of bees like the mailbox was full of bills. A divorce ate up a man's *time*. The little lying cunt sitting there with her expensive bitch lawyer, the judge looking at Dave Edmonds, the hero of that game at Cloverdale High, like he'd look at a squirming thing under a rock. Emergency room photos. Affidavits from "friends," as if the cunt had any. She'd whored it up and fixed him good.

He didn't realize he was muttering to himself. A tall, chubby woman in a long blue wool coat passed, giving him a strange look, and he didn't even notice her. She glanced back twice, her round forehead creasing under an expensive mahogany dye job, and vanished into the left-hand door.

A short while later, a portly man in a white short-sleeve shirt and a pushed-askew tie came out. His nametag read *David Douds, Manager*, and his faded hazel eyes, while tired, were still sharp. He scanned the parking lot, and hurried back inside.

Dave Edmonds kept pacing, and feeling the heavy handle in his right pocket. It was warming up, because his palms were sweating.

Sooner or later, they would have to come out.

Chapter Nineteen

OLD CONCRETE

"I DON'T LIKE it," Rick Talbot said, morosely, blinking his sleepy, bloodshot eyes.

"You don't like anything." His partner Louie leaned back in his busted-down office chair. One of these days, the thing was going to give out, and his partner would go ass-first onto the floor. If he could find it, under the moldering paperwork and other detritus stacked against the back of Callahan's desk. Callahan and Ramirez were out working a domestic; another asshole with a gun had decided it was time to ventilate his estranged. At least there weren't kids involved.

"I just want to know what that guy was doing on the road."

Louie Vantarello sighed, mopping at his brow with exaggerated care. He was dark-haired but balding, and a hard little pot belly strained his shirt, but the rest of him was just as lean and agile as a twenty-year-old. And about as mature, too. Still, he was a good partner, so he took it from the top, one more time. "Eric Sturmen. Thirty-five, address on Portside, antiques dealer. Worth a tidy bit, all of which is going to charity. No connection between him and—"

"Judith Edmonds, Judy *Altfall*, recently divorced, ex-husband a jackass. Was going to visit her sister, left early and took the scenic route." Talbot, sad-eyed and blond as a golden retriever, ran a hand over his buzzcut. It was getting too long.

"No connection," Louie repeated.

"No connection we can *find*." Annoying, but he had to say it.

"Maybe he was out looking for antiques." Louie snorted.

Talbot tented his fingers in front of his nose. It helped to bat this back and forth, and it also helped that the Homicide floor was relatively quiet at this hour. Everyone was either out getting a bite or pounding some pavement. Or, like Callahan and Ramirez, at a scene. Spring fever, everyone got antsy, and the casualties rose. "What, old concrete? When was the last time that end of the county got a revamp?"

Louie wagged his eyebrows. They hadn't got the 'balding' memo, and were luxuriant enough he could probably grow them out and do a comb-back. "Probably the last time Captain got laid."

"Or you. So. Freak storm." Talbot held up a finger. "Strangers." Another finger. "This Sturmen fellow got a call from a number we can't trace. Tells his boyfriend—"

"Hate crime?" Louie theorized. "Goes to meet someone, gets beaten up and dropped off? Looking to flag down the minivan…"

Talbot pressed his fingers against each other a little harder. "That's assuming. Altez said he didn't seem too upset. Just had to go, be back in a bit." Altez was the boyfriend, a little Argentine number with big brown eyes, a boyish-smooth face, and a long crop of black hair. He looked like a greyhound, all skinny muscle and nerves, especially in the…well, it had to be a kimono he'd been wearing. Maybe he'd been wearing a pair of falsies too, or had implants. Apparently he and Sturmen had been a thing for multiple years.

You saw all types, working this job. And you always had to rule out foul play first. The trouble came when you couldn't rule it out *or* prove it. Those cases left a squidgy feeling in the guts and a tickle in the back of the brain that kept a man up at night.

Louie kept leaning back in his chair. "Can't tell much from the body. Imagine that, getting fried by lightning. And the kids, too."

"Forensics says the kids might have asphyxiated in the car fire." The autopsy photos were enough to make even a seasoned detective queasy. Kid cases were the *worst*. And the mother, her big eyes still and wounded, just staring with incomprehension, sitting on the hospital bed.

"Hell of a thing."

"Yeah." Talbot contemplated the top of his desk, not seeing the phone, the strewn paper, the ancient computer monitor. Budget cuts bit deep these days. "What about the blue at the scene?"

"Coincidence. Sent out to look at that damn stream, from all the runoff. It's on the roster every spring. Same blue is going out in another couple days to check it, too."

Probably hoping he wouldn't come across another burning car down there, too. "The only thing is—"

Louie finished the sentence. They'd been over and over it, and the fact that Louie hadn't sworn at him, even good-naturedly, meant Talbot's partner was just as uneasy as he was. "—how did Sturmen *get* there? It just doesn't feel right."

The boyfriend was ironclad; he'd left ten minutes after Sturmen to go to work at the Cooper Building downtown. Security cams and coworkers saw him all goddamn day, until he left at seven PM. According to everyone, they were a relatively happy couple. There hadn't been any suspicious financial crap, either. "Car's still in the parking garage. Maybe Sturmen got jumped on the way there, taken out to the End?"

"That would be one sick fuck, transporting someone out that far."

Which would mean premeditation, but any asshole smart enough to subdue and transport someone would know the river was a better choice for sinking remains instead of dropping them in the middle of the road. Not to mention that Sturmen had been alive when lightning hit him, or so the M.E. swore.

Talbot's stomach growled. It was time for lunch. "Rendezvous? Something he didn't want his boyfriend to know?"

"Leaving the car meant he wasn't going far. Unless he was picked up, yeah, but it's not on the cameras."

"Sturmen's exes all amiable. Business fine, no rivalries anyone can think of." Talbot ran down the list of their interviews mentally, again.

"Captain wants this one stamped and forgotten." Louie's sour expression said he understood that particular request. Still, it nagged at both of them.

Nothing to hang anything on, just a freak accident and something in Talbot's bones telling him it wasn't *right*. It stank to high heaven, he just couldn't figure out how. "Boyfriend won't be too happy about that." The little guy had been calling every day to check if progress had been made.

"What'll he do? Christ."

"Come on." Talbot shook his aching fingers out. "Let's get some lunch. Chinese sound good?"

"Sure. You gonna let this one go?" Louie didn't sound hopeful.

"No fucking choice, unless we get something else."

Talbot's phone shrilled, his cell buzzing in his pocket at the same moment. He winced, reached for the handset, and punched the button. "Homicide, Talbot speaking."

Louie's chair thudded down. His partner stood, pulling down his sleeves and picking up his suit jacket. It was sunny, but the wind held a promise of more rain.

A few minutes later, Talbot slammed the phone down. "Chinese is gonna hafta wait. We've got another one."

"Fuuuuck," Louie groaned, with feeling, and as usual, Talbot agreed.

Chapter Twenty

Reasonable Imitation of Class

Half of winning any game was the waiting. Marlock, his hair slicked back and his London Fog nicely belted, saw them step through the market's doors from his perch in the coffee shop every grocery store had to have nowadays. He blended right in, between the good coat and the shiny travel-cup meant for fancy java and environmental snobbery. He took his time, taking a last swallow of cold acidic brew he'd made in the hotel room this morning, folding up the *Wall Street Journal* and tucking it under his arm. Getting a basket and cruising for a little lunch would keep them in sight, and he would be even more invisible. Most of the customers were high-end granola housewives; there was a lot of tanning-bed orange and expensively done white-bread dreadlocks. Agnes the blonde looked like she belonged here, between her sleek hair and her yogic thinness; Jude, even in what was obviously her sister's jacket and a pair of jeans, did too.

It was amazing, really. You could always tell when someone came from class, even if they were dirt-poor when you met them. It was something about the way they carried themselves, especially women. Even on limited budgets, they made different choices. Something as simple as how they used a soup spoon, or tied their hair in a messy chignon instead of a ponytail. The way they tucked their knees aside when they bent to retrieve something, the way their hands moved. Years ago, you could tell them by their gloves, even if they only had a threadbare pair.

After so long, he could give a reasonable imitation of class, if he had to. It was still kind of pleasant to see a dark-haired woman who had been born into it push a shopping cart in her sister's wake. Or it would have been, if Marlock hadn't been able to feel the pain leaking out of her. It was a steady low grumble, a seashell-sound, an almost-audible vibration. That lucent clarity moved with her in an egg-shaped field, and the normals around her leaned unconsciously in her direction. The sister actually had to nudge people out of the way, and cast a few eyeroll glances at some of the oblivious shoppers.

Jude kept her head down. She very carefully did not look at any of the strollers, or the toddlers settled into grocery carts and buckled carefully. Each time they passed a kid, though, that vibration would pulse a little.

Jesus. What was the sister thinking, dragging her out like this?

Don't get all excited, Press. He drifted, not too close, not too far. Nobody gave him a second glance, but his Mark was a quivering warmth on his back, reaching around his ribs. She was putting out a *lot* of glow, and he was soaking it up even at this distance. Didn't look like she was burning up, either. He was itching to get a look at her Mark, see if he could find any hint of Sturmhalten in it.

It didn't really work that way, but he still wondered. Had she figured out something was going on? Finding a tattoo you were *damn* sure you hadn't had before a near-death experience was bound to trouble you, even if you were used to weird occurrences. Grier had often lamented there was no way to tag potentials before they triggered, and even Marlock had looked at him like he was insane.

That was part of the reason he left the intel sector to work this case. Ends justified means, sure, but only to a point.

Fuck that morality shit. You've got a job to do. After a while, even a cold, calculating bastard could have some qualms. If you didn't mind doing dirty work, you had to at least make sure it was in service to something reasonably clean, somewhere down the line.

The thought that he really didn't like Phil Grier or America enough to keep killing for them was a little troubling, but easily pushed aside, because the girls were at the checkout now. There were a couple bottles of wine in their cart, too.

Which one of them drank the red, or were they equal-opportunity imbibers?

There was no self-checkout. He could have convinced the card reader it had an approval, but he paid in cash instead. Saving his energy was probably the best choice. He counted out the bills just as he noticed a manager, shirtsleeves flapping, hurrying for the automatic doors. Tagging behind him was a round, unsmiling woman in blue, and her worry and self-importance pinged in Marlock's head like bad radar.

Fuck. The idiot probably can't blend in.

It didn't matter, though, because the girls were just about finished. He smiled at his own checker, vaguely aware of the niceties he was mouthing. Something about the weather, and being able to get into the office late. *Come on. Delay the sirens a little.* The busybody in blue had probably twigged onto little Davy, and if the manager approached the asshole he'd have civilian casualties. Which, you know, eggs and omelets. But still, it would be *messy*, and fresh dead bodies were the worst.

The girls headed the way they'd come in, and Marlock followed. Nice and easy. Rain had retreated, one of the quick changes spring did in this part of the world, and sunshine glared through the glass doors. The next few moments were critical.

The blonde kept talking. Something about asparagus not really being good until April anyway. Jude shrugged and said something Marlock didn't quite catch, because the sound of the automatic door whooshing covered it. Agnes—Christ, he bet she *hated* that name—laughed, a pretty, bannering sound tossed into late-March sunshine.

After that, it happened fast. A yell, a sharp ear-rattling crack, and Marlock dropped his shopping bag, blurring forward. A car alarm began to blare, and Agnes's bright new-penny laughter turned into a terrified yelp.

Jude Altfall turned. She saw the familiar form sprinting for her, and instead of flinching or cowering she stepped forward, letting go of the cart and darting in front of her sister. Then she stopped cold, arms spread a little, as if she dared the motherfucker to shoot her. A little disdainful *come on* motion with both her hands, but Marlock plowed past her, crunching into Dave's midriff. The gun skittered away, not firing again, and the portly manager—his nametag read *Douds*—stepped on Dave's hand. The big man howled, a cheated sound, and Marlock snapped a glance back to see Jude, haloed in rich golden spring sunshine, gazing down upon both of them with the Madonna-like serenity of shock.

Chapter Twenty-One

NOT WORRIED

A DARK-HAIRED blur tackled Dave Edmonds, the rotund front-end manager from the Laurel Market vomiting to one side with his nametag knocked askew, her ex-husband spewing spit as he screamed, a silent cop car bouncing into the other end of the parking lot, almost taking out its transmission with a high nasty scraping sound. They apparently didn't know you had to coax your car up *that* hillock.

Dave's eyes rolled, his face a reddened, distorted mask. Jude stared, caught in a glass ball of sadness and resignation. On some level, she'd been expecting him to show up with a gun for a long while, and maybe it would even be for the best. Aggie was behind her, Jude knew that much, and the only clear thought in Jude's head was *keep Aggie back there, Dave found a gun, well that isn't a surprise, he always threatened.*

"KILL YOU!" Dave yelled, but it looked like the other guy had him pinned pretty tight. "YOU

CUNTWHORE BITCH KILL YOU KILL YOU!"

Cops piling out of the car. Sirens getting louder. The manager shouting, wiping his mouth with the back of his hand. One of the cops stepped in the gently-steaming pool of vomit.

Nervous people threw up, it was just what they did. How would you clean it up out here? Cat litter, and maybe a hose? It would have to be the non-clumping kind of litter, right?

Jude blinked. The world went away for a few moments, a blankness filling her.

When she opened her eyes, they had Dave handcuffed, one cop all but kneeling on his back as he thrashed. The dark-haired businessman who'd tackled her ex-husband stood to one side, his hands up until the cops sorted out he was an almost-hero. Aggie, her arm over Jude's shoulders, making sounds Jude heard from very far away. *Oh my God, are you hurt, are you…Jude, Jude look at me, look at me…*

The businessman ran his hands back through his dark hair—a little too long for the office, really, but maybe he was in a tech startup or something. One of the cops found Dave's gun and stood near it, glowering.

"KILL YOU!" Dave kept yelling, and Jude's head was full of a strange buzzing. It was part of his style, the sonic assault as well as the physical, and sometimes Jude had felt this curious detachment, something inside her curling up and letting him rage outside. It was pretty much the same as everything in her turning sideways. Thankfully, though, there was no searchlight inside her head. She simply…observed everything, and felt only a mild surprise that she hadn't, after all, been shot.

They bundled Dave into the police car, and his thrashing tantrum made the car's springs squeak. He threw himself back and forth, still screaming, and Jude heard her own voice giving soft replies to the cops' questions. One of them had a very red face and an aggressive blond buzz-cut, taking up a spraddle-legged stance that blocked her view of the car. "You're safe, Miz Altfall. He won't bother you no more."

Oh, that's a lie. But you probably don't know it. "He always got out before." She said it kindly, apologetically, knowing it wasn't this guy's fault. The engine of the car holding Dave turned over, coughed, and started; she could still hear his muffled cries. One of the cops either had a cell phone or a slim digital camera, and was taking pictures of the gun where it lay in the crosswalk.

Will they have to listen to him screaming all the way to wherever they're taking him? This wasn't really like Dave, she decided. It was more like him to wait until he knew for sure she was at Aggie's, then break in and find her sleeping. Like he had at Ash Lane, but that wasn't breaking in because he still had a key, right? That's probably what he thought, that it was his house and he owned everything in it, including Jude.

No, this was not like Dave Edmonds *at all*.

"I have a copy of the restraining order—" Aggie, digging in her purse with one hand.

Jude wondered where the groceries were. It didn't seem to matter much. Nothing did. Her skin felt funny—cold, and loose. Everything around her was too bright. The pavement was doing strange things under her feet.

The hero, the front of his coat—London Fog, and a nice one, she saw, in the same mad way she had noticed the weave of the hospital blankets or the pattern on the linoleum in the ER after she'd left Dave—damp from the pavement, had strange eyes. Very dark, iris blending into pupil. Maybe she was hallucinating, because something dark also moved around him, and it reminded her of things she didn't want to think about.

Like lightning, and shadows, and the van rocking under gale-force winds. *Who's behind him?*

The businessman kept *looking* at her. He pointed at her, too, and the cop questioning him craned his head to look.

"She's going into shock," Mr. Businessman said, and Jude tried to shake her head. She was *fine*, really she was, she just...

What just happened? She stared across the parking lot. Where was the grocery cart? *Why am I still alive?* Car roofs gemmed with leftover raindrops glowing in the bright sunshine, and the world went away again into a gray cloud.

"Jesus—" Aggie said, in a very small faraway voice. Everything was telescoping away. "We need an ambulance, we need a—Jude? Jude, honey, open your eyes. Jude, talk to me."

I should be dead. Jude found that she'd shut her eyes, and willed the gray blanket to surround her. Thank God nobody was hurt.

"No you don't." Someone talking, breathing on her ear. "Don't go checking out now."

Her left hip twitched, as if something was tugging on the skin. Maybe the bruise there...

The same queer, flat, inner certainty that told her the searchlight in her dreams was a malignant white finger spoke up. *That's not a bruise, Jude.*

"Come on back, doll." A funny twist to the last word, as if he said it a lot. "Everything's fine."

Her eyes opened, sleepily. She blinked up at him. It was the businessman.

His irises were really quite dark, and the olive of his skin tone was almost sallow in the spring sunshine. A proud nose, and his dark hair didn't look like it was supposed to be slicked back. There was something cruel around his mouth, and a shiver went through her. Circles under his eyes, fresh-shaven cheeks, and eyebrows that needed some taming. His hand was warm, even through his driving gloves.

Who wore those, anymore? And how could she feel it through her sleeve?

"I can't believe you just *tackled* him." Aggie pulled at Jude's other side, everything in her tone shouting *I'm grateful, but watch it, buster.* "Where did you come from?"

"Just getting my lunch for later." He let go of Jude's arm, slowly. "They drove over it. Shit."

He sounded so bereft a laugh rose like a burp in Jude's throat. Everything around her came back into focus. *Jesus.* "I'm sorry," she offered, dismally. How many times had she said that after Dave found fault with a dish or a server's attitude and began ranting in a restaurant? Or when he made those horrible jokes in front of her increasingly fewer friends? Or when he showed up at an elementary school, polite at first but then raving and frightening the entire office—except Principal Saffron, probably.

This is in a whole different league, Jude. Then again, thinking *what would Principal Saffron do* was probably a really good coping mechanism. Probably better than anything Jude could come up with on her own.

"Sorry? For what?" The guy glanced over his shoulder; brake lights on the car carrying Dave flashed briefly, jewel-bright against the sunshine. "He had a *gun*. Why are you sorry?"

There was no way to explain, so she simply shrugged, helplessly.

"Ex-husband," Aggie said. "Hers."

"A real winner." One of the guy's eyebrows lifted a little. Jude's knees felt strange—not weak, but like they might bend backward, perhaps. Like they weren't quite fashioned like everyone else's and had only just realized it.

"That's why he's ex. I'm Aggie, this is Jude."

"I'm Pinkerton." He shook hands with Aggie, and for once she didn't sweetly smile and drive her brutally short nails in. Which meant he hadn't tried the macho squeezing game.

"Miz Altfall?" The blond cop bustled over as an ambulance nosed into the lot. "The EMTs will want to check you guys. Can I get the number off that restraining order?"

"I'll take care of this," Ag muttered. "You, Mr. Pinkerton. You want to take her over to the EMTs? Don't argue, Jude, you've gone transparent." Just like that, Bossy Aggie appeared, and began *arranging* things.

The businessman—Pinkerton, what a name—curled up one corner of his mouth in a smile that tried to reach his eyes but didn't quite make it. "Is she always like that?"

If she thinks she can get away with it. "Since she was born." Jude tried not to feel bereft. Now she had to make small talk with a bystander who'd had his day ruined by Dave. "I'm sorry. He...God."

"It's not your fault. But I guess he probably tried really hard to convince you everything was." Usually, people sounded awkward when they said something like that, meant to comfort her or just smooth over the embarrassment. Mr. Pinkerton just sounded...neutral.

I don't want to talk about this with a complete stranger, thanks. "Are you all right? He had a *gun*." The woozy gray feeling began to come back.

"He did. Looked like a .38." As if it was no big deal someone had been waving a firearm in the Laurel Hill Market parking lot. "He threatened you, too, and squeezed off a shot. Attempted assault, attempted murder, deadly weapon involved, resisting arrest—a whole laundry list of charges."

Thankfully, that gave her another subject to throw into the small-talk arena. "Are you a lawyer?"

"Hell no." He had her arm again, a soft touch cupping her elbow. The grocery cart, forgotten, had bumped against the curb, hopping up and beaching itself.

A sudden desperate desire to get everything in the car filled her. "I have to…look, can you help me? Just to get the…get everything in the car. The groceries."

He stared at her for a moment, as if she'd just asked to fly to the moon. Her eyes felt like they were swelling, and the world wavered for a moment. The tears did not brim over, but she still wiped at them, angrily, and wished her hip would stop twitching. It didn't hurt, it just felt like the skin had started moving on its own. Kind of like the eyelid-pop Mom got when she was tired, passed down to Aggie and Jude.

"You're worried about the groceries?" That hiked both of his eyebrows up, and loosened that cruel mouth of his a little.

"Not worried." It didn't matter if he looked at her like she was crazy, Jude told herself. She hitched her purse higher on her shoulder, and stepped away from him. Maybe the thing on her hip was healing. "There's nothing wrong with me. You tackled him, *you* should go get checked out." With that done, she put her head down and started for the cart. It was a cool morning, but the sunshine would spoil the perishables. Best to get them into the trunk, especially since she and Aggie might be here for a while.

Cops always took forever.

He had longer legs, and got to the cart before she did. "Okay. Where's your car?" He pulled it back, neatly freeing it from the curb, and his expression was set as if there was something distasteful about three brown paper bags and a gallon of skim milk.

Maybe he's vegan. It struck her as oddly funny. She didn't dare laugh, but at least shoving down uncomfortable hilarity made the tears go away.

Chapter Twenty-Two

BAR ANY DOOR

WITH A FEW minutes' work you could bar any door, even a flimsy hotel piece-of-paper-shit. There were some times, Marlock told himself, that dragging any furniture that wasn't bolted down into a barricade and settling down with a bottle of Macallan was not only a good idea, but the only reasonable response to a clusterfuck like the one shaping up here.

He'd lifted the grocery bags carefully into the back of her sister's Volvo, and every time he'd looked at this new Marked, even just a sideways glance, he felt a stab in his anemic conscience. Paper-pale, obviously hovering near shock, she was focusing on unimportant trivia. And he'd enabled it, partly because he'd set the whole situation up, and partly because that clarity, that *heat*, spreading out from her felt like a warm bath on his own Mark. She didn't seem to notice the greedy gulping, even when she took the empty cart and walked away, leaving him at the open trunk. Which he stupidly closed, as if it made any difference.

She even put the cart all the way in the return, carefully stopping it before it banged into the railing at the end, and turned to check on him, shading her eyes against the spring sunshine. Chestnut and gold in her messily pulled-back, curling dark hair, her wrist bent at just the right angle to look fragile, and the thin stupid voice masquerading as his conscience piped up again. She reeled him in just like an expert playing a fish, or a planet snaring a passing moon.

Then her eyes rolled up and she swayed, and that was how Marlock found himself half-carrying her to the ambulance that had just thrown its doorwings open and was looking for any injured. They put her in the back and took her blood pressure, threw a blanket over her and put her on oxygen. She didn't resist, but whenever one of them said something about going to the hospital she moved as if she would get out of the damn ambulance, and Marlock didn't blame her.

She must have seen enough of the hospital to fill her to the back teeth.

The sister was formidable. She smiled sweetly, but there were terrier teeth behind that neutral lip gloss. The cops were falling over themselves to make it easier on the nice ladies, and Marlock barely even needed to present ID and a subtle bit of pressure to keep them from wondering too much about him.

Preston Marlock should have been happy. He should have been fucking *overjoyed* that it had all worked out so neatly, and the secondary suggestions he'd implanted in the goddamn ex-husband would kick off any time now. Instead, he was in a cheap hotel room with a bottle of amber alcohol and the sneaking suspicion that everything was going to get tangled beyond repair.

Why? The woman was a prize. A new Mark with enough power to light up both coasts—not only was she the perfect bait for the Skinner, but she could *also* solve a few more of his problems. As long had he had some contact with her, he wouldn't have to feed his own Mark in…other ways.

There were more nasty bumps on the horizon though, ones Jude Altfall couldn't mend. Like the familiar, unwelcome, itchy feeling at his nape that somehow, somewhere, someone he knew had been alerted to his presence. He hadn't plugged into the locals except Lawson, but one or two of them must have figured out Sturmhalten had been murdered by now, and they had to suspect someone would come around asking questions. The old man wasn't precisely social, but it was known he had one or two friends.

That was manageable, though. The idea that maybe someone else, someone Marlock hadn't spoken to in two years, might have a zero on him was enough to put him on edge. He always used to be able to tell when Grier had an eye in his direction. Working with someone so closely, you got to anticipate them.

If the agency was in town, they would trip over their own feet *and* his. Not to mention they might decide, again, that the Skinner was interesting enough to *study* instead of ventilate. There would go Marlock's vengeance. The thing he was living for, right?

He decided not to use any of the hotel glasses; they wiped those fuckers with Pledge and putting stank-lemon in a Macallan '64 was one thing he could do without on his list of sins. So it was his travel mug, rinsed carefully with a bottle of distilled water and dried with a few unbleached paper towels, that accepted a few inches of God's amber grace. Whereupon Marlock wedged himself in the most defensible corner of the room and took the first sip.

After the third slow sip he loosened his tie, and let himself exhale, long and slow.

Why are you doing this? The last phone call before he'd gone dark. Grier, the asshole, had almost sounded desperate. *It's outside your brief, Press, come on!*

Handlers and controls were always thinking you could put limits on chaos, like bumpers in a bowling alley. When you got on the ground and started tagging and bagging, or got sent into a slaughterhouse just to find out what was inside, you were disabused of those notions pretty goddamn quickly. Chaos spread like oil on water, that was why they called it *entropy*. It just kept going.

There was no good reason for him to think the agency was in town. Just a feeling. Which was worrisome enough, but not the real problem.

The real problem was, he didn't need a top-up. An hour with Jude Altfall, and not only was his Mark sleepy-full, but the rest of him was suffering uncomfortable sensations. Like a pale, emaciated ghost of a feeling that could be described, roughly, as *guilt*.

You couldn't afford that kind of shit. Not if you expected to stay loose and operative in enemy terrain, and bait a killer into showing himself.

Christ, Preston, she just lost her kids, you pointed her ex-husband at her—that gun was in your hand, really—and now you want to traumatize her some more by using her in a trap?

Well, he didn't *want* to, but he was *going* to. Jude Altfall, with her pretty nose and wide, dark, wounded eyes, might end up on the pile of dead bodies the Skinner sat on top of, whatever Mark she'd gained scraped off her body by the sick fuck. What would he do with it? Who knew? Did it matter?

Press could start going down the list, maybe. Even getting drunk wouldn't stop that recitation once it got started. He wouldn't even start with the one he'd been brought in on; he'd dug up what he believed were the first victims himself, before he left the agency.

Wanda Krysizak, twelve. Josh Ames, seven. Imri Aman, nine.

"Fuck," he breathed, and took another sip, exhaling to feel the burn all over his tongue, in his cheeks, down his esophagus, and through his nose for good measure. The Krysizak murder was the first one he could find, and it had been a messy one. The Skinner got excited with some of the female Marked. He'd started with children, probably because they were easier to overpower *and* likely to be disbelieved when they acquired a Mark. A kid's first instinct would be to hide the strange, small symbol, especially after a traumatic trigger.

"Stop it," he told himself. "Don't start that shit." Not when he was so close to catching the bastard.

It didn't matter. The names kept going inside his head. He knew, when he got to the end, he would be forced to add Erik Sturmhalten to the list.

Soon, probably, he'd be adding Jude Altfall's name, too. Unless he was fast, and lucky, and the agency stayed out of his way.

Preston kept drinking. The names kept coming.

He wasn't going to be able to sleep. But with his Mark warm and satisfied after being close to Jude's, it wouldn't matter.

The rasping pain of that recognition, he acknowledged bitterly as he kept whispering the rosary of murdered souls, was one thing he couldn't bar *any* door against.

Chapter Twenty-Three

LOOSE ENDS

BEING IN THE high-ceilinged, large, but oddly womblike collection room usually soothed him. No windows, but the arched ceiling was frosted glass and on sunny days the warm glow was soothing indeed. At night, the vault was dark velvet. Glass cubes, each with the acid-free bed for its carefully treated, irregularly shaped treasure, marched in neat rows with enough room for him to wander between in any direction. A labyrinth of regimentation and chaos, a reminder to stay on the path and also to look at the scenery. They hummed uneasily, a mostly inaudible vibration that could lift goosebumps up a modern Neanderthal's back.

When the collector bothered to think of the vast mass of human-shaped waste that had no idea of the true state of the world, *non-evolved* was the best term he could think of. The markings, by their very existence, were proof of evolution and of God's smiling upon the chosen few at the same time. It was a shallow man indeed who could not imagine the two coexisting. The stories of angels and miracles—or demons and supernatural vengeance—were merely symptoms of superstition.

Sometimes, as he strolled among his captive treasures, hearing their dissatisfaction and longing rise and fall in the deepest part of his ears, he thought about the beginning. When you had more money than sense, you went to extremes. Skydiving. Hang gliding. Deep cave-climbing. Safaris. Sooner or later, the odds caught up with everyone.

The ultralight had stalled, earth and heaven changed places, and he'd awakened amid the wreckage with his ribs on fire with pain and the snake, drawn by his body heat, rearing on his chest. Its wedge-shaped head swayed gently, tongue flicking to check the air, and he had put his hands on it, while the rattling buzz of its warning filled the shattered teacup of his skull. The hot beautiful wire of strength flooding him, as the snake writhed against his grasp, and the sudden *knowledge*. He hadn't doubted his sanity for a moment. There wasn't room for doubt when the entire world told you, in no uncertain terms, that you'd been chosen.

The media had called it a miraculous escape. His retreat into philanthropy was credited to the accident. Really, he had simply found things he liked better than making money, although chasing lucre was necessary to pursue his other goals. The hunt took more and more of his waking thoughts, more and more of his energy.

He found himself before an empty glass cube, resting his right hand on its top. Temperature, acidity, humidity all controlled, but the bed was empty. He preferred to watch his quarry until the larger markings retreated into smaller, more powerful ones, but he also took a select few just after they had appeared. This cube's treasure had belonged to a foul-mouthed boy fond of lightning, but the collector had wanted the grander prize, the more powerful one. Sacrificing the lesser to gain the greater usually worked—nothing was so effective against one of them as a marking of their own kind. Fascinating, really, all the different forms they could take. He wouldn't have believed it before the accident.

The skin along his ribs was raw. Refining the process had involved quite a few missteps, but now his method was assured. Trial and error had granted him this collection, the markings upon the preserved hides moving slightly as they sensed his presence. Quick work with a blade, a dip in the solution, then the merciful slash across the throat if the subject had not displeased him.

Those who struggled, or who cost him more effort than he judged them worth, were not so lucky.

But now…now, something was different. This particular subject had somehow robbed him, and perhaps had transferred all that lovely power. All that *potency*, wasted on a non-evolved stranger.

A stranger who might have seen the collector's face. He grimaced, then smoothed his expression, patting at his hair with his left hand to make sure the thick blond mop was still in place. Bad enough to have one's acquisition stolen, but stolen by someone who could never understand the *use* of such a gift…well. It was enough to infuriate a lesser man.

His fingers drummed against the top of the case. The hole in his collection wasn't precisely gaping, but it irked him.

Mr. Bell would bring him whatever information could be gleaned after dinner. Then, the collector thought, he would decide. Of course, he might have to tidy up the loose end. It was upsetting, to think someone had seen his face at the moment of his non-triumph.

Erasing the witness might be necessary. It might even, he reflected, be satisfying.

A few moments later the vault was empty, and the collection of Marks on their beds of stolen skin quieted.

Chapter Twenty-Four

THUM-THUMP

JUDE STARED AT the brown, sagging lump. "Why am I doing this, again?"

"Because it will help you feel better." Aggie smacked a different lump of clay onto the wheel. "And because I don't have a pug mill yet. When I do, it might deprive my work of *authenticity*, but until then, I need some of that wedged."

"This is your thing, not mine." Jude poked at the clay with one fingertip. It was cold, and damp. Two scraped-clean wedges stood on the work table, and Aggie bent over the wheel, the floorswitch under her experienced foot.

Her workroom was chilly, probably because it was part of the old garage. The kiln projected outside, a tax-deductible monster since Aggie was technically a corporation. There was precious little profit—even at the ridiculous prices her ware sold for, she only worked until she broke even, then took a vacation and sold backstock until the next quarter. It kept her out of trouble, she often said with a gleam in her hazel eyes, daring Jude to mumble something under her breath like a big sister should.

After the divorce, Aggie had even floated the idea of Jude working with her. *We could pay you a salary, you know, to make it official. And that will solve daycare hassles, and—*

We would kill each other, Jude had remarked, but what she really meant was *Dave knows where you live*.

Aggie might have even clued onto that. In any case, Jude had lucked into the job at the big-box store across the freeway. She had been making it work, goddammit, until that morning with the pink slip in with her paycheck. Which she still hadn't deposited. She had her doubts the bank would take a rain-soaked, smoke-smelling scrap of worthless paper.

Only half the LED overheads were on; the big window on the side of what had been a third of the garage was crowded by a box hedge ruthlessly trimmed level to its bottom, because Aggie liked natural light. The door out to the short gravel path to the greenhouse was open, letting in the cool juicy scent of grass that had just started growing again and the faint good smell of leftover apple blossom. Jude glanced habitually at a kid-sized worktable Ag had put in for Ess and Sy, scraped clean but with their last two efforts—Essie's coiled vase and Sy's improbably complex, lopsided "dinosaur" figurine—standing forlorn. The immediate panicked *where did they go, they're too quiet* kicked in right on schedule.

Then, right on schedule too, the sick thumping her stomach, and the bitter taste in her mouth.

"Come on, Jude. Help me out. Try it." The wheel hummed, and Aggie bent, her hair falling to one side and her pretty face a picture of concentration. Jude watched the curve of a cup flower under her sister's competent fingers. It looked easy, but Jude's own efforts had produced nothing but lopsided mutations.

The only thing I ever did right was my kids. And I didn't even do that very well.

She sighed, tore off a chunk of clay about the right size, and began wedging.

Slice the clay along the wire, smack one half down and the other atop it. The important part was the throw—just hard enough, an efficiency of effort forcing the air bubbles out. Cut in a different direction, slap it down again. Over and over, getting into a rhythm as soon as you could and checking on each cycle to see how many little air pockets remained.

Slice. *Thum-thump.* Slice into three, *thum-thum-thump.* The last piece always sounded different than the others. Jude tried to empty her head, to think of nothing but the clay.

It didn't really work.

Dave's face, contorted with hatred. The sound the gun made as it skittered off along the pavement. Lucky it hadn't gone off again, lucky the first shot had been pointed at the roof of the grocery store. Lucky someone had tackled Dave. Lucky to be alive.

Lucky, lucky, lucky all over. Except not. She was thirty, her children were dead, and she had miraculously survived *twice* now. Bucked the odds.

At least I'm rational enough to know God is a monster, if He exists.

Their tiny hands, the half-moons of minuscule fingernails. Essie's expression the first time she tasted baby food instead of breastmilk. Simon's face squinched up as he filled his diaper—for the first few months, no baby is smiling at you, they're just happy to have let a load out. Then the first time they *look* at you, a whole other person behind those small eyes, moving those perfect little fingers. They had been so different, too. From the moment they had slid out of her, shrieking with indignation, they had been like night and day.

Like her and Aggie. Had her mother ever felt that marveling wonder, that sense of utter terror? Tiny little lives depending on you for *everything*, even their own breath. So small and fragile, and the world was so harsh.

Thum-thump. Cut. Slap and slap again.

Something she'd never had a chance to ask her mother. It was probably good her parents were both gone; they didn't have to see this.

Simon's sunny chortle. Essie's seriousness; the smile that would light *her* face was like dawn, gradual and disbelieving at first, then wider and wider until complete, incandescent joy had won out over her solemnity. The first time it snowed, and Simon burst into tears as the cold kisses touched his face.

Thum-thump. Thum-thump.

Other memories crowded in. Both children crying, Essie silently and Simon at top volume, snot streaking his lip and bubbling from his nose, Dave slamming the front door and her head throbbing because he'd bounced it off the floor again, her stomach aching because he'd kicked her, and her children had seen it.

Her son needed to know, so he asked *her*, because Mommy was where the answers came from. *Why is Daddy mean?*

Hesitating, caught between a pandering but safe lie and the dangerous and hurtful truth, but Essie had a quick answer. *Shh, we're not supposed to talk about that.* Hugging Simon, her daughter's face almost an old woman's, and Jude jolted into the realization that she was not protecting them enough.

Not protecting them at *all*.

Thum-thump.

The clay was nice and homogenous now, but she kept going. She stopped slicing it, and instead picked it up, ramming it back down on the worktable's canvas cover. The thick-legged, heavy-topped table quivered each time she did. Lift. Smack. Lift. Smack.

Again. And again. The table shuddered, and someone was making a low sound under the thrum of Aggie's spinning wheel. An animal-moan, full of pain and shame and inarticulate hatred.

Sometimes, in the deepest, blackest corner of her soul, she had wished she didn't have children, that she could just pick up and leave Dave. Just drop everything, get a backpack and go, instead of being nailed to a man you'd thought was a prince in shining until you figured out princes were mean, petty shitheels. Then, as always, the sinking, sneaking suspicion that somehow it was something about *her* that had turned a prince into a shitheel struck, sinking its fangs in.

The searchlight trembled inside her head, but Jude let out a sharp short sound, and it shattered, batted away along with the awful sense of being watched.

Thum-thump. A low, keening, hurt noise, an animal's moan.

It was her. *She* was making that noise, and it only got louder as she kept lifting the clay and slapping it down, little bits fraying at the edges and breaking off, smearing onto the table. Eventually she wasn't even lifting it, she was simply slapping and awkwardly punching, while that noise grated up from her chest.

Who was the bigger monster, her for daring to dream of freedom from her responsibilities, or God for answering the wish?

She couldn't tell, and after a while the sound shuddered to a stop and Jude found herself staring, entranced, at a sadly abused splattering of clay all over Aggie's nice clean worktable. Her hands hurt. Her neck hurt, her teeth gritted against each other, her ribs and shoulders and back and legs hurt. The pain was all through her, and this didn't even scratch the surface of it.

Her left hip was warm, though. It was about the only damn thing on her body that *didn't* ache.

She stared at the patterns of torn clay, her body aching and paradoxically hollowed out, a cup to pour a whole pitcherful of black tarry guilt into. Throwing a cup or a bowl was about building walls up around nothing, Aggie often said. It was the empty space that made it usable.

Nothing in her would turn sideways now. It had all come home to stay inside her chest.

"Go get cleaned up," Aggie said. "I'll be up in a few."

Jude should have stayed to clean up the mess she'd made. But she dropped her head and obeyed, shuffling for the door as if she'd grown elderly in just the past hour. The humming of the wheel followed her, burrowing into her head and her cracked, bleeding hands.

Chapter Twenty-Five

Rewards

THE MARKET WAS behaving oddly, and the collector could not find the reason. Nevertheless, he was tranquil, letting the information stream pass through the monitor and away. So many times, the problem was one of *proportion*. A combination of rising high enough to see the entire stream and carefully combing its source to see which pebble was diverting it required a relaxed, intense focus.

Which was broken by a quiet chiming, just as he lost fifty percent on Conphris shares for the day. A tiny downtick in the overall scheme of things, but still irritating, *especially* as he was not to be disturbed during the last few hours of his chosen markets.

He toggled the switch. "Yes?" No warning in single, silken word, but any of the staff would *sense* his displeasure. Or at least, they should. He was goddamn well paying them enough.

"Sir." Mr. Bell's quiet, careful voice. "I believe you'll want to see this."

The irritation mounted, but he closed his mental hands around it and imagined the creak-snap of a tiny hyoid under them. When he could be gracious again, he touched a different switch, and his office door unlocked with a soft heavy sound. "Come in. Would you like some coffee?"

"No thank you, sir. I apologize for the disturbance, but I think it warranted."

We shall see. "I trust your judgment, Mr. Bell." It wasn't quite a lie.

The tall, spare, dark man accepted the compliment with a grateful nod. He had a desk just outside this particular office; the secretary in this building was a blowsy blonde in the outer room whose efficiency nevertheless exceeded expectations eighty percent of the time. It was, when dealing with female employees, the best that could be hoped for, and her slavish devotion was matched only by the other four head secretaries in his other four offices. Especially the Hong Kong branch; *that* middle-aged minx had never married, and he was sure she cherished a film-worthy crush on her distant round-eye employer.

Mr. Bell, perhaps sensing he was on thinning ice, got straight to the point. "The witness was attacked by her ex-husband in a grocery store parking lot. A bystander tackled the ex, who had purchased a Smith & Wesson .38—"

"Saturday Night Special," the collector murmured.

Mr. Bell nodded. "The police report was flagged by our systems. I requisitioned and reviewed the surveillance footage from the grocery." He opened an anonymous, heavy-duty file folder, and extracted a printed sheet. "This is the bystander."

The collector gazed at the piece of paper. He glanced at the information flowing through the three large monitors to his right again, and noted the markets were behaving again, several shares he had anticipated rising smoothly in a flurry before another close-of-session. Slightly pleased, he returned his attention to the picture. Mr. Bell had framed the face nicely, even though it was in grainy black and white.

The same long nose, almost-cruel mouth, and dark hair. The man in the picture had shaved and slicked his hair back, but he was still recognizable. "Now, sir," the collector said, musingly. "Yours is a familiar face."

Mr. Bell did not speak just yet, though the collector could tell he had more. He studied the face intently for a few moments more. No, there was no question. It was *him* again. The ghost dogging his footsteps. "Any information?"

"His identification was for a Scott Pinkerton, thirty-four, investment counselor."

"And deeper digging met a blank wall." The collector drummed his fingertips on his glass-top desk precisely once each. Same old story. This ghost had a multiplicity of identities, all leading nowhere. Which was very interesting.

Was that a slight smile on Mr. Bell's bland face? "Yes. Except for one very interesting ping on the cross-tracers."

"Oh?"

"It led me to a blind hole, sir. But the dimensions of the hole were visible."

A momentary irritation at being expected to decipher an underling's riddle surfaced and was pushed savagely away. Bell was a marvelous asset, and it was not the man's fault the collector was on edge. "Which means?"

"I believe this man may be wanted by a government agency or two."

"Which ones?"

Now Mr. Bell handed over the remainder of the file, anticipating his employer's desire for it at that precise moment. "Some very well-funded ones, sir, but I cannot tell more. I believe it may be advisable to use contractors in this situation."

The collector made a slight *tsk*ing noise. It was a good suggestion. It could muddy the waters, or it could bring him the witness with a minimum of fuss and personal danger. He flipped through a few pages of neatly written observations he would go over at leisure later, and found a picture of the witness, along with a short printed biography at the bottom of the page.

An unremarkable curly-headed woman, after an unremarkable bad divorce, driving her rusting minivan along an unremarkable road. And stealing a very valuable piece of *his* collection, or possibly just surviving the frittering away of said valuable piece. Sturmen's personality would certainly point in the direction of him stubbornly wasting all his power instead of giving it to a collector who had *clearly* overmatched him in wits, cunning, and strength, even if said collector had a weaker marking grafted to the skin of his ribs.

He had been looking forward to wearing Sturmen's marking so *much*.

"Very well," he said, as if Mr. Bell had spoken in argument. "Engage the contractors, then. No trace can lead back to us, Mr. Bell."

If his employee was offended at the implicit mistrust of his ability, he did not show it. "Of course not, sir." He waited for a moment, to see if the collector had anything else to add.

Which, this once, he did. "If this goes well, there will be a reward."

Mr. Bell betrayed no craven groveling or greed. "Yes, sir." The words were brief, gracious, and grateful. "Thank you, sir."

What would I do without you, Mr. Bell? Still, it never did to trust too thoroughly. He had selected and trained more than one assistant, and…rewarded…each one in turn. Once this matter was successfully concluded and the collector's questions answered, it could be time to consider a changing of the guard, so to speak. "Thank you."

He watched the man leave, and turned back to the markets to find they had recompensed his foresight and patience again. Money was so *easy*. It was a good thing he had more complex affairs to keep him occupied, or he might grow lazy.

And that, the collector mused, simply would not do.

Chapter Twenty-Six

JUST HIS LUCK

MARLOCK'S NAPE WAS itching like a sonofabitch, and a ghost of a hangover still clung to his liver and temples. It had been a while since he'd gone into the burrow, and he couldn't even kid himself that it had just been a temporary dip in a pool of self-loathing. No, he'd gone under and started swallowing, and as a result, his time window for secondary contact was melting *and* he felt like a pile of dead dogshit.

Go over it again. "Pinkerton." He put the rental car—a nice late-model Taurus, silver-gray and with about as much pickup as an anemic goose—into park and blew a long exhale out between pursed lips. "It's Scott, Scott Pinkerton." *Because I'm a regular old gumshoe, when I put my mind to it.* "I have a copy of the police report, and…I just wanted to make sure everything was…all right."

The key was going to be projecting concern, not creepiness. Hence, the flowers—not a cheap bouquet, but not a top-of-the-line either, just daisies and a couple sunflowers. There had to be a reason she'd put sunflowers in the graves. "Well, you know…he could have shot me too. I didn't really think that much." Just the right note of self-deprecation, a little boyish charm. And here he was, practicing his lines in the car like a stupid kid before a high school date.

The timing was right, too—late afternoon, but not late enough to get dark. Westering sunshine dipped the end of the street in gold, lined each budding branch. Street parking instead of going up the driveway—was that right? He frowned, thinking about it. On the one hand, the Taurus looked respectable enough. On the other, pulling right into the driveway might make them nervous. Might make them feel blockaded.

No, he decided, street parking was best. It was what Scott Pinkerton would do. This ID was already burned, since the cops had it, but it wouldn't raise any flags and he might as well use it while he was intersecting with the girls. Secondary contact, time to gain a little trust, and maybe ensure their cooperation later if shit got ugly.

It sounded neat and clean-cut. Only he was sure it wasn't going to end up that way.

It never did. Especially when you were nervous and hungover.

Walking up to the front door instead of sneaking around the back was an uncomfortable experience. Their driveway was a semi-circle, but one half of it was barred from the street by a large wood-and-wrought-iron gate probably older than either Altfall girl. There wasn't a fountain in the middle, but there was a garden space, crocuses poking through a mat of mulch and opening shy cups to the cool breeze. Someone down the street was mowing whatever postage-stamp of yard had survived the winds of rising property values, and the vivid tang of just-growing-again grass mixed with thick, reddening sunshine and the tall, severe farmhouse towering over him to produce a weird feeling. Not nostalgia, because he'd never even dreamed of living in a place this big.

He kept trying to find a word for the feeling as he edged up the driveway, keeping himself to a steady, polite pace, the flowers held like a shield and his expression settled into the thoughtful, hesitant almost-worry he'd practiced in the mirror before knotting his tie and setting out on this stupid, high-risk gamble.

The sister's Volvo was tucked to the side under an arbor covered in vines just beginning to green. Its hind end watched him just like the garage doors did. Marlock kept going, steadily. Usually he could slip right into a cover and method-act his way through. Normally it would be fine, just one of hundreds of operations, a goddamn cakewalk.

He was almost to the pair of doors above the steps. They were doozies, a big red-painted mouth. He would bet one half was permanently bolted shut, and judging by the wear on the sturdy rubber welcome mat set in front of the right side, he'd win the bet hands-down.

What the fuck am I doing? Clutching a bunch of wilting green stems, dying when they were cut and now dying even faster because the hand holding them sucked at all the energy it could find to keep itself going.

There was a name for what he was doing, and it wasn't intel. It was pure fucking stupidity, and greed. He wanted to get close to Jude Altfall again, and feel that warm, delicious buzz. He'd bet it could even flush his hangover away. And he wouldn't have to worry about taking too much. She *radiated* the fucking energy, just like the sun. She didn't even notice.

An onlooker would notice him slowing, however, and finally stopping a good six feet from the front steps. Cracks in the driveway teemed with moss, but it was obvious Cheerleader Agnes had someone come out and pressure wash every once in a while. The place was in good shape.

Did the cheerleader like sharing space with big sister? They seemed pretty tight.

Stop fucking around. The best thing to do was about-face and double-time back out to his car, and toss the goddamn flowers in the gutter on the way. Tuck the car somewhere nice and out of sight, then come back and find a spot to watch the house because his nape wasn't even itching anymore, it was full-on cold, insect feet scraping down his back in rivers. Pretty soon his gut would start to tighten, right before the tango began.

Trouble, headed this way. Hadn't he hoped for that? It didn't feel like cops, and he was pretty sure the cheerleader didn't have a stalker. It would be just his luck to save both Altfall sisters from douchebags in a week, and find out the Skinner had struck again somewhere else while Marlock was spinning all four tires with his thumb up his ass.

The doorbell was surrounded by a wrought-iron thing like a jester's head. You had stick your finger in the grinning mouth to ring it.

It would serve him right, he thought bleakly, if the metal jaws closed with a snap and he lost a phalange tip.

No answer. They were probably gone. Maybe he was lucky, and nobody was watching him being a complete, utter, total shitheel of a moron.

Footsteps. The door shuddered, and Marlock froze.

Chapter Twenty-Seven

An Optimist

"Now this is funny." Louie looked up as Rick trudged into the office. Blunt fingers scratching at the right side of his potbelly, Louie had a splotch of chocolate sauce on his tie. The man couldn't keep his clothes clean if his life depended on it.

"What, your face?" There was no heat to it. Talbot, wearing even more of a hangdog expression than usual, hung his coat on the hook glued to the side of the metal file cabinet. One of these things the damn thing was going to pop off. "Goddamn coffee."

"Right there." Louie pointed at the desk, and his chair squeaked menacingly. "As if I didn't know Betts loaded you up before you left home. Remember the Sturmen case?"

"Mhmnn." One cup of coffee was never enough, even if Betty Talbot made it thick enough to eat a spoon. She'd been in the Marines, and her cooking remembered it. Every day he was goddamn grateful she hadn't divorced him yet, but this morning had been double.

"Guess what the ex did." Louie was freshly shaven, but he was in hiking boots. Looked like he expected footwork today, goddammit.

"What ex?" Talbot blinked. There were yellow sticky notes all over his half of the desk. God *damn* Louie, did he have to do that? Voicemail worked better, for fuck's sake. But Louie couldn't let a goddamn phone ring. He always picked up.

"Edmonds." Patiently, as if he wasn't rolling his eyes at Rick's slow start. Hare and tortoise— Louie jumped ahead, Rick plodded. Between the two of them, the close rate was good, but sometimes Rick's stomach lining informed him it wasn't optimal to keep going on this way.

His wife called Louie *the other woman*. Kind of funny, especially the way Betty's mouth twitched at the corner whenever she said it to irritate him. It was what passed for a gentle ribbing in the military, probably. You could even find a brand of it in the station breakroom. Flipping shit got to be a habit, even in a marriage. "Oh, *her* ex. Okay." He grabbed his coffee cup—a silver canister Louie rinsed for him every morning, since the fucker always got here first. Maybe when he retired, he'd slow down. "Whafuck, then?"

Louie scratched at his belly again, but meditatively. "Showed up at a grocery store with a .38 and tried to shoot her."

"Woman's having a hell of a week," Rick observed, a little ungraciously. "Did it work?"

"Nope. Bystander tackled him, Copes and Messinger brought him in for booking. Real winner, a psych case."

"Huh." Rick took a gulp of coffee-and-creamer. Louie didn't understand, even after five years, that *coffee* did not need *milk* or anything even *approaching* dairy products.

"Screaming. Frothing." Louie's eyebrows were up. "Hell of a thing."

Rick looked at the whiteboard between the file cabinets. Sometimes they taped up a map on the opposite wall and pinned locations there, trying to figure out patterns, movements. Pictures of victims or witnesses sometimes made it up on the wall, and there were a few sketches. John and Jane Does, cold cases, their flat gazes a terrible accusing weight. "Grief, maybe."

"Could be." Except wife-beating assholes didn't really grieve for anything but their own fucking inconvenience, Louie's tone said plainly. They often went after their kids, too. You saw a lot of that, on the force.

Rick took another hit of coffee. He could *feel* the blessed caffeine soaking in. One of these days he was going to tell Louie to can the fucking dairy. Or nondairy, whatever. "Woman should buy a lottery ticket." *If it wasn't for bad luck, you'd have no luck at all.* That was the old adage, wasn't it?

Louie snorted. "An optimist. Sturmen's boyfriend called again."

"Shit."

Louie's thoughtful nod said he concurred completely. He leaned back in his chair again, and the mournful squeak it gave rasped across Rick's last nerve. Homicide was beginning its morning stretch-and-yawn; murder didn't take many nights off. "Full moon coming up too. Gonna get crazy."

"Yeah." Rick shook his head. "We're gonna have to close that one, Lou. It stinks, but we gotta."

"I know." Louie's chair thumped down on all four legs. "Maybe he flew out to Bath End."

"Yeah." Talbot stared at the file folders stacked next to the sclerotic monitor. Budgets were tight, and people kept killing each other. Every day, it was an avalanche of shit, and they were shoveling with teaspoons. "Maybe he fucking did. Let's do the paperwork, I want to catch the next asshole."

Chapter Twenty-Eight

The Situation Warranted

AGGIE SWIRLED THE oil in the wok, a deft wrist movement, and flicked the hood fan on. The flame under the wok was steady and blue, and Jude concentrated on matchsticking the carrots, the santoku's handle familiar and weighted precisely right. It was nice to cook in the old kitchen again, she supposed. Nice to hear the grumble of the fan, nice to hear the soughing of the gas stove, nice to glance at the window and think *Dave is in a holding cell for tonight, at least.*

It felt like a reward, and it shouldn't have.

The onions went in, and Aggie began to hum, her usual cooking melody. The Forbidden Rice was already done in the cooker—little purple beads, supposed to be reserved for Emperors. Essie might eat a little stir-fry, but she wouldn't touch strange-colored rice. Simon would happily chow down on the rice—purple meant fun, in his lexicon—but he would never touch anything with onion in it, and

Aggie was of the opinion that you could not have a stir fry without a bit of onion and red pepper.

It was too quiet. Two little noisemakers should have been sitting at the breakfast bar, coloring or playing with toys while Auntie and Mommy cooked, firing questions at both adults, elbowing each other, chattering about their day at school. The glass of chilled white wine next to the scarred cutting board was another reminder—she wouldn't have let Aggie pour it for her, since she didn't drink, and *especially* if she had to drive home.

Home. A funny word. This was Aggie's house. The apartment would be cleaned out and re-rented by the end of the month. Everything from said apartment, except her clothes and the smoke-filled, wet ruins of her purse, was now in a storage unit over on Crell Boulevard. The house on Ash Lane had gone to Dave in the divorce; if he went to jail it would go to the bank. Years of hard work and sleep deprivation, all erased in moments on a winding county road.

The carrots went into one of the prep bowls. Aggie was mad for prep bowls. *Mise en place is everything*, she always said. *And so are scrapers.*

Spatulas, Jude would always mutter. Her sister was always buying *those*, too. One of these days, the cabinets wouldn't be able to accept any more prep bowls, and there would be an explosion.

Scrapers, Aggie would reply, with an eyeroll. *Spatulas are different, Jujube.*

Funny how you could stand in a room and have a whole conversation with a memory. Jude made sure the bean sprouts were rinsed, and the water chestnuts. Aggie was in full-on experimentation mode, and woe to anyone who interrupted her flow.

"Get ready," Aggie half-sang, crooning to the wok as she squirted a little more peanut oil in. Sometimes she cooked with the blues on, sometimes with Cash, Cline, and Williams. When she was in the mood to make tabbouleh, it was gamelan music. *They just seem to go together, don't they, Jude.* Tonight, though, it was a cappella night in the Altfall kitchen.

The doorbell rang, its Westminster chimes floating through quiet halls, picked up and echoing in the kitchen as well.

"Oh, *fuck*. Jude, can you—"

"Just keep your eye on the wok," Jude replied, and laid the knife down. The sink was full of plastic chopping mats and other bowls, and the mixture of onions, garlic, and fragrant chili paste would linger against the countertops and fill her nose tonight, sleeping in Granma Lefdotter's iron bed. Down the hall, past the living room on the left and the study on the right, the big drafty foyer alive with good smells and the tinkling of the chandelier, her feet cold even through Aggie's old pair of wool and leather slippers.

She went on tiptoe to check the peephole, and for a moment she thought it was Dave. A man, with a fistful of yellow and white, and her heart leapt into her throat and began pounding so hard she gasped. Then she recognized something in the way he stood, and a curious floating sensation took over.

Two deadbolts and the chain, her fingers still shaking from the adrenaline shot, and she cracked the door a little to see the hero from the parking lot. He'd half-turned, as if expecting a chilly reception or maybe just thinking they weren't home. He had a bunch of daisies and sunflowers in one hand. She couldn't remember his name, and how the fuck had he shown up at Aggie's door?

She peered at him, and a long awkward silence was only broken by Aggie's full-volume beginning of *Waltzing Matilda* in the kitchen.

Dark eyes, and his proud nose. His hair was still pushed back, but not as aggressively slicked as yesterday's. Same very good coat, but his shoes weren't wingtips. They looked like hiking boots, but that was probably more comfortable after a hard day at the office. Crow's feet at the corners of his eyes, and a shadow of stubble—he'd bristle up early.

And he was holding *flowers*.

"I, uh." His Adam's apple bobbed. "I have a copy of the, the police report. And I don't want to be creepy, I just thought…I thought…" Was he *blushing*?

Jude's mouth was hanging suspiciously open. She closed it, and glanced behind him at the driveway. Maybe he'd parked on the street, which was odd but…well, if you didn't want to be a *complete* presumptuous turd, you wouldn't take up someone's driveway. The kind of guy who would throw themselves on a man with a gun might also park elsewhere.

"I can understand if this is a...a bad time," he continued. There was some message in those dark eyes, one she couldn't quite decipher, and all of a sudden a dinner alone with Aggie, each of them studiously avoiding looking at the empty chairs at the table where small people should be, seemed like the least appetizing thing in the world. Sitting at the breakfast bar because neither of them could face the thought of the table and wouldn't admit it out loud seemed unappealing as well.

Jude gathered herself. "Oh. Yeah. Do you like stir fry?"

He blinked, twice. Opened his mouth, closed it, finally found a word. "What?"

"My sister's making stir fry. Come on in." She stepped back, trying for a welcoming smile, and maybe wasn't doing too bad. Something about it must have been off, though, because the man held out the flowers, stiff-armed, as if he was allergic to them.

"I can't. I just wanted to make sure everything was okay. You seemed pretty upset."

"Yeah, well." *My ex-husband was going to shoot me. Have you just figured out I'm a trainwreck instead of a distressed damsel?* "The situation warranted a bit of upset."

Aggie's warbling cut off. "Who is it?" she yelled from the kitchen, and for some reason, the hero winced.

"Here." He shoved the flowers at her. "I didn't mean to interrupt. I'm sorry." Then, of all things, he turned around and headed down the driveway.

Jude stood in the doorway, her hand dangling limply. Daisies and sunflowers. Cheerful flowers, and she sang the song to the kids all the time, about the eyes looking up at the sun and the sun smiling back, a world full of flowers all because of a smile.

I don't want to think about it. The pain came, right on schedule, and a persistent sense of something strange was holding its clawlike hand.

She watched him make a hard right at the end of the driveway and vanish past the wall, and her hip was twitching again. The bruise-mark wasn't getting any lighter.

"Okay," she told the driveway and the crocuses, as the sun dipped and daylight dimmed. "Now that's a little weird."

When she shut the door, she even hooked the useless chain on, too. Shaking her head, she retreated down the hall. "Aggie, you're not going to believe this."

And I don't even remember his name.

Chapter Twenty-Nine

WELL-PROVIDED FOR

OF COURSE ERIK would have liked the building, it was a big steaming heap of Art Deco. *The twenties,* he had often said. *What a time to live.*

The interior was redone, probably with Erik's not-so-subtle guidance, carpets in just the shade of tasteful blue he'd prefer and sconces lovingly restored, not to mention the scrollwork on the grille-door to the lift.

Marlock took said lift, pressing the top button with a slight feeling of misgiving. You had to have a key to go that high, but it was no big trick to jiggle the lock when you had a Mark full-up from the agony and sweet pouring light of one Jude Altfall. There was no lift attendant, and that was a mercy. History plodded on, and he didn't have to deal with yet another oblivious civilian shit-scraper.

This was going to be unpleasant. Maybe it was penance for daring to walk right up to her door. *The situation warranted a bit of upset.* A half-rueful almost-smile, those big wounded eyes, and her hair all messy curls. The clarity leaking from her—did she invite strangers in for stir-fry every day? He should have been overjoyed. He should have gone right in and done his best to charm both of them. It would have made everything easier.

Instead, he was here, in a cranky antique elevator, and the farther it rose from the ground the more his stomach balled up. It didn't help that he knew he'd have to do this sooner or later.

The lift slowed, the inner doors opened, and he didn't have to walk through the tiny parquet-floored receiving-hall and knock at the only door on this level. A penthouse, just the place for watching storms. How many times had he knocked on that reinforced door and heard Erik's irritable *"Komm, du Bastard,"* from the other side?

No, Cat had heard the lift, probably, because she stood in the open door, her broad hands working and her Adam's-apple bobbing up and down. She had the thick, fringed lashes most women would kill for, and her legs weren't bad. You could see a slice of one through the opening of the battered, quilted silk kimono hanging on her shoulders, and a nasty jolt hit Marlock's solar plexus just as her deep, nasty-yellow grief socked into his Mark.

It was Erik's dressing-gown. *What a civilized custom*, he'd said. *Yeah, you can scratch your balls with ease*, Marlock had replied.

"Press." Catalina's familiar, throaty voice. "*Dios*, I thought..."

Did you think it was him coming back? "Hi, Cat." He'd stopped dead, just outside the lift. It wouldn't go down again until he closed the grillwork. "I, uh…"

"You're about to ask if this is a bad time." That faint hint of an accent, her chin rising a little. Defiant, maybe. You could see the shadow of her other form, heartbreakingly young in a polo shirt and jeans, and Marlock could hear Erik's benevolent tone. *Go eat your hormones, Cat. The men are talking.*

"Yeah, well, I never show up with good news." As she had pointed out endlessly the last few times he'd seen Erik.

"At least you're honest." Blinking furiously, she stepped backward, catching her bare heel on the kimono's hem. Erik had been much meatier. Taller, broader at the shoulder, but both of them were narrow-hipped. "I thought you would come."

"He was my friend." He heard himself say it, numbly. It was hard to think with that delicious stew of emotion rasping along his Mark, and a familiar feeling bit him in the guts again. It wasn't precisely shame, but it was close.

"Oh, *bueno.*" Catalina's voice broke, but she just stalked angrily for the kitchen, leaving the door wide.

Inside, it was Erik all over. High ceilings, hardwood floors buffed to a high gloss, plenty of space on the walls framing certain objects. A Japanese silk-scroll painting of a heron standing in water, spearing a fish with its beak. A reproduction of El Greco's *St Philip*, an original Klimt full of gold and blue no auction house or museum had ever seen. The lugubrious met the ornate and stopped for a drink in Weimar, that was Erik's interior decorating, and Marlock had listened to him expound on philosophies of aesthetics in mud-filled trenches while shells exploded overhead all through the dark years of victory and defeat alike.

Two years ago the old man had seemed much more relaxed. Cat was the reason. *I fear I must marry, as every old man who wants some comfort.*

Christ. Even the furniture here was painful, because he remembered Erik picking the pieces out or telling him the provenance of every stick. *Kiln-dried, you know. It's best.*

Press swung the door shut, locked it. Bent to take off his shoes, and that was when it really hit him. Erik would never again sniff at the plebes who tracked street-trash into their homes. He'd never give a long-suffering look and point at the small cabinet where slippers for his few guests were kept. The man who remembered the trenches, who was there that Christmas night when singing rose to the frozen sky and no crack of gunfire disturbed it, the man who knew what it was like to live Marked and slowly realize old age wasn't part of the package anymore…

A good chunk of Preston Marlock's own life was gone, because there wasn't anyone else left alive who remembered it.

So, Press padded into the huge flat in sock feet. Opening the cabinet was just a step too far.

The floor plan was open, living room and library/salon space on either side of the kitchen, small breakfast nook tucked alongside and the dining room behind antique folding doors on the right that were almost never closed. Two bedrooms on the left, each with a restored Corbreba oak door carefully hung and glowing with beeswax. Small stands held statuary, and the only thing missing was fresh flowers in every cut-crystal or marble vase.

Catalina had probably thrown them all off the balcony. The flowers. Maybe the vases too.

The kitchen had been redone, Corian countertops mimicking sandalwood, warm oak cabinets. New sinks, and the balky gas range had been replaced with a sleek top-of-the-line model, probably for a professional kitchen if its size was any indication.

There's no reason not to live well, Press.

The sideboard in the dining room was open, ranks of bottles inside glowing like jewels. A bottle of water-clear schnapps stood on the new countertop, and Cat was reaching into one of the new cabinets for another glass. Her hand trembled, and her grief held a darker, roasting edge now.

Fear.

She almost dropped the French cut-glass tumbler. Set it on the counter with exaggerated care. Her eyes were red-rimmed, those lashes matted, and her cheeks were hollowed out. Her lips were pale without the heavy carmine stain she dabbed on with a tiny brush from a tiny bottle.

It was, by far, the most feminine she'd ever looked.

"I'm not here to hurt you," he finally said, awkwardly.

"As if you could." But the tremor in the words said differently. Cat knew. Not everything…but enough to make her cautious. "It was another one, wasn't it. Another one of *you*."

There wasn't any point in lying. "Yes."

She poured a generous measure for herself, another for him. He would have preferred Scotch, but oh well.

"And?" she persisted. She very carefully kept the counter between them, so Marlock had to lean over a bit and reach to get his drink. Playing it safe.

"And I'm looking for the motherfucker that did for him, Catalina. When I find him it's not going to be pretty."

Some of the tension went out of her shoulders. She sagged, and it occurred to him that physical violence wasn't the only thing she was afraid of right now. "And no," he continued, "you're not in danger."

A quick restive movement. She'd played *futbol* in her youth, and it showed. "You're sure?"

Coward. But who wouldn't be, if they knew what the Marked were capable of and had no goddamn carnivorous tattoo-thing on their body to protect them? "I'm sure. And I know Eric's left you well-provided for. So there's that."

She had gone rigid again, and stared at him. A muscle in her cheek twitched. The glass in her hand squeaked a little as her fist tightened. "*Conchudo.*" Her accent thickened.

"I don't mean it badly." Marlock lifted the glass, took the schnapps all in one bolt. It was a hell of a dram, and it burned all the way down. Erik would have sniffed at him for swilling like a pig. He could drain off all that raw emotion of hers, so she could get some rest. It might even be a kindness.

Erik had hit him with a lightning bolt a couple times, just to see what had happened. They'd both been drunk on this very type of schnapps. The crackling bolts had tingled pleasantly. It was the only time in his life Marlock could remember laughing so hard his belly hurt.

That seemed to finish everything up. They stood, on either side of the counter, as the now-soulless husk of a beautiful apartment echoed around them. Marlock studied Cat's face. She stared at his nose, blinking every once in a while when the salt water welled up. His own eyes were grainy. The liquor sent up a fuming burp or two, but he grimly held onto them, exhaling politely through his nose.

If Erik was alive, Press wouldn't bother keeping a belch or two in. Playing the prole to the Junker aristocrat, a game they both enjoyed.

Cat poured herself another round. She tilted the bottle toward him—it was older than her by a long shot, for fuck's sake. The label was bleached past recognition.

He shook his head. "Cat?"

"What, *pelotudo*?" Daring him to be an asshole, to say something cruel. He could. Hell, if Erik was here, both of them could start in on her, and finally Catalina would leave the room and slam the door. Why she stayed for it was anyone's guess. But there was also the times she cuddled against Erik on the couch, her dark head on his shoulder, and the old man had seemed…

Content.

"I...you know we can do things." He took a deep breath. "Do you want to keep knowing? I can make you forget." He wished he hadn't refused the bottle. Getting drunk again tonight would be a blessing, but he had to go back to the goddamn Altfall house once it got good and dark.

The itching at his nape just wouldn't let up. Trouble coming, and here he was, fucking around with something that had nothing to do with his mission. He couldn't even be a decent man here, in front of a grieving little bitch who had turned Erik's last years into relatively happy ones.

"*Dios*," Catalina managed. Sounded like a scared little boy with a rock in his throat. "*El me amo*. You won't take that away."

"I won't, I wouldn't. I was just *asking*." He regretted taking his shoes off, turned on one sock-clad, slippery heel, and headed for the door, carefully not glancing at the bank of windows looking over the city, the glimmer of water in the distance. Dusk had dropped over sunset like artillery smoke over a burning city, purple gathering in corners and shadows turning darker, deeper. The two chairs were set there, both battered leather recliners older than Catalina as well. He remembered Erik having them delivered in New York one smog-choked afternoon, and fussing at the workmen to have them placed just so.

Now we may sit and talk.

He was at the door before Catalina spoke again. "Marlock." The blurring of the vowels, the burr in the R. South America had been kind to Erik more than once, and this little piece of it…well, she'd made him happy. Or as close to happy as a Marked bastard like Erik Sturmhalten could get.

"*Senora* Sturmen." It really cost him nothing to say it. Maybe that was kindness, of a sort.

"He left something for you, too. In the will."

Goddammit, Erik. Practically immortal, but he kept his legal identities updated. When you had a Mark, you never knew. Practically immortal didn't mean immune to disaster.

"Keep it for me," Marlock tried to make it sound like a request. "When I kill the fucker that did for him, I'll collect."

"*Dios mio*," Cat muttered again. "*Gracias, senor. Que el Diablo te lleve.*"

"He already did," Marlock said, and grabbed his shoes. He didn't bother to put them on, and just as he shut the front door, he heard the tinkle and spatter of breaking. She'd hurled his glass after him, too.

Yeah. His throat ached, his shoulders were rocks, his neck was a rusty iron rod. Everything on him hurt.

That was about as well as it could have gone, really. Now he had other work to do.

Chapter Thirty

Package Pickup

IN THE MIDDLE of the night there was a faint scratching sound, like a cat politely asking to be let in. The workroom, full of the scent of wet clay and a thin subtle perfume from the spray of blowsy apple-blossom in a vase on one of the worktables, was otherwise silent. Most people were really careful about locking their outside doors, but they forgot garages were easier to get into than anything else. Once you were in, hardly anybody locked the door between the car-house and the people-house.

The tool was very simple—a vacuum seal, an arm, a little locking diamond point. The skritch-scratch weakened the glass, and a quick, deft wrist movement would pop it free. The man in the dark stocking cap waited, secure in his professionalism, glancing at the garden behind him with a quick catlike movement. Sometimes he even thought of himself as feline, a creature of night, sliding through small spaces, all velvet until it was time for claws.

This was not his usual job. He might not have taken it had the reward not been considerable. The only tricky bit would be getting the package to the van outside, but the syringe in the small case at his hip would help with that.

The other inhabitants of the house were expendable, but if the package went undelivered, the fee was canceled and the half he'd already received due back. He couldn't decide if the hiring party was an amateur or just overconfident.

The wind rose, rustling trees that hadn't stretched their fingers out yet. Upper-middle-class neighborhoods like this didn't have any real security to speak of, except dogs. Even a fucking parakeet could turn a job sour, but he was assured there was nothing in the house but the package and the expendables, of which there were only supposed to be *one* but it was best to plan for plurals.

While he waited, he slid his warm gloves off, and broke out the latex ones. You could even take *those* babies on a plane, claim you were allergic or something. An old drinking buddy of his used to swear he'd once finished a job with a pair of them, knotted together, around a choking expendable's throat. It was probably bullshit, but the story was hilarious, especially if he did his impression of the—

Instinct brought his head up. The man in the stocking cap half-turned, scanned the garden again. No floodlights out here, even. It was like they were *begging* for a home invasion, or something. Nothing out of place, just inky shadows he'd recently slipped through, the gravel paths all silent now. It took time and patience to move silently over gravel, but it helped when it wasn't fresh. Weeds cushioned a lot of the noise.

He went back to the suction cup and the diamond sharp, feeling the bite as it pushed into the glass. Breaking windows was *messy*. You wanted something quiet, something not easily detectable—sometimes, he even broke the window from the inside on the way out, just to give whoever came across the scene a headache. When he dropped off the package, maybe he'd head to Macau. You could pick up work around the casinos there, boring but enough to keep you in skittles and poontang.

He was almost ready to make that one, small, wrenching movement to pop a circular piece of glass out—big enough he could reach carefully through and unlock it, there wasn't even a sensor on this door, for Christ's sake—when instinct made him hunch his shoulders, again. It was stupid, there was nobody there—

Except someone *was* there, a shape made of blackness with hard flat glitters for eyes, and the only reason the man in the stocking cap did not scream was because the muscles of his throat and the flat pan of his diaphragm refused to work. His eyes squeezed shut, and clawing pain ran down his right side, a strange, bowel-loosening, *draining* sensation.

"Well, hello, friend," a soft, persuasive, male voice breathed in his ear. "Let's go back to your van and have a chat, shall we?"

Chapter Thirty-One

It's Vertigo

THE BODY WAS beginning to stink. They went quickly once they were drained, something about the cell bonds weakening. Marlock sat in the driver's seat, measuring spaces on the wheel between his fingertips. To the coroner, it would look like this guy had a heart attack. If Marlock wanted to be extra careful, he could run the van off the road and hike back to town.

He hadn't decided yet.

Half an hour to dawn. The sky was graying in the east, and a hush through the treetops said all the birds knew it. He was gambling that no other shady asshole would be creeping up to the Altfall back door. Because this guy, sure as shit, was *not* the Skinner. A wiry blond military dropout with a couple barely contained drug habits and a certain reputation for transporting body-sized things from one place to another, this man had taken the job through an anonymous deep web exchange; that much he had told Marlock between gasps. He didn't know why someone was willing to pay a hefty sum to have a girl transported to a motel and photographed, because it didn't matter. Maximum deniability and maximum insulation of the paying party.

In this case, said paying party was pretty certainly the Skinner. Marlock had taken what information he could from the gibbering, broken man before mercifully turning his lights out.

Now, Marlock had his gloves back on. It would be a simple matter to prop the asshole in the driver's seat and send it down the short but very steep edge into the chuckling stream below. It answered one nagging question—the Skinner wasn't sure if Jude had a Mark or not, which had some interesting ramifications he didn't want to think about right now.

He should get moving, he decided, because the next steps were very clear.

Get Jude. Find the Mark on her. Use it as bait. Draw the Skinner out—because once the killer knew for sure she had a Mark, he would want to attend to taking it off personally. The question of what he *did* with them was one Marlock had decided not to think about a long time ago. Knowing how serial killers operated, they were probably trophies. Stood to reason there would be an unhinged bastard with a Mark of his own out there to match the unhinged fucktards without.

There were unhinged assholes everywhere. Just look at *him*, sitting in a van with a dead body and preparing to dangle a civilian in front of the Skinner.

He knew, before he even reached for the lock, what he was going to do first.

After the stink in the white van with its maroon stripe down the side, the predawn air was bracing-sweet. His feet made small noises on the pavement. The road snaked along the side of a very large hill, its craggy face just as sheer as the drop on the other side. Marlock tried to imagine driving along, maybe with the radio on low, as if you knew this road and liked it. As if it was pretty, with the greening trees on either side. Even in winter, there would be a sort of stark beauty here. It would give someone time to think, driving along. If you didn't have any peace anywhere else, you might decide on a whim to take it, then drop south and approach Laurel Hill through a tangle of surface streets getting progressively more and more gentrified, rings in a tree stump heading for the core of downtown.

The yellow line was faded, and now that he was out of the van the guardrails looked a little rickety. His eyes adapted, pupils swelling, the road clearer and clearer.

There was still a scorch mark. Marlock's skin tingled all over, faintly. *Two* scorch marks. The one where Erik must have been standing, and a long, fractured zigzag leading to a larger but paler one, where the heat of the burning minivan had been intense enough to mark the concrete.

Marlock stepped directly into the smaller one. The chill was only because it was an early, early morning in spring, he told himself. It wasn't because he was standing where a...

Might as well say it. Where a friend died. Erik was old-school.

It had been Sturmhalten he'd gone to when he left the agency two years ago. They had talked all night while Catalina slept, in the rambling way of men who had seen both war and peace together, and found nothing much to recommend either. Erik was having a jealous fit over Cat and some young waiter, and the anger portion of that night had been Marlock taunting him about it—and Erik taunting him in return. *Can't fuck a woman without killing her, can you, Press?*

No shiv went in as deep as the truth could. The anger was a gate to get through, and they did it just as they always had. Afterward, he told Erik what he was going to do.

I'm going to hunt this fucker down.

Do you know why? Erik had countered.

"Yeah," Marlock murmured, his answer from long ago. "Somehow it got personal."

How many years since he'd gotten the news? *Can the Ripper hunt. We're sending you overseas. There are other threats that need your attention.*

The hell there were. Watching Phil Grier's face as the news came out of his handler's tight, prissy little mouth. Knowing, with a deep, dull certainty, that it suited the powers-that-be to let a killer get away with it. At the time, he'd just been furious. Now he wondered, as he had with increasing urgency over the last two years, if the agency knew who it was, but left him alone for some reason or another.

He hadn't admitted as much to Erik, but the other man would have been an idiot not to guess. Just like he would have been an idiot to go meet this asshole. How had the Skinner lured him out? A challenge? The dueling scars on Erik's face, the thinner scars on his hands as he made coffee.

It isn't age that kills you, Press. It's vertigo.

What were the chances of a potential coming along then? If Erik hadn't thrown his Mark, maybe he would have been able to fight the guy off.

Marlock closed his eyes. He turned around, once, aimlessly. Then, head down and eyes open again, he paced along the fracture-mark to the larger scorch. Maybe that bitter tang in his mouth was *her* grief, *her* fear.

It's not. You know what it is.

He was going to have to take advantage of whatever trust he'd gained from Jude Altfall. He was going to have to deliberately break that trust, and throw her into deep water, hoping he'd be able to get a clear shot at the shark. If she survived, she'd never want to see his fucking face again.

Just add her to that long list of people who don't, Press. Move on.

He scuffed one toe on the scorchmark. That would be the driver's seat. Which meant just behind her, a few feet away…

Sunflowers, falling silently into a grave. Jude, her dark eyes firing, mouthing *go to hell, Dave*. She'd stepped in front of Aggie, too, spreading her arms despite the gun in Dave Edwards's hands. A real Mama Bear, protecting her little sister. How much grief did one woman need, for Christ's sake?

It didn't make any difference. The Skinner was coming, whether Marlock stayed here to babysit or not. He might never get another chance, and then what would every single fucking horrific thing he'd done during the long pursuit be for?

Absolutely nothing.

So it's decided. Pick her up. You can even use this motherfucker's van.

Marlock tilted his head back as dawn came up, birds waking from both winter and night to make a racket in the treetops. Funny how you could find wildness so close to concrete canyons and teeming hives of humanity.

His face felt odd, because his mouth was open, everything contorted. He wanted to scream, but it couldn't get through the iron fingers on his throat. He was a complete asshole, his only friend was dead, and he was about to put an already traumatized woman through hell. The Skinner would probably kill both of them; he was either a powerful Marked or had some weapon Marlock couldn't figure out.

After a little while the urge to howl ebbed. He made a single papery sound, more like a croak than a scream, and that was it.

Preston Marlock headed back for the maroon-striped van, his jaw hardening and his stride lengthening. The birds, taking no notice, continued caroling for the joy of dawn.

Chapter Thirty-Two

Concentration

LATE THAT MORNING, she decided it wasn't a bruise.

Jude squinted at the mirror. It was too damn bright in here, though Aggie said she hadn't changed any of the bulbs. Her head felt funny, probably because she'd forgotten her coffee on the breakfast bar, just left the steaming cup sitting there for an hour while she roamed the house, a weird sort-of-static filling her head. Aggie was in her workroom, and Jude had no desire to join her. She'd made up her mind to do some cleaning, but the mop and bucket was just outside the bathroom door, forgotten as well.

She just couldn't settle on something and finish. Her brain simply…wandered away. The egg pan was soaking in the sink, and Aggie had told her in no uncertain terms *don't touch the stove again for a while, okay? Or any knives. I'm going to have to chip this clean with a chisel.*

Jude, her hair rat-nested because why bother combing it, stood in her bathroom, her jeans unbuttoned, looking at the mark on her left hip.

It looked more like a tattoo than ever. It wasn't a lightning mark, she'd Googled those on Aggie's laptop. Those electricity-maps looked like delicate tree branches, and this mark was dark and definite.

"It's impossible," she told herself. "I'd notice if I got a tattoo. Right? I'd remember that."

That was the trouble, living with Dave—doubting your own sanity was a given after a while. He would have hit the roof if she'd gotten a tattoo, right? After she left she didn't have money to blow on that sort of crap. Plus, the needles...she hated needles. So did Essie.

The world grayed out again, came back. She found herself in the living room, her jeans unbuttoned and the old rotary phone set on their mother's favorite chairside table looking up at her. Was it ringing? Picking up the handle was hard, because for a moment, she couldn't remember where the fuck she was, or even what you said when you answered a phone.

"Hello?" she whispered into the receiver.

Nothing. Not even a dial tone. Because, of course, *that* antique hadn't been plugged in for years.

Jesus Christ. She set it back, gently, as if she was Mom after a gossip session with one of her ladyfriends. When Jude was a girl, she thought it was all one word, because that's how Dad used to say it, all in one breath. *Your ladyfriends*, he would say, smiling, and Mom would mock-bat gently at him with one gloved hand.

What had she been thinking about?

Oh yeah. The tattoo. Her fingers zipped and buttoned, habitually. God. She couldn't keep a thought for more than a few seconds, and she'd left the mop upstairs. Had she even loaded the dishwasher, or turned it on? There was a maid service, of course—Aggie still used the same company Mom and Dad had—but it was ridiculous not to do certain basic things oneself, really. Even Mom had vacuumed before the maids were due, just to be sure.

Mom refused to dust, though, saying it ruined a lady's complexion.

It wasn't a fresh tattoo, either. There was no hint of scabbing. It looked like it had *always* been there. Even the color was strange—way too dark, darker than any ink she'd ever seen. Even kid grocery clerks were getting them now, for Chrissake. Even Essie's teacher had one, a tiny, couth lotus on her slim ebon ankle; Jude remembered glimpsing it on Parents Night under the pantyhose and smiling a little.

Jude groped blindly for the leather couch. It had been in Dad's study, but Aggie liked it out here, where the big living room windows could look over the driveway and the crocuses, the wall and the greening trees. Soon the leaves would be full-size, and the crocuses would have retreated. The tulips were already up, too.

She sank down. The pain came, a sharp stab in her chest, again. That Parent's Night she had been so nervous, expecting Dave at any moment, but Essie and Sy had been overjoyed to show her their doodles, their teachers, their friends. Principal Saffron had casually walked them to the minivan, chatting about this and that, and Jude suddenly realized the woman had been keeping a sharp eye out, too.

Was Dave still in a holding cell? He could probably make bail, and if he did…

God, the yammering in her skull just would not *stop*. She found herself rocking back and forth, slight fidgeting movements. Couldn't sit still, couldn't stand still, couldn't get any thought past the gate, just all over the map. Was this what it was like to have ADD? There was nothing about losing your goddamn mind in the pamphlets Ms. Carr had given her. Except "trouble concentrating." Well, this certainly qualified.

She stared, unseeing, out the window. They still got carolers at Christmas, and last year Essie had begged to go door to door with them, singing her heart out, her solemn face flushed with cold and joy. Jude, mouthing the words with no breath or noise behind them, had shivered and trudged until her daughter got tired, then carried her back, and promised Simon that next year *he* could go, wincing at the thought of carrying *him*, too.

Aggie liked handing out paper cups of hot cider, and…

"Jude?" Her sister's voice, from the kitchen. Another noise, too. Splashing water.

Christ. I think I left the tap on.

"Jude? Honey?"

"I'm sorry," she called, dismally certain there was a lot more than a water bill to be sorry for. "I'm in the living room." Her peripheral vision caught movement on the driveway, but when she looked there was nothing but the crocuses, and maybe she was hallucinating. That would just put the capper on the whole damn thing, wouldn't it.

Who wouldn't go crazy, under all this?

The water turned off. She could *hear* the static-sound of Aggie's worry, and the prospect of having to explain that she just couldn't keep her mind on anything and, by the way, she had a possibly hallucinatory tattoo she couldn't explain, loomed in front of her on a dark wave.

Afterward, she was never quite sure what had happened first—the sound of wood and glass breaking, the sudden burst of bright light inside her head, the splintering jolt against the front door…or Aggie's high, choked, desperate scream.

Chapter Thirty-Three

A Very Bad Day

MARLOCK PARKED HIS rented Taurus a block away, rehearsing different lines likely to draw Jude out of the house. He couldn't drain her, but the syringe from last night's visitor would come in handy. Or he might not have to use it, if he could get her to come willingly. He could invite her bowling. Out for coffee. Out for lunch. Out for a rendezvous at a motel with a murderer. His nape started itching again, and his cell buzzed insistently in its padded pocket. He wouldn't hear the ringer through the buffer sleeve and the padding, and without the buffer he'd drain its batteries without meaning to.

It was Lawson. "Guess what, you spooky sonofabitch."

It was hard work to unclench his jaw enough to speak. "Not in the mood, Johnny Law."

"Not interested in Dave Edmonds?" A rasping chuckle—God *damn* the man, he was going to smoke his way into another set of tumors. Would he call and beg Marlock to pull them out again, or did he just want to commit suicide one stick at a time?

Marlock's nape tingled unpleasantly, the sensation growing. He restrained the urge to scratch. The van from last night was in a tangle of scrub brush just before urban density rose again, at the very last dogleg of Bath End Road. Someone would find it and heart attack would be the verdict, there was no reason for anyone to connect him to it. "I'm about to go into a meeting, Lawson." *About to commit a felony too, if you really want to know. Maybe even more than one.*

"Found him dead in the psych cell this morning. Hell of a thing, his ex losing the kids and him going nuts like that. Had some sort of seizure and swallowed his tongue."

"Tragic," Marlock said dryly, but his heartrate began to pick up. His eyes narrowed, darkening a bit. From here he could see almost to the Altfall driveway.

The hind end of a black van—they were everywhere these days—receded down the street, its brake lights growing vivid as a cloud passed over the sun. There was a whole mess of dark clouds coming in, and Marlock wondered if the residents of this city ever suspected a guy who could remember trench warfare would sometimes stand on the roof of a skyscraper downtown, or the roof of his very own apartment building, and conduct storms without a baton. Just his hands moving and the lightning-glow filling his eyes and teeth.

Do you want to fly, Marlock? Sturmhalten would ask every once in a while, with that crazy twitch of a smile. The answer was always no, but sometimes he'd wondered what it would be like. The power did what the will directed, and once you Ascended a few times, the sky was almost literally the limit if you could shape storms.

Lawson lit another cigarette—quick flick of a lighter, a tortured inhale. "Pillar of the community, everyone's gonna miss him. His next of kin certainly did."

You mean someone gave birth to that shithead? "Oh?" A minivan hit by lightning, a van now resting in the creek, and a black van idling along Jude Altfall's street. *Huh.* He shook his head a little, irritably, his hair a little too long. Time for another trim, if he could fit it into his schedule between breaking a law or two. Or twenty.

"Showed up to identify the body as soon as it hit the morgue, and start the paperwork to take it away. Some cousin from Louisiana." Lawson's tone was hard with suppressed glee. He probably thought he was giving Marlock bad news.

Maybe he was. "Figures." But it didn't. Davyboy hadn't said anything about family visiting, and Louisiana was a ways away.

"Yeah, except now the body's gone. Coroner's throwing a shitfit. Remember that little asshole at the morgue?"

"I do." Marlock didn't like where this was heading.

"He swears—get this—that the body's just vanished."

The van up the street braked, more definitely, as if it had just found the address it wanted. Movement from its side, hidden by the line of oak trees. The itching on his neck became pain, tension spilling down either side of his spine. Jesus Christ. A daylight snatch and grab. High-risk, especially for a team. Were they insane?

Shit. Shit shit shit.

"What, it got up and walked out?" He forced himself to sound casual. "What was the kid smoking?" *I didn't plant anything deep enough to make that motherfucker get up again.* And since he hadn't, that only left a couple other possibilities. None of them were good. Nor was the van, rocking a little on its springs as it unloaded.

"Yeah, well, figured you'd want to know."

"Thanks. Your check is in the mail."

"Fuck off, Marlock. I got eyeballs crawling all over me because I picked the weirdest case of the year to get curious about. Try not to ever call me again." Lawson hung up.

He would have liked to sit and think about this turn of events, but there wasn't time. Either these assholes were amateurs, or they were being very well-paid. Someone had decided to use belt and suspenders when it came to having a look at Jude Altfall. It was an old trick—get a couple different teams working on a contract, with slightly different timing structures so you either wore down your target or had a convenient patsy. Or both.

There was always the chance they'd bungle each other, too. Especially if someone wandering by made a habit of being a spanner in the works.

He didn't have time to worry. Marlock crossed the street at a lope, pulling at his gloves. They came off as easily as ever, and he stuffed them in his trouser pocket. His coat was back in the Taurus, because it would weigh him down, and his outline blurred like clay in running water as his Mark woke up, tingling in double anticipation as he stepped into the blur. There was going to be murder, and he was going to see Jude again.

And these overgrown kidnappers were about to have a very bad day.

Chapter Thirty-Four

GALLOPING INSANITY

IT WAS SO *bright*, like a flashlight in her face. She tried to run, but the best she could manage was an arthritic shuffle. It was a nightmare, her limbs weighed down and the world turned to a cold, sterile glare. Later, she remembered the jarring as her feet slapped the hardwood floor in the hall, her shoulder glancing off the wall and knocking down the daguerreotype of Great-Grandfather Altfall's sternness. Granma Lefdotter swore the man smiled and laughed all the way to the grave, but you couldn't tell it from that fading chemical collection of shadows and lines.

Kitchen. Dazzling light, a vague confusion of jumbled motion, Aggie's hair a bright scarf as she fell, her head just missing the corner of the butcher-block island. Big dark shadows with deformed faces, a sound like popping corn and shattering ceramic at the same time, a sudden chill as outside air poured into the warm kitchen.

An iron bar hit her in the stomach and Jude folded in half, all her breath *whoosh*ing out as if Dave had decided she was being uppity or he'd taken down too many beers. If he just had one or two he'd be friendly—

The world turned over, and Jude found herself flat on her back, her head ringing, her eyes watering, and a grotesque black bugface leering down at her. A crouching man twice her size in black with white splashes—riot gear? Police? The bugface was a gas mask, why would they need a *gas mask* it was ridiculous—

His gloved hand reared back, a tiny glittering star caught in the thick fingers, and she heard another popping sound.

Gun. That's a gunshot.

"*Aggie!*" she yelled, and began to thrash, because the man kneeling above her had his knees braced on either side of her hips, and was trying to jab at her with that tiny starlike thing in his hand. It was a needle, and this had to be a nightmare, it had to be. A hallucination, like the goddamn searchlight.

Thump. A solid meaty sound, Aggie's pained little cry. The man on top of Jude was yanked back, and a smear of black loomed above him. It wasn't another man in riot gear, it was a streak of pure bubbling darkness, and her left hip turned hot.

"I don't think she likes you," someone said, a low velvety male voice, and the darkness had claws. It stretched, and the man was not just lifted but *ripped* upward, the star-thing flying free and smacking the ceiling with a small glassy sound of breakage. More breaking sounds, this time like sticks crunched in half inside cotton padding, and she realized what it was.

Bones. Snapping.

The black smear *shifted*, and a familiar face swam up out of its inkpool darkness. The long nose, the bitter mouth, and those crow's-feet at the corners of his dark, dark eyes. He looked familiar, but she couldn't for the life of her remember where she'd seen him. "Stay down," he said, fiercely. "You hear me? *Stay down*."

Then he was gone, the smear moving too quickly for her to track, and Jude rolled onto her side, crawling on her belly like a preschooler playing Happy Inchworm. She made it around the kitchen island, and Aggie was there, lying on her back and blinking rapidly. Her sister's head was at an odd angle, and bright red dappled her chin.

Blood. Aggie's mouth was bleeding.

Soft, slithering sounds. Choked cries of pain. It was oddly *quiet*, and Jude reached Aggie, patting at her sister's shoulder, trying to figure out if she was bleeding anywhere else. Her left hip burned, burned, and as she grabbed her sister's shirt to try to lever her up, Aggie moved, sense returning to her wide blue eyes. Her little sister twitched, her neck making a strange popping noise lost under a short, muffled cry of pain from somewhere else.

Aggie looked, in fact, just like Simon when he was scared, all wide eyes and glaring freckles against translucent milky skin.

Jude curled over, closing her sister in a terrified hug, and the heat in her hip eased. Aggie was saying something, but Jude couldn't hear over the sudden rushing in her ears. She rocked Aggie back and forth, clutching with hysterical strength, until she realized her sister was saying *let go, let go, you're hurting me.*

Bit by bit, her arms relaxed, and Aggie's hands were there, pushing aside Jude's tangled hair. She examined Jude's face, then glanced aside, a quick flick of her golden head before erupting into wild motion, scrambling for the sink.

He said to stay down, Jude thought, opening her mouth, but the sheer galloping insanity of the whole morning hit her from behind and she could only produce a small dry whispering *uh* sound.

Aggie clawed at the cabinet door to haul herself up, fished in the sink, and dropped back with a bruising jolt and the morning's dripping, crusted egg pan, heavy enameled cast iron, in her fist. She put her back to the cabinet and motioned to Jude. "Over here," she whispered, frantically. Her lip was swelling; someone had clocked her a good one. "Over here!"

Then what? I don't think you've thought this through, Ags. Jude froze, a sudden instinctive certainty roughening the skin between her shoulder blades.

A hand sank into her hair and *pulled,* a flare of excruciating pain from her scalp all the way down her neck, and Aggie lunged upright, screaming and waving the egg pan. Jude grabbed for her own head, finding gloved fingers and clawing at them, a brief flare of red pain as one of her nails ripped down to the quick. It was pretty useless, Aggie staggering toward them with the pan hefted and the guy who had Jude's hair had something in his other hand, and the present looped over into the past and Dave's contorted face as he pointed the gun.

There was a snapping and a crunch, Jude's hip heating up again in the middle of the confusion. The fingers in her hair relaxed, spasming once and pulling terribly before falling free. The man who'd grabbed her—he was in black and a gas mask, too—fell backward, but Aggie was already on top of Jude, and she swung the egg pan with deadly certainty.

Crunch.

Jude collapsed, Aggie fell on her, and to top it all off, the hero from the parking lot landed on them both.

Chapter Thirty-Five

Causing Mayhem

One moment Marlock was fine, at the top of his game, the deep painful joy of causing mayhem against several heavily armed jackadoos and moving too fast for their confused only-human reflexes filling him just like the hot greedy gulps of energy. Harvesting each of them in turn took too much time, so he was oilslicking, grabbing just enough to incapacitate and using it flagrantly. One of them, dying from a hemorrhage but too stupid to know it yet, blundered down the hall while he dealt with the rest of the front entry team, and he might have hesitated to turn after the scumbag if he'd known he'd get hit on the head by one of the goddamn civilians he was *protecting*, for Chrissake.

The impact cracked something in his head, and for a short, terrifying while nothing would work. Arms and legs gone, everything gone haywire, and his vision speckled with strange dots and blurps that were too irregular to be anything but something pressing on the brain. He could still *hear,* in a faint faroff way, and there was a hazy sense of something moving.

Christ. So this is how I die. Even the hunger, the old familiar endless hunger, and the rage had deserted him. He could heal, he was pretty durable, but that required focus, and he couldn't quite figure out where to direct the power. His ribs seized up with pain, his Mark biting into his skin, and for a moment the horrifying idea that he'd fallen into a carefully prepared trap overseen by the fucking Skinner loomed in front of him.

For his second time dying, though, it wasn't all that bad. Just...disconnected.

"What are you doing?" A woman's voice, familiar, a terrified whisper.

"I don't know." Another frightened whisper.

Then the sunlight came from nowhere and clove him in half.

It peeled away layers of darkness, that sword of golden light, boiling through nerve and muscle. His skull creak-crackled, fragments reassembling themselves and slivers popping back into place and fusing. Pressure on the brain receded, the swelling vanishing, erased. His Mark stretched, glorying in the flood of pure light, and his eyelids fluttered against a glittering clarity.

"Holy *shit*," the first voice breathed, and he recognized it. It was the sister. Cheerleader Aggie. She'd hit him with something, hard enough to smash his skull in.

Which meant...

The light came back, digging in and repairing, easing down his skin, sinking into his muscles, filling him with fresh air and fresh bread and the smell of laundry dried in the sun. It was *sunlight*, he realized, and the symmetry of it trembled just inside his mental grasp before fleeing, steam disappearing on a hot sidewalk. A final jolt, as if making sure his heart was still going, and the light retreated, leaving him temporarily blind.

"Aggie?" Jude, rasping. She sounded very young, but her voice was still so, so sweet. "I…you see that, right? *Right?*"

"I see it." Awestruck disbelief. "I just don't know what *it* is."

"It happened…in the hospital, too. The little redheaded girl." Jude's tone trembled on the edge of hysteria, and there was an audible gulp as she swallowed. "It wasn't just a dream."

"Oh." The cheerleader sounded pretty calm, all things considered. Maybe he shouldn't have thrown himself into this, the blonde yoga coach could have probably beaten the shit out of two teams of hardened mercenaries with whatever crockery was to hand instead.

Marlock found himself flat on his back, his arms outflung and the sour taste of almost-death in his mouth. His eyelids fluttered again, and his vision came back in stages. He stared at a misty middle distance, suddenly aware he was lying on something soft and slanted. Movement in his peripheral vision, he twitched, and Jude Altfall's face swam into focus.

Her hair was a mess, she was deathly pale, and the clarity haloed her again. Her shirt was torn, there was a bruise rising on her cheek, and she looked…

God. "Wow," he heard himself croak. "Hi."

Jude stared at him. Her sister's face came into view, a pale moon, behind her. Looked like someone had socked her a good one, her mouth was all bloody. "Jude…what if he's *with* them?"

"I don't think he is." Jude studied him, her eyebrows coming together like she was trying to read a word nobody had ever defined for her. This close, the heat of her legs through her jeans mixed with the stunning, overwhelming clarity around her, and both filled his head with something unsteady and dangerous.

Aggie was having none of it, thank you very much. "We can't rule it out."

Smart girl. Marlock found his arms and legs were not only obeying him again, but they were full of pep. He felt, in fact, better than he had in years. His throat was dry as salt pan, though.

"I'm going to call the cops." Aggie swayed on her knees. It was probably going to take a couple tries for her to get to her feet. The bright blood on her mouth smeared up her cheek.

"No." It came out hard and fast, and he was staring at Jude so maybe she'd think he meant *her*. So he tacked another couple of words on. "No cops."

"Oh, *great*," Aggie moaned. But it was Jude who was processing this way better than the usual civilian.

"Why no cops?" she asked, in a small, cracked little voice. Her throat was probably as dry as his.

Her lips were a little chapped, but they still looked very soft. "And why...how...*you*..."

Well, maybe she wasn't quite as calm as she looked. But she was holding up really goddamn well, considering.

It was time. There really was no easy way to have this discussion. "Tattoo." He cleared his throat, and made himself as heavy as he could, because he was lying on her legs and even if he hurt her, he wanted her to stay right there, and keep looking down at him. And *listen*. "A tattoo you can't remember."

"What the *fuck*—" Aggie began, but Jude shook her head, glancing at her, and wonder of wonders, the blonde quieted right down.

Her gaze swiveled back down to meet his. "How do you know?" Very softly, still dazed. Was she even taking any of this in?

His internal wince was familiar, and just as painful as it had ever been. This one was going to hurt even more, though. Once she saw his Mark, any chance he had was out the window. Like he'd have any chance at all, really, but this once he would have liked to have a few minutes of fantasizing about it. "Because I've got one too. We can tell each other, Jude." A deep breath—this was never easy. "We're Marked. And you're in danger."

"No shit." Her tone shouted *I think I've figured out that much, sir*. She moved a little, as if to get him off her knees, but he stayed put. His ribs were burning with her nearness, and half his back. His Mark had no doubt grown.

Hers probably had, too.

Despite the situation, his mouth wanted to twitch. No doubt most of the guys had gone for Aggie, but anyone with any sense would snap the older sister up in a heartbeat. The crashing realization of what he was about to do hit, thunder before lightning for once, and the fresh green smell of approaching rain blew in through the kitchen's shattered back door.

He didn't have his gloves on. He could probably touch her. She didn't look drained in the least.

What would it be like, to feel someone else's skin after all these years?

He inched his fingers down, found his shirt was still untucked. His suit jacket had come off to take care of the van's driver outside, he'd pulled the vehicle into the driveway to keep it off the street *and* just in case he needed to carry bodies to it later. Had one of the neighbors called the police? Most of them were bound to be at work, right?

"I got stabbed," he heard himself say, dully. "Almost died. That's how it works, a potential almost dies. Who knows how many of them *actually* kick the bucket? There's no way of telling a potential from an ordinary, we know that much. Anyway, when I came back, I had a...a Mark."

"I'm calling the cops," Aggie said again, but she didn't move. She also didn't sound very determined, for once.

He pulled at his shirt, to free it from his belt. He could smell her. No perfume, just a hint of soap and the raw, beautiful, soft scent of a living woman. If he closed his eyes and inhaled he could fix it in his memory, but he didn't want to. It would only hurt more later, and he would probably remember it anyway. Things like that didn't go away.

Cool air touched his navel. He pulled the shirt up, wondering if it had bloodstains. They both inhaled, sharply, and a familiar hot shame went through him, harsh as a cheese grater.

Because he could tell it was moving, scales that looked horribly realistic crawling along his skin. The curls were reminiscent of scorpion-tails and claws; they sensed interest and attention—and the warmth flooding out from Jude. It *had* gotten bigger, curving around his torso and spreading strange, sickening fingers down his belly. It would grow, branching and twisting, until it covered his trunk and his legs, then spread from his shoulders and down his arms. The last was the neck, and once it reached his face he'd do something drastic, pulling on the Mark for all it was worth, because he *hated* having to wear surgical bandages all over his fucking head.

When it had even crawled under his hair, the Ascension would hit again, and it would shrink to its original size, as big as his palm and much more densely powerful, probably on the back of his shoulder next.

Sometimes they chose the scar from the killing wound, other times they just picked a spot on the body and began to grow again, a little more slowly.

The first Ascension always hurt like hell. Jude would miss that, though.

"Oh, my God," Aggie said, quietly. "Jude…"

"I have one." Jude's pupils swelled, giving her a dreamy look. "On…on my hip. I…after the accident…" She made a little movement, as if to uncover hers, and Marlock had to move. He spilled off her lap but stayed recumbent, to make himself seem less threatening. Her quick fingers unbuttoned her jeans, and he found out two things.

One, she wasn't wearing panties. Not even a thong. She half-turned, shyly, and pulled her shirt down to cover up anything unmentionable.

Two, the Mark was on her left hip, and it was beautiful. No wonder there was all that clarity surrounding her—it was sun-shaped, not a star but *the* star, the thing everything in the world depended on. At the end of its rays, tendrils curled like thornless rosevines, sweet and harmonious.

The Mark just showed what was inside. Once she understood that, she'd understand about his. You couldn't look at Marlock's for very long without getting queasy. The spurs and scale-shading did something to your vision, some atavistic warning thrumming through the visual nerve.

Hers, though…you could get lost in the curves, in the endless motion. Lost in the light, in the glow of a sunny day.

"But you…" She fastened her jeans again, and Marlock was conscious of a trickle of sweat sliding, exquisitely slowly, along his neck. "You have scars."

"Yeah." He was a regular Frankenstein's monster, stitched up so many times it was a wonder the Mark could crawl over the thickened tissue.

"I *don't like this*." Aggie, blinking furiously, was going to make the shift into *don't believe my eyes, because I don't want to*. "I'm calling the cops."

No, you're not. But tapping the sister and knocking her out wasn't going to win any points with Jude. "Yeah, sure. Whoever set this up has plenty of cash, probably has an ear or two down at the station. They'd *love* to hear from you." Now was the time to uncoil, and start brushing himself off. "And they'll probably want to keep *you* in a holding cell, too, while they figure this out. This is an awful lot of firepower to bag two girls. They might start to be suspicious, especially with recent events."

Jude stared at him. A small vertical line had appeared between her dark eyebrows. It was a thinking look, and it probably meant trouble.

"That's why you tackled Dave," she said, finally. "You knew I was different."

"The man in the road that afternoon was my friend." Nothing like the truth for serving a purpose or two. "Someone killed him, and I'll bet they're after you."

"The man in the…"

Aggie boiled over. "This is *insane*." She began patting at her pockets, and fished out a sleek silver smartphone. Marlock set his jaw. If she began to dial, there would be problems.

"Everything is." Sadly, softly, but Jude was still examining him with that small trouble-line on her forehead. "There was someone behind him. That man. In the road." She scooted back, something grinding on the floor under her knees.

A broken plate, probably. "A shadow. He...the lightning..."

Thankfully, Aggie just held the phone, her hand dropping, irresolute.

"His name was Erik. He was my friend." He brought himself up to a crouch. It was *amazing*. One minute he was brain-bleeding on the floor, the next he felt like he could run a marathon. "And if you want to call the cops, fine, but I'm not waiting around for them."

The cheerleader jumped on that one in a hurry. "How do we know *you* didn't set this up?" She swiped angrily at the blood on her mouth.

Jude's hands dropped from buttoning her jeans back up. Her eyes were a little glazed. "Why would he do that after tackling Dave?" It was a quasi-logical objection, and the idea that both these naive little girls were probably going to end up dead or traumatized into a lunatic asylum hit him full-force.

It wasn't a pleasant thought, and it wasn't the kind of thing Marlock was used to thinking. You couldn't dither about the incidental costs on a mission. It fucked you up and made you less effective.

"Oh, so, he's a marginally *okay* kind of stalker? There's..." Aggie glanced around. "There are *dead bodies* in *our house*, Jude!"

"Your house," Jude corrected, very softly. "Nothing's mine anymore." There was no hint of anger to the words. Just sadness, and resignation. Her hair was that wild because she hadn't combed it, probably. What had she been doing before they busted in? Crying? Thinking about her kids?

Fuck. This is going to get messy. Marlock settled back in his crouch, still trying to stay small, not to overwhelm her. It was *already* messy. That ship had sailed.

"What are you talking about? It's *half yours* too." Aggie made a small, frustrated noise. "Do you think I'd throw you out, you idiot?"

Jude's slight shoulders hunched, a heavy weight visibly settling on them. "What the hell's going to happen next, for God's sake? I...I just can't *even*, Ag."

"Well, fuck the rudder, but I can't either." It had the quality of a private joke, and Jude's shoulders eased. She leaned toward her sister, and Aggie hugged her. Put together like that, they were about the size of one of the gorillas who had come stamping in to waste the sister and spirit Jude away. He decided not to tell her so in explicit detail, but he needed to light a fire under them, and get them used to doing what he said.

"I hate to break this little party up." Marlock made it particularly harsh, each word a bullet. "I'm getting the hell out of here. If you're smart, you'll come along."

Jude blinked at him. "Aggie's right. We have to call the cops." There were thoughts moving in those large dark eyes, and that bruise on her cheek made his own face ache.

Marlock ran his hands back through his hair. *Calm down. Think. Think like him. Is he going to try again?* "If there's no dead bodies, do you still have to call them?"

She worked this around in her head for a moment, visibly struggling to catch up. "What are we going to do, bury them in the garden? Jesus."

At least she's thinking. "No. Not Jesus, doll." His lip curled. *Just me.* "Go upstairs and get cleaned up, ladies. While you're at it, think about how we're going to patch that door. But for the love of Christ, don't call the cops. I don't want to die in this shithole city."

They stared at him, and there was that flash of hurt in Jude's dark gaze. The vulnerability. If he was Dave Edmonds, he'd probably want to kick her, just for looking so goddamn helpless. It wasn't what a real man would do, but Marlock was feeling pretty goddamn Pinocchio right at the moment. He had a sudden, vivid fantasy of just draining Agnes on the spot, then chasing Jude through this big, comfortable house and getting his bare hands on her, pulling all the energy he could until he burst like a bloodfat tick.

They couldn't call the cops anyway. The mercs had cut the landline, and Aggie's cell phone was now empty of its charge, courtesy of a few moments of concentration on Marlock's part. If there was a cleanup crew, they would have to get the fuck out before *it* arrived and Marlock had to deal with yet more shit. Why he wasn't just stabbing Jude with the sedative from the asshole the other night and leaving Aggie to deal with this mess was beyond him.

"Go get cleaned up." How much simpler could he make it? "You don't want to see this."

Chapter Thirty-Six

SAME HALLUCINTION

IT WAS QUIET again, but this wasn't the familiar peace of the house Jude had grown up in. This was a new, fragile silence, with sharp teeth underneath. Heavy mechanical jaws, just waiting to snap closed. Aggie peered out the front window, scrubbing her hands together as if they were still wet from their hurried cleanup. "What the hell's *that?*"

"It's the van they came in." The parking lot hero stood next to the fireplace, his arms crossed and his lean, olive-skinned face set as if he was sniffing something awful. Maybe he was, but all Jude could smell was disturbed dust, fresh air from the broken kitchen door…and fear. *That* copper stink, at least, was familiar.

There was no trace of the bodies. She didn't want to wonder what he'd done with them, and she didn't want to *ask*, either, but he saved her the trouble.

"That's where the bodies are." He sounded pretty level, all things considered. Very calm. His eyes were back to regular-dark, instead of *black*. Still, it was…unsettling. Just like the way he stood there, weight evenly balanced even though his arms were crossed, no slouching. It was a military posture, and that was concerning. *Was* he military? Or something else? What the hell was going *on*?

"How often does this sort of thing happen to you?" She leaned against the doorway, her knees not wanting to hold her upright. *Don't make him angry, Jude. He's probably not very nice when he's angry.*

"You don't want to know." Broad shoulders under that ripped suit jacket, and his shirt underneath was spattered with dark fluid she did *not* want to think about. "Now, girls, the best thing is for me to take Jude somewhere—"

"Oh, no you don't." Aggie took two long angry strides towards him, her ponytail bouncing. You could tell she meant business when she tied her hair back with a scrunchie. The only thing that would have been more troubling was a ballet bun. Her lip looked a lot better, once all the blood was washed off. The swelling shrank almost fast enough to see. "My sister is not going anywhere alone with you."

"Your sister is standing right here, Ag." She took a deep breath. Her cheek ached, but the bruise didn't seem that bad either. She didn't want to think that maybe it *had* been bad, but the…the thing on her hip…

She braced herself, took a deep breath, and tried again. "Look, mister…" That brought her up against a wall. "Look, I'm sorry, but I, um…I can't remember your name."

They both stared at her. Aggie's cheeks turned pink, probably because she, for once, couldn't remember something Jude had admitted to forgetting.

"It's okay," he said, steadily. His dark hair was wildly askew, and the disconnect between his ramrod posture and his general dishevelment was jarring. "I gave the cops a fake one anyway. It's Marlock."

Was that a first name or a last one? He didn't add anything else, so Jude decided to forge ahead. "Okay, Mr. Marlock. I, you know, there really isn't any graceful way to say this. I'm very grateful, of course, and—"

"But you'd rather not be any more involved." He nodded, and the sarcastic curl to his thin lips was definite now instead of just implied. Almost a sneer. "If I had a nickel for every time I heard that, I'd be a rich man."

A slight bubble of irritation warmed her throat. Which was good, because it also gave her rubbery knees and her flip-flopping stomach some much-needed bracing. "I was about to say, I'm very grateful, of course, and I'd like to know a little bit more about this…this thing, this…*mark*. And about your, um, your involvement with this whole series of…unfortunate…"

She ran out of words, because the lip-curl had turned into a smile. It wasn't a kind expression, or a particularly forgiving one, and either his pupils had swollen or his irises had turned to tar again, because his eyes looked like ping-pong balls with large black dots on them. It gave his gaze a nasty, directionless quality she wasn't sure she liked, even if he had shifted just a couple degrees and aimed that nose of his at the front window. A cool breeze touched Jude's hair, riffling the tangles—she hadn't bothered to comb it, even. Just washed her face and hands, and pulled on a sweater. Not to mention a pair of trainers, because if something else happened, it was better to have shoes on than not.

"Class," he said, softly. "Pure class. Listen, Jude—can I call you Jude?"

How very polite. "You might as well," she managed, faintly. Had he heard Aggie call her that, or—

"Okay. Jude, you've just seen things ordinary people don't. You're searching for some kind of rational explanation. There isn't one. Some people are just *marked*, that's all. Nobody knows how, or why. It's not the sort of thing they write in the history books." He delivered the last sentence with a whiff of irony, as if he considered the oversight silly but unavoidable. "I'd love to go through everything I know, and teach you how to use what you've got. It's just not a good idea right this moment, because whoever paid those assholes is going to get really antsy when they don't send pictures of you, or show up with you gagged and trussed like a turkey. I'll help you, but you've got to do what I tell you."

"Awfully convenient, you showing up like this." Aggie took another step, this time towards Jude, and the protective bristle on her was familiar and depressing. It should have been Jude bristling like that.

Big sisters and mothers were supposed to know what to do. They weren't supposed to be just as terrified as their tiny, living, breathing responsibilities. *More* terrified, because there was nobody to look to for answers, nobody to rely on. It was all up to the mothers and big sisters, but somehow when they were handing out the owner's manual for this sort of life Jude had missed the event. Even the Mommy Voice had deserted her. Jude squeezed both her hands shut, forcing her nails into her palms.

Even if you bit them all the way down, there was enough to hurt you. If you really tried. One of her fingernails had ripped during the whole thing, and it stung because her palms were sweating.

The sting gave her something to focus on. Good enough.

"Yeah, well." His eyes had returned to normal, a slight difference between iris and pupil that made him look a *lot* more human. "I was in the neighborhood, because I was working up the balls to ask your sister to coffee."

Jude's jaw dropped. Or if it didn't, it felt suspiciously loose and wobbly, like her knees. The daisies and sunflowers he'd brought were lying amid shards of one of their mother's favorite vases in the kitchen.

"Coffee." Her hands relaxed a little, then a little more. "You were going to tell me about the, uh, the marks, over coffee?"

"If I could convince you I wasn't crazy." His face slammed shut like a door, no hint of a smile left. Nothing but that straight poker-bluff calm. "Would you have believed me?"

"Holy shit," Aggie breathed. "I think he's serious."

Marlock pitched forward slightly, glancing at the front window again. "It would be really nice to stand around chatting, but I don't think it's a good idea."

She realized he was watching, maybe for another vehicle to roll up. Maybe for someone else to appear. Someone in a gasmask and riot gear, perhaps?

Jesus. "Just…just give me a second for this all to sink in." Really, though, Jude suspected none of this was going to be absorbed. There just wasn't room for it inside her aching head or her clogged chest. "I…why would someone…"

"It was just luck, Jude. If you hadn't been a potential, you'd've probably died in that accident. But you were, and—"

That was what she'd been overlooking. Jude's eyes finally opened all the way. Everything seemed clear and sharp, now. "You've been following me."

Did he wince, ever so slightly? "I just wanted to—"

"That *accident*? Your friend, right? He had one of these, one of these marks, and somehow it happened to me?"

"It's called a boon. It can transfer, when…look, that's not important right at the moment. You were just in the wrong place at the wrong time."

"My kids died." Saying it out loud hurt, but the pain was eclipsed by a hot, prickling feeling running up and down her arms. "It wasn't an *accident*."

"You lost your kids, I lost my friend. Okay? Now can we talk about getting you somewhere safe?"

The blood drained from Jude's face. She could *feel* it, her skin whitening, and Aggie made a horrified little sound suspiciously like *uh-oh*.

She drew herself up, as tall as she could, and realized the prickling heat was anger. "It's not the same thing, Mr. Marlock." Enunciating every word very slowly, very crisply. The breeze down the hall had warmed up.

"Uh, Jude?" Aggie whispered. "You're…you're *glowing*."

Marlock's eyes had narrowed, as if he was staring into a bright light. "I'm sorry about your kids," he said, very quietly. Very reasonably. "But unless you want your sister dead too, we'd better get out of here. I had no idea the Skinner had this kind of cash to throw at problems, and it's not a good sign."

"The Skinner?"

"That's what he does to his victims, Jude. He takes their Marks." Still squinting, as if staring into a sunny sky. "While they're still alive."

"Question?" Aggie half-raised her hand. "How do we know you're not—"

"Don't be a dumbass. Why would I have killed a bunch of…you know what? Fuck it. Deal with it on your own, dolls." He jerked himself upright, peeling his shoulders away from the mantel Great-Uncle Beauregard had carved, and stalked for Jude.

No, not for her. For the front door, Jude realized. He had to get past her to do that, though, and her hand shot out as he passed, closing around his wrist above the cuff of his driving glove. His skin was warm, and he froze. He didn't look at her, staring instead out into the hall, but his Adam's apple jumped, convulsively.

"Okay," she managed, around the rock in her throat. "Okay. What do you want us to do?"

Because she was out of ideas, because she wanted her sister to live, and because he'd not only tackled Dave but he'd also fought off men in gas masks and, well…the scorpion-curved arms of his tattoo, Mark, whatever it was. Those lines were just as dark as the not-tattoo on her own hip. Unless they were all three having the same hallucination, this guy was Aggie's best chance of surviving.

She didn't, she realized, care much about her own.

Chapter Thirty-Seven

I'VE GOT YOU

WELL, AT LEAST some things never changed. Aggie still hated following someone else in heavy traffic. "Jude?" Now that they were out of the house, she couldn't believe she'd been talked into leaving so easily. The black van loomed in front of them, carrying a cargo of death and that man.

Marlock. First name or last name, he didn't say, and she hadn't thought to ask.

Jude, in the passenger seat, sat pale and composed. Well, maybe not *composed*. Maybe just in shock. She'd only seen that set, blank look on her sister's face three or four times in her whole life, and each time it made a squidgy sort of panic threaten deep in Aggie's belly.

Like opening the front door to find Jude on the step, little Simon sup-sucking with tears and Essie clinging to her mother's leg like she was shipwrecked and there was only one raft. The bruises beginning to glare on Jude's face, and

Aggie's suspicions vindicated. How bad was it that her first feeling had been *I knew it, that bastard*?

Instead of something, well, a little more *helpful*. Because Dave had been a bastard in high school too, but Jude always sounded so *sure*. Just like she had when Aggie was a kid and her big sister was the font of all wisdom their parents chose not to disburse. Aggie had thought, well, big sister knew best, and in any case, it was her life, and maybe adulthood and fatherhood would turn a bastard into a reasonable human being.

Yeah. Right.

Do your deep breathing, Ag. She inhaled, smoothly, filling her stomach. They were heading down the hill, parallel to the freeway on Simonds Street. He was a good driver, not sliding through any yellow lights to leave them adrift in a rented Taurus.

His rented Taurus. There was probably paperwork in the glove box she could check, but she needed both her hands clamped on the wheel. Otherwise, they might start to shake, and *that* was not a happy thought.

She tried again. "Jude? Jujube?"

Her sister stirred. "Hm?" A soft, inquiring noise. A very mom-ish sound—*I hear you, but I'm not actually listening, just confirming that you matter.* She'd heard Jude make the same sound during the kids' chatter at the end of a long day. It generally meant she was asleep on her feet. Worn out by long hours and single motherhood, getting thinner and thinner, and refusing any sort of help. Refusing to even move in with Aggie.

Nothing's mine anymore. Did she really believe that?

"Talk to me." It sounded selfish. The black van ahead of them turned on its left turn-signal, and she followed suit, checking her blind spot and easing into the lane after it. Was Marlock watching his mirrors? If she suddenly yanked the steering wheel and floored it, would he curse? Would he try to follow? He was in a van full of dead bodies, for God's sake. What if they got pulled over?

What if she could get him pulled over?

"About what?" Jude didn't even sound mildly irritated. Just flat, and terribly calm.

"Are you okay?" A banal question, but Jesus, what else could she ask? The green arrow showed up and they turned onto Kafflin Way. The buildings down here were tagged with graffiti and some had boarded up windows, and the farther they got along Kafflin's straight shot on the riverbank the worse it would get, until they got to the waste land near the edge of the industrial section. Where the fuck was this guy *going*? He drove like someone used to the city, too. Where did he come from?

Those horrible, moving lines on his body. The scales. The way they twitched and rippled. Aggie was having a lot of trouble even *thinking* about it, and she believed in energy and intent and all that. You sort of had to, teaching yoga. Now it was staring her right in the face. The marking on Jude's hip—not a bruise, not a tattoo, because it didn't look right.

Nothing about this looked right.

"Yes." Jude paused. "No. I don't know."

"All right." The absurdity of it hit her. Of course Jude wasn't going to be *okay*. She might never be okay again. There was the incontrovertible fact of her sister *glowing*, her skin luminescent, even her clothes turning bright and hyper-saturated with color. And that guy's head repairing itself, bone making weird popping noises as it fused, and—

Don't think about that. Focus on the now. Bizarre. The whole thing was utterly, completely *bizarre*. Maybe it was a practical joke? Who would be so cruel? Dave? He didn't have the money to hire people to pull off a stunt like this. Or the brains, frankly.

"Do you have your pain pills?" She had to say *something*, for God's sake. All those years of meditation and yoga, and now, when she really needed to be calm, her heart was pounding, her palms were damp, and screaming and throwing up her hands seemed like a good option. Or, at least, a way to break the tension.

The van accelerated, and she obediently pressed the Taurus's gas pedal, keeping pace, following at a safe distance.

"I…" Jude bent, slowly, and grabbed the purse Aggie had given her. "I'll check." The cheerful yellow was nothing like her sister—she preferred more muted joys.

Or did she really? Ever since childhood, Jude had been the responsible one. The sane one. The one who just seemed to know where the Band-Aids were, how to balance a checkbook or write a term paper. After Mom and Dad's accident, she'd been the one to call the funeral homes, sign papers, take care of details. Effortlessly gliding through the safe lane, while Aggie stopped to pick dandelions on the meridian. Jude had explained birth control to her, had taken her to Planned Parenthood that once and held her hand, and made Aggie's grilled cheese with the crusts cut off all the damn time.

"I have them," her sister said, softly. "Why?"

"Take one. You're due." *And boy howdy, I'm thinking you need one right about now. I could use one myself, just to calm down.*

Jude didn't even argue, just obediently popped the lid on the bottle and shook one out. She glanced around, her curly hair swaying—and oh, how Aggie had prayed for years for her hair to develop just a little of that beauty, even just a subtle wave.

"You'll have to dry-swallow it." *I should have grabbed a bottle of water.* If *she'd* been the one in the passenger seat, Jude would have thought of it.

"Yes." Jude nodded. That quiet voice, absent and thoughtful. It wasn't her regular, practical, stubborn sister at all.

Sooner or later, even little sisters grew up. Aggie tapped the brake as the van slowed, and when it turned off Kafflin she followed. The riverbank came close to the street here, and there were overpasses looming above, creating pools of deep shadow even on a sunny late-spring afternoon. It was always evening in this part of town, a weird, unsettled gloom.

We shouldn't be down here. The van slowed even more, and Aggie found herself doing her deep breathing again. She'd taught Essie how to exhale all the stress and focus on her breath. Sometimes, when she watched the kids for Jude, she pretended they were hers, and their trustful shining faces always turned up like flowers looking at the sun. She was an adult, their auntie, and of *course* she knew what to do.

She hadn't, though. She'd just been winging it. What if...it was crazy to even think it, but what if Jude had been winging it all her life?

"Go on, honey." Aggie's grip loosened on the wheel, became natural. Maybe she could reach over and look for paperwork in the glove box. Would that freak Jude out, though? "It will help."

Jude obediently palmed the pill to her mouth and settled back in her seat, staring blindly out the windshield. The van's brake lights showed up, rubies in the dark, and when it finally bumped up over the curb and onto a slice of gravel and weeds she realized what he was going to do—leave it here. There were hulks of other cars tucked in odd corners here, too. Pretty smart, Aggie wouldn't have thought of it.

She could turn the wheel and get them out of here. She *could*. They could go to the police—except this Marlock guy was right. Anyone with the money to do this sort of thing...and now she was an accessory. So was Jude.

Great.

Would it matter that they were innocent? Maybe, but the last thing her sister needed was to sit in a cell while the bungling asshole police who couldn't even keep her safe from Dave Edmonds tried figuring things out. The restraining orders hadn't done any good, and Jude was quiet about everything, but Aggie *suspected* a whole lot more. If she was right about that, what else was she right about?

It was Aggie's turn to take care of her big sister. It was about damn time.

"Did it get down?" she asked.

Jude nodded, silently. There were tear-tracks on her sister's face.

Aggie reached over, took Jude's left hand, and squeezed gently. Just like Jude had squeezed hers when dropping her off for finals that one weekend in high school. *Everything will be fine, Ags. You've got this.* She'd sounded so certain. Aggie had clung to that certainty, never even thinking about how much it might cost her big sister to sound that way.

What if Jude hadn't been certain at all?

"Everything will be all right," Aggie said, and she found she sounded just as sure, just as calm, as Jude ever had. "I've got you, Jujube."

Her sister just nodded. There was a shadow at the driver's side, and Aggie jumped as Marlock appeared out of thin air, tapping twice on the window with his knuckles. Little white scars clustered thickly all over the hard bumps, bone thrusting through skin. A guy with hands like that probably did a lot of punching.

Christ, they were trapped in a bad horror film, with a man who could do awful things. And they were *trusting* him.

"I've got you," Aggie repeated, and rolled the window down. "What now?"

"Now I drive." He sounded like he did this every day. "Get in the back."

Chapter Thirty-Eight

BROKE THE MOLD

THEY WEREN'T STUPID, Marlock reminded himself, now in a fresh suit and sprawled in the one lone chair the room could boast. Just civilians, and civilians asked questions. "Now we sit tight and try to get some sleep."

Jude Altfall stood in the middle of a cheap hotel room on Pontselvie, hugging herself, cupping her elbows in her hands. Even transparent-pale and messy-haired, she still gave off that same indefinable air of *class*. "When they find the van—"

"There's nothing there to tie us to it. That's why we took it down by the water." *And left it unlocked.* "It'll be stripped by dawn." The mass of decaying organic ooze inside would be loathsome, but hard to identify. Driving with freshly dead bodies was unpleasant at best, and he'd had to keep *pulling* at them to break them down past the point they would begin twitching.

Marlock squashed a small thread of irritation. Would it be too much to ask that they just trust he had their best interests in mind?

Of course, they were smart not to. He didn't. Still, it rankled.

"Fingerprints, or fiber evidence—" Aggie wasn't about to let it go. She perched on the edge of the queen bed with its dusty peach coverlet, her blonde head cocked a bit as if she couldn't quite believe she was expected to *sleep* in such a rundown place, even if it had hot water and a dearth of cockroaches.

"You think anyone would have sent those guys if they were irreplaceable? Besides, I wiped the van. They won't find a goddamn thing. Now please, quiet the fuck down. I have a headache." He didn't, but he wanted some goddamn peace. He needed to think, since he'd gone and done something stupid.

"Aggie?" Jude kept hugging herself. Tense arms, big eyes, her breasts pressed together under that blue sweater with its wide scoop neck. "You've still got dust in your hair. Why don't you take a shower?" Her throat moved as she swallowed, a vulnerable little movement that just brought home how fragile her neck was. She was skin and bones, really. The picture on her driver's license had much softer, rounder cheeks. Normally Marlock didn't go for the ultra-skinny look, but—

"I'm not leaving you alone with *him*." A disdainful little sniff. So the cheerleader thought he was dangerous or something?

Good.

Jude, however, just shook her head. "If he wanted to hurt either of us, he could have done it a million times by now. Go get cleaned up so *I* can get cleaned up. Mr. Marlock, can we get room service or something? I think everyone's probably hungry and a little worn out."

Just like a mom, maybe. Making sure everyone was fed. Christ. *It's not the same thing*, she'd informed him. Goddamn right, losing Erik wasn't like losing a child, but…Jesus. Could you ever make that sort of judgment, though? Death was death, no matter who it happened to.

His wrist still burned. Skin on skin, and she hadn't immediately let go of him with a cry of disgust or passed out. She'd fucking *touched* him. Casual as you please.

He'd tried a few times over the years, of course. Even if he was careful, only baring the minimum and wearing a condom, there was still the moment when the Mark took what it wanted. The first time he'd been lucky, the girl just passed out. The second…

Don't think about that.

He couldn't help it. Jude had *touched* him. A slight, soft pressure, the first time he'd really felt someone's skin in…God, how long?

Doesn't matter. Come on, Press. Get back on the horse. "Food." He nodded, slowly. "Yeah. Good idea. Give me a minute, I'll go out and get something."

"Is it safe?" She hugged herself even tighter, and he couldn't really think with her there radiating all over him. She was too pale, trembling, and her eyes had a glassy sheen he didn't like at all.

He tried to imagine them dealing with the drained, too-light bodies. Aggie would probably puke, Jude would probably just look green. "What?"

Her blue sweater was a little too big, but she made it look intentionally relaxed instead of sloppy. "Is it safe? For you to go out?"

She was asking *him*? Jesus Christ, when they made this one, they broke the mold. "Better than either of you traipsing around. Just give me a few seconds to think, okay?" Not to mention get the rock out of his throat and the pressure below his belt to subside. A man learned to let off steam in other ways, but there was nothing quite like the original, and how much of a bastard was he for thinking about that at a time like this?

"Okay." She half-turned, looked at her sister. Invisible woman-signals flashed between them, and Aggie hauled herself up from the bed with an elderly sigh.

"Fine." She tossed her golden head and grabbed a small green carryon bag. "I'll save you a towel."

Of the two of them, Aggie was the one who had thought to pack; Jude had just looked dazed. Marlock had caught her trying to put the kitchen door back together, for Christ's sake. Trying to fit the splinters together, glancing at the frame with quick little furtive movements and hunching her shoulders as if struck each time.

The bathroom door shut with a precise little click. Which left Marlock alone with Jude Altfall for the first time, if you didn't count him throwing flowers at her and running like the coward he was. The curl in her hair was all luxuriant silken tangles, and that stupid pointless warmth of her was all over him, plucking at his skin, bathing his Mark in warm oil. She'd seen it, so she knew how ugly he was. Why was she looking at him like that?

Why the *fuck* had he brought her here, instead of just sitting tight and waiting for the Skinner to come collect her personally? He could have made a case for staying at the Altfall house, but he hadn't. He'd hustled her out of her familiar surroundings and into this chintz-cheap room with dun curtains and that peach duvet on the queen bed. Why the fuck had he done something so stupid?

You know why, Press.

Why was she just *standing* there? It got on a man's nerves, being stared at like that. "See something you like?" He lifted one corner of his top lip, showing his teeth. It would turn his face into a monster's leer, just like the rest of him.

Was that slight movement a flinch, or a recoil? Her jeans were a little too big, and had frayed at the heels. There wasn't a dent on her left ring finger; he wondered if the ex had ever bought her a ring or if she'd just taken it off with a sigh of relief one day.

"Thank you." Her arms tensed, probably to keep her from flying apart from the sheer impossibility of the situation. "You didn't have to stop Dave, or make sure we were okay. Really. Thank you."

Well, wasn't that the best way to make Preston Marlock feel like the low end of a shit-filled pool. It wiped the snarl off his face, that was for sure, and he either had to shift uncomfortably in his seat or start telling her a few home truths, and he didn't want to do either. She was dealing with this way more gracefully than *he* had, that was for goddamn sure.

He'd gone kind of crazy when his Mark triggered. Of course, that was probably the best way to handle prison, but—

Those were uncomfortable memories. He was going to have a whole new set of them soon, he suspected.

So he stood. "Uh. Yeah. You're…I'm gonna go get us something to eat." He found the room key in his trouser pocket, tossed it in her direction. She almost didn't catch it, and even that awkwardness was oddly graceful. "You…uh, are you a vegetarian?"

She shook her head. Her hands were limp now, the hotel door key dangling from her right. A ghost of a smile touched her pale lips. "I wondered if you were vegan. In the parking lot."

What? "No, I'm a good old-fashioned carnivore. Lock the door after me. When I come back I'll knock twice, then wait a second, and knock once. Okay?"

"Why not shave and a haircut?" Her chin lifted a little.

Yeah. Definitely broke the mold. "Too cliché." He tried not to feel amused, and got out of there before he started smiling.

It was raining, a warm spring shower, and there was a mutter of thunder approaching. What he needed was a payphone, but what he had was a few prepaid cells. It was annoying to have to use one of them up, but it couldn't be helped. He tucked himself at the end of another hotel hallway, next to the ice machine.

First time, nothing but automated voicemail. He tried again, and a third time. *Come on, you asshole.*

Finally, on the fifth, he got lucky.

"*What?*" A deep, roughened bullhorn, amazing from such a reedy man. Maybe it hid in his potbelly? There was a faint hint of an accent, too, heavy on the consonants, handling the vowels a little strangely.

"Boo, motherfucker." Marlock pitched the words low and polite.

Cloth moving. Had the man been in bed? "Press?"

"It's me. How you been?" He didn't care, but it was nice to ask, wasn't it?

"How have I...you cocksucking freak, it's late—"

"I don't want to call back."

"Two years you've been gone, and now you want to—"

"Phil, come on. I need help."

"Oh, of course you do, why else would you be calling *me* up out of the blue, you shady sonofabitch?"

"I'm not gonna apologize."

"Of course not. I would be shocked if you did, dickwad." Breathing heavily, now. "What the fuck do you want, Press?"

Phil Grier was a foulmouth little rule-checker, but he'd once been Marlock's handler.

And the agency would be very, very interested indeed to hear about Jude Altfall.

Chapter Thirty-Nine

SAME SMILE

THE COLLECTOR LEANED forward, considering the top of his desk as he placed his elbows precisely upon it. "I see." He was, all things considered, very calm. Another day had ended with losses, this time in a sector of the New York markets he hadn't foreseen. There was an uncomfortable dampness on his nape. "You went through the usual channels to procure the contractors?"

"Yes, sir. They were both recommended by your approved parties." Mr. Bell looked slightly pale, as well he should. His tie—a very understated blue—was a single millimeter askew. It was, given the circumstances, an acceptable deviation.

The collector suspected his own tie was a little misaligned as well. "Is there any police interest?" *That* was the important thing right now. He didn't want undue curiosity on the part of the authorities.

"None, sir. Both parties are very apologetic. It's as if the active elements simply vanished."

"Unlikely that both would abscond with the money." He fought the urge to sink back in his chair. His desk was not as neat as it should be, since the working day had not ended.

"Yes, sir. Both are ready to refund the payment, pending your response." Mr. Bell was probably extremely grateful *he* had not supplied the recommendations for the contractors.

"Hm." The collector steepled his fingers. "This requires thought. Would you pour me a drink?"

"Scotch, sir?"

"Yes, and one for yourself, if you're so inclined."

A slight respectful bob of Mr. Bell's dark head. "Thank you, sir."

The collector stood and paced for the Kohle chairs before the window, stood near them and clasped his hands. Stared thoughtfully through the floor-to-ceiling glass. The view was just as stunning as it was every other evening, but it somehow left him unmoved. Very disturbing developments.

In his collection was a certain piece of stretched skin marked with eye-patterns, over and over in repeating fractals. It was perhaps time to plumb its possibilities. Just thinking about it made him restless, in the same way the prospect of an attractive and available woman made less-evolved men slightly…aroused.

"Sir." Mr. Bell settled the glass of amber liquid in its proper place, on the porous stone coaster on the small table next to his employer's favorite chair.

"Please, sit." The collector motioned toward the other chair, and Mr. Bell thanked him quietly. He settled, but did not sip at his own glass of Scotch. Faultless manners, really, waiting for his betters to take the first drink. When he was forced to put Mr. Bell to pasture, it would be a sad day. Before then, though, there was much to be done.

The collector lowered himself gingerly into his own seat. After he made a few decisions, he could go back to work, perhaps with a little more tranquility. "If we were to double the payment…"

"They would no doubt be more assiduous, sir, but it may not be wise."

"True." The collector sighed, deeply. The Altfall woman should be tidied up, once he made sure nothing of Sturmen's lingered on her. His shadowy pursuer, too. As Mr. Bell had said, the dimensions of the hole his identity was buried in were very interesting. Were higher authorities watching the collector? Unlikely, but…he couldn't discount it. "What do you think of our ghost, the fabulous Mr. Pinkerton?"

"I re-examined his traces. He may be a private citizen like yourself, sir. Money can buy identity, or the lack of it."

The collector nodded as if he'd thought of that already, even if he hadn't. "Another collector, perhaps." *Now that would be prey worth hunting.* "Still, I'd like to be sure. It wouldn't do to have too many lions at the waterhole."

"No, sir."

They enjoyed their Scotch together in silence, and by the time his glass was empty, the collector had reached his decision. Mr. Bell collected his employer's glass and stood, ready for orders.

What a find the man was. It was a pity. "Mr. Bell, I want both the woman and Mr. Pinkerton. Alive and well. If they are delivered to the lakeshore property in that condition, I will triple the fee and add a bonus. If they are delivered in any *other* condition, both the go-betweens will refund quadruple the fee. And if they only manage to bring the woman, they will be paid the rest of the original amount."

"Yes, sir." Mr. Bell did not remonstrate, or ask him if he was sure. He simply turned and glided away.

The collector settled back in the chair, preparing to enjoy the spectacle of the lights across the bay. Work could wait until full dark had fallen. A thin, cruel smile played over his face as he loosened his tie.

He might have reconsidered his orders, and Mr. Bell's usefulness, if he had seen his employee wearing exactly the same smile.

Chapter Forty

DRASTIC

AT LEAST THERE was plenty of warm water in the shell-pink motel bathroom. It never seemed to get hot, though, even when Jude turned it all the way over and stood, trembling, under the spray. At least the water pressure was good, stinging needles jabbing at face and breasts and belly. The skin around the tattoo-thing got pink, and the spaces on the inside. But the black lines didn't change.

It had gotten bigger. It looked like a part of her skin, like she'd been born with it or got a tattoo so long ago it was well-healed. She poked at it with a fingertip and shivered at the sensation—a rippling under her skin, and her eyes stinging.

Jude. You're glowing.

The unreality of it hit her, through the thick chemical veneer of the pain pill. This whole thing was a nightmare. Maybe she *had* died in the flames of the van, and this was hell. A hell perfectly tailored to her, a lovely little personal afterlife. Who needed screaming in hellfire when you could be dropped into something like this?

After a while, cowering in the shower seemed pointless, so she turned the water off. Aggie had left her a towel, true. At least it was relatively clean, smelled of bleach, and she could wrap the still-damp one Aggie had used around her hair. And Aggie had packed clothes, too. Which was good, because the jeans Jude had been wearing were filthy with plaster dust, and now that she looked at them, crumpled on the yellowing linoleum floor, it was probably likely they had blood on them, too, from the gas-mask attackers.

Her brain struggled with the memory of the ink-black smear that was Marlock, moving too quickly to be real. The horrifying distorted faces, gas masks like giant insect heads, and the sound of bones breaking. The worst, though was that bubbling streak of darkness on the air, his face surfacing from it when he told her to stay down.

See something you like?

Why would he help her? Just because they both had these things-that-weren't-tattoos?

They get bigger as you use your power. They show what you are.

Well, his was full of spikes and scorpion-tail curves, moving lazily against his ribs, reaching around his back, moving slightly like scales on the side of a large basking creature. A glimpse of black hair on his chest when he pulled his shirt up, but what you couldn't look away from were the silvery, long-healed scars. Thin, thick, ragged, smooth, they were everywhere on him. There was one on his left eyebrow too, hair-thin but still there, and once you'd seen the others all you could do was wonder where they came from.

Where *he'd* come from.

Voices through the thin door. Jude began to get dressed, and her ears must have dialed up to eleven, because she could hear them.

"I don't like you." Aggie sounded combative, which probably meant she was scared. Well, Jude was scared too. Mostly, though, she was just exhausted. Nothing made sense anymore.

"That's okay, kids usually don't." Marlock, and the sound of crackling paper. "I hope you like bacon cheeseburgers, because that's what I brought."

More bristling from Aggie. "What do you mean, kids usually—"

"Sweetheart, you have no idea how old I am. And besides, Jude's probably always been a substitute mother for you. It's all over her."

"What's all over her?"

"Responsibility." Well, Mr. Marlock certainly had a snappy comeback for everything.

"Yeah, well, that's how Dave roped her in."

Jude flinched, yanking the clean jeans up and zipping in a hurry.

"That so?" Nothing but mild interest in Mr. Marlock's tone.

"Yeah. She never could resist puppy eyes."

Oh, hell no. You two are not going to dissect me like this. Jude yanked the T-shirt over her head and hurried to open the door, letting out a cloud of steam. For such tepid water, it certainly generated a lot of vapor. "You're back." She scrubbed at her hair with Aggie's leftover towel, but she could tell it wasn't going to do much good. "So, if you're done talking about me like I'm not here?"

"Ears got better, huh?" Marlock grinned, a wide, white, toothsome grimace, as he settled three bags full of greasy Shack burgers on that table. "That's good. You're learning to focus. It can heighten your senses."

"Superpowers." Aggie probably would have been standing with her arms folded, if she hadn't been holding a drink carrier. The familiar red and white cups with the domed lids…

Burgerdoodle! With mayo and a chocklik shake, please?

He'd gone to the Shack. That's right, there was one on 175th. She swallowed, hard. Her face must have changed, because both of them stopped. Aggie got pale, and Marlock straightened slowly.

"Jude?" Aggie sounded a little lost, to be honest. A little *scared*.

"I just…" A long shaky breath left her, words refusing to form until she could fill her lungs again. "I…was going to take them for burgerdoodle. The…Simon, and Essie. That's what we were talking about, when…when it happened."

"Oh, God." Aggie almost dropped the drink carrier. If one of them was a chocolate milkshake, Jude decided, she was going to go back into the bathroom while they ate.

"Shit." Marlock grabbed for the bags. "I'll get something else."

Oh, Lord. "No. No, it's all right. You just...you go ahead. I'm not hungry."

A single shake of his dark head, his hair holding little dots of water. Fog must have risen from the river, like it did on some spring nights. "Bullshit. You'll go into shock if you don't eat. I'll get something else."

"*No.*" The Mommy Voice came out in full force, and she wondered if she'd shouted, because Aggie swayed a little. "It's *fine*, really it is. It's just a little...strange, that's all."

His mouth thinned, relaxed, thinned again, and Jude realized that if he got angry at her for yelling at him, if he thought she was getting, in Dave's words, *uppity as fuck*, it could get very ugly in here.

Very ugly indeed.

"You mean *painful*." He tilted his head a little. His driving gloves made small noises as his hands tightened. "You mean it hurts."

Well, yes. As a matter of fact, it does. "You could say that."

"Marks don't get rid of that." He held her gaze, his eyes doing that getting-darker trick again. He didn't look like he was going to explode, though. "I wish they did."

"Yeah." She sounded like she'd been punched, again. "Great. Good to know."

His gloved hands moved, quick as a wink. He subtracted the drink carrier from Aggie with one swift, economical motion. Waxed paper crinkled and crumpled; and he headed for the door. "Lock this after me. This time I'll knock four times, then two."

"Mr. Marlock—" It was ridiculous, to make him waste all that food. It was too late. The door shut, a little harder than necessary.

Jude's knees were a bit wobbly. Aggie, one hand falling to her side, had the other one pressed to her mouth. "Oh, honey," she said through her fingers, and took a step past the rickety pasteboard dresser holding a heavy, old-fashioned TV. "Come here."

For once, Jude didn't swallow the tears. She sagged against her sister, trying to control the hiccuping sobs, and Ag stroked her hair again and made soothing noises.

All the time, Jude stared at the darkened television screen. It blurred and wavered as her eyes filled and emptied, and yes, she decided, she was in hell.

This *mark* he was talking about—she'd seen what it had done to his injuries. The little redheaded girl at the hospital, too. If there was any justice in the world, it would have saved Sy and Essie. Or the flames would have eaten Jude as well as her babies.

There was no justice, and now men with guns had burst into Aggie's house, and the whole crazy, impossible thing was just building and building.

If this kept going, she was going to have to do something…drastic.

Chapter Forty-One

Borrowed Eyes

UNDER THE HIGH, frosted glass done, the collector's breathing echoed in ragged bursts. The marking writhed madly, sinking in capillary-claws, struggling to overpower him and wreak a terrible vengeance upon its tormentor. It took resolve to conquer them. Willpower. Forcing his will upon each pattern was a better, cleaner, surer high than cocaine, or heroin, or anything else the non-evolved could name.

It was pure *power*, and it was the only thing that gave the collector a hard-on anymore. Even sex paled beside this *magnificence*, though the mechanical insertion and movement was still useful. It kept the head clear and the nerves aligned.

Underneath the ragged square of skin he pressed to his side, the writhing protean tentacles of his own marking strained, hungry to gulp down whatever it could of the other skin's pattern. He forced them both to behave, harsh breaths echoing against the other glass cases. Normally, he used the smaller room with the bank-vault door, but he was impatient.

He needed to know. His hair, wet with sweat, flopped against his forehead as he fought the convulsions.

It was always a risk. They did not last forever; one of the hazards of such a collection was that each item only carried a finite charge. Miracles, yes, but each use drained them. Eventually they would turn into snot-thick clots of rotten tissue, all their usefulness gone. He'd discovered this the hard way.

It only made sense to acquire them. *He* could use them properly. The sorry sacks they were originally attached to were only vessels to nourish them until he harvested the finest specimens. This marking, with its many blinking eyes, had belonged to one of his most difficult acquisitions.

At first, the eyes could not find what he sought. They stared into a deep black well, and the slithering sounds in the depths had troubled him until he decided they were simply the marking thinking him an easily frightened fool. The markings were fractious, always. Restive.

Angry.

He'd lost more than one before he discovered the secret: the bearer must be alive when they were cut from the flesh beneath. None of them had ever given up the miracles willingly.

The darkness thinned, became membranous. For some reason, the first thing the eyes showed him was an image of a flimsy beige door, a scarlet, throbbing lip-print on its filthy surface. The number *8* glowed bronze above it, and as the shadow retreated swiftly, he found the eyes could slip through the door.

It was a dark room. Hotel, perhaps—the clunky furniture and pattern on the short nylon carpet seemed to say so. Bodiless, the collector turned this way and that.

Two forms on the bed. He squinted, not with his physical eyes but with his borrowed ones, looking *underneath*.

Light. Pure golden light, a glowing sun. It scorched him, drove him back toward the door. His borrowed eyes fought his control, and he drew back, *back*, through shoddy corridors and beyond the papery walls. A listing sign in the parking lot—*The Holden Inn*, with *Vacancies* buzzing below in red neon. A dark blot in the parking lot, but it moved away so quickly he was sure it was only a passing occlusion.

A savage joy filled the collector, for now he knew.

He would have to question her, before he took what she had stolen. The collector hooked his fingers under the elastic skin, peeling it away from his ribs. His breath came hard and fast, sweat standing out in giant clear drops over his naked body. His erection throbbed painfully.

Oh, when he had her at the lakefront house, he could amuse himself for a short while before the *denouement*. He'd earned it, and so had she. The next hunt would certainly not be so interesting.

He finished tearing the skin away, and his quick hands re-pinned it on its acid-neutralizing bed. You had to keep them at the proper pH—too basic, and the collagen structure would be weakened, too acidic, and the stretched hide would turn frail as lacework.

Skin was so delicate and so strong, all at once.

The collector closed the glass case, waiting until the light inside turned to a row of greens, temperature and humidity control normalizing. He reached down, cupped himself lovingly.

No. Not yet. He had to find his robe, then inform Mr. Bell. Sometimes the eyes could look through *time*, as well, but he didn't want to risk it. The sooner, the better.

Then he would have that lovely light, and whatever marking it was attached to, right where he wanted it.

Chapter Forty-Two

A Ride Coming

THE BLONDE DIDN'T even sleep quietly. She muttered and murmured, tossing and turning, while Jude lay on her side, breathing so slowly he restrained the urge to check her for a pulse. He'd brought back Chinese, and found the sisters sitting next to each other on the bed, lights on, the television on with no sound and their faces eerily blank in the blue light. They were holding hands, too, all four interlaced, and they leaned against each other like they remembered being in the crib together.

He suspected that image would stay with him for a very long time. What would it be like, to have someone you could cuddle against like that, taking strength or at least comfort from closeness? Both of them had red-rimmed eyes, and blinked at him like he was a stranger.

Well, he was. But at least he'd brought Chinese, and they'd both eaten. Jude was a whiz with chopsticks.

Of course she was. She even smiled a little, solemnly, tapping them together to show him how to hold them a better way.

Stupid fuck, Marlock. What the fuck have you done?

It didn't matter. When he felt the little tingle along his nerves that meant there were creepers around, he would slide out and away. The agency would pick up Jude and her sister. It wouldn't be comfortable, but it was a damn sight better than anything the Skinner would do to either of them.

He squeezed his eyes shut, his legs stretched out in front of him. The chair wasn't comfortable, but that would keep him awake. *I'll watch,* he'd informed them. *You sleep. You'll need it.*

Aggie hadn't given him a lick of sass, even.

Two years wasted. Because he just couldn't do what needed to be done. He'd never have a better opportunity to draw the Skinner out, and he'd thrown it away. Why?

Because he was a dumb fuck who let sentimentality get in the way of the mission. Now, when he recited the rosary, he'd have to add more names—all the dirty deeds he'd done while chasing this motherfucker down. All for nothing.

He'd already written the note, scribbled on hotel stationary. They were both dead to the world, worn out after a day no civilian would be feeling too perky after. Jude had lain awake for much longer than her sister, probably worrying about something. She'd turned on her side, and he wondered if she was looking at the faint shadow of him against the window. The thought was kind of pleasant, actually, unless she started being able to use her Mark to go stepping inside his head.

It wasn't impossible. Very little was flat-out impossible, once you had an Ascension or two under your belt. She didn't even know what Ascension was. Babe in the woods. He could teach her. Oh, yes, could he *ever*. And once she figured out a few things about him, it would be a heave-ho out the door.

Stick around. The agency would love to get you back.

Oh, wasn't that seductive. He could junk the Don Quixote bit and ingratiate himself with the agency *and* with her. Good cop, bad cop—he could let the agency be the bad cop for once. She was ready for anyone who could tell her it was going to be all right, she was numb with grief and traumatized, it would go down easy. Even a monster like him couldn't fuck *that* up. She was ready to cling to anything.

Even to a wreck on the dark side of the fence, a man who just wanted to use her.

Yeah. Go ahead, Marlock. Do it. Just sit here.

A tingle ran along his nerves. It brought him up in a hurry, patting his pockets—he had everything, yes, and the rest of his stuff was in the rented Taurus. Time for him to soft-shoe off the stage unless he really, truly wanted to be here when they came in and whisked Jude and her sister away.

It felt weird, a searchlight pressure passing overhead. Roving. Maybe they'd gotten a Mark who could project, or maybe they'd just triangulated his throwaway cell. Someone was looking, peering through cracks, zeroing in.

He shut his eyes. *Just a second, okay? Just for a second or two. Think about it.*

Who was he fooling? He'd been doing nothing *but* thinking about it, trying to turn it some way inside his head that would make it stick. He could even, if he thought about it, find some way to make the rosary go away. Just shove it in a box, or decide he'd had a two-year bender on the sweet, killing liqueur called believing yourself a better man than you actually were.

He'd justified worse to himself. Even Erik knew that.

Except Erik didn't know anything, now. He'd thrown his Mark at a potential, maybe to save her, or maybe as a fuck-you to the Skinner.

And now he was dead.

The searchlight was turning in narrower and narrower arcs. Now was the time.

Fuck it. He found himself at the door. He slipped through, into a hallway full of stinging fluorescent light, the rug with an uneasy writhing pattern that was at least second cousin to the one in *The Shining*. What a kicker of a story *that* was.

He concentrated, the skin on his hand moving uneasily, and the deadbolt inside the door *chucked* shut. Shook his fingers out—it stung, Jesus, that was uncomfortable. Found himself pressing his aching fingertips to his mouth, mashing them hard enough he could feel his incisors through his lips. The searchlight hesitated overhead; he *felt* it, a pressure against eardrums, teeth, the backs of his knees. It slid past him, and fastened on the room behind the door.

Marlock pressed the kiss on his fingertips against the plywood. It was the closest to her he was ever going to get, from now on.

He wasn't even trying to be a good man. He was a fucking toad, because he was *scared*. Not of the Skinner, though that asshole was something to be cautious about.

No, he was terrified of Jude Altfall's eventual realization of what, and who, Preston Marlock really was. Seeing that pretty face of hers twist into a mask of disgust. Class was class, and he wasn't.

Not even close.

He ran his hands back through his hair, and his stride lengthened. He shouldn't even watch from a distance to see them pick her up.

Marlock hit the stairs at a run. He'd take the Taurus and check into another motel near the freeway, get some rest so he was sharp for a long drive tomorrow.

The girls had a ride coming. And he had a job to get back to.

Chapter Forty-Three

JUST TALENTED

JUDE ALTFALL DREAMED.

The van rocked slowly, the howling wind turned to a low groan. She had time to see the lightning come, a solid bar of it from the sky filling the figure of a man with pure incandescence. His hands stretched out, and something inside her turned—not sideways, precisely, but inward. Or in some direction there wasn't a name for, a flash of recognition, and the white fingers clawed along the pavement, scorching chunks and throwing small rocks free like popcorn. It reached the van, and Jude threw her arms wide, her body pitching violently.

Hit me. Don't hit them. Leave them alone.

The same old song. Dave had started in on the kids. Little things, pokes and pinches. Everything inside her rose up in rebellion. Confronting him, even though she knew she shouldn't. Don't you ever touch my daughter again.

His fury. The world upside down. Later, the emergency room, Aggie at the Laurel Hill house with the frightened, timid kids, and Jude bending over in the scrubbed-down curtained cubicle, trying to muffle the sobs, can you tell me who hurt you, Mrs. Edwards?

Oh yeah, she could. She did. She tried.

Hit me. Leave them alone.

When you got right down to it, that was motherhood. Stepping into it was like picking out a comfortable sweater, one you'd never had before but knew every inch of because your whole life you'd done what was best. What was expected. Smoothing over, supporting, helping, taking care. The relief, in marrying Dave, thinking maybe, just maybe, it was her turn to be taken care of.

Selfish Jude. No wonder it had turned sour.

The raindrops on the van's windshield flashed. Their tiny cries were lost in the impact, and Jude fell spinning into darkness, knowing it was a dream and she would jerk awake at any moment, because that's what happened when—

Falling. Something wasn't right. She wasn't waking up.

Bright white pierced the hole she floated in, a searchlight from a twisted, blackened tower. A sterile white glare.

There you are, you bitch. You *stole* it.

Falling. Those scythes of light cutting closer, closer, and when they touched Jude—

—jolted upright, sweating, ribs heaving and a bubble of something hot and foul in her throat. Beside her, Aggie made the soft sounds she usually did while sleeping. Not quite snores, but too heavy to be called sighs. Ag could fall asleep at a moment's notice, and she could be counted on to doze right through a nuclear attack. It boggled the mind, but then, so much about her little sister did.

She'd been born cheerful, where family legend had it Jude had come out watchful from the beginning.

Just like Essie had. Now Jude wondered if it was a first-child thing, or if she, like Essie, had seen...things.

Her hands shook, tiny pale branches caught in a windstorm. No, Mom and Dad had loved each other, and neither of them had ever raised a hand to their girls. They didn't need to, between Jude's desire to please and Aggie's good nature. Which just made Jude falling for Dave a personal failure rather than a continuation of family trauma, right? Never quite measuring up no matter how hard she worked reaching its natural conclusion.

The room was full of predawn hush, indifferent curtains blocking the cold gray glow of the window, hanging limp and lifeless. There was the small table, with the plundered cartons of takeout stacked neatly. The bathroom door was almost closed, golden electric light outlining its edges. Maybe he was in there.

Why would he be in there with the door open? Maybe that was some sort of bodyguard thing. He never said *exactly* what he did for a living. If it involved knowing what to do with dead bodies and supernatural tattoos, it was probably a doozy of a career.

Jude rubbed at her face, thin skin over bone, the crusts on her eyes proving she'd leaked in her sleep, too. She glanced at the bedside clock. Six-thirteen.

On a normal day, both the kids would be up, getting ready for school. A regular morning was only thinly controlled chaos. Get the kids up, get the cereal for them, pour juice, throw on the clothes she laid out the night before over the one chair in their living room, make up the two mattresses in the one bedroom because making your bed was a good habit and made you more successful. Get the kids dressed, check their shoes, make sure they had their raincoats, make sure she had everything she needed in her purse, check their backpacks, calm any morning fidgets and adjudicate any morning disputes. Check out the window, scrutinizing the slice of parking lot she could see, with the brown and white van in her one appointed parking spot clearly visible. Check the peephole before opening the door, ushering the kids downstairs, always ready, always on edge, because Dave could find them.

Instead, here she was in a hotel room, not hurrying to get through the morning and gulping a mouthful or two of juice to fuel her through the drive to their school. No kids. No husband. No house. Nothing but her sister.

She'd even ruined Aggie's *house*. Normally it took skill and dedication to fuck a life up so thoroughly. Jude was, apparently, just *talented*.

The heat was on. That was why she was sweating. There was no sound from the bathroom. Of course, you could sit in there forever with very little noise, attending to personal business, right?

There wasn't even that subliminal sense of someone breathing. Mommy Radar, Aggie called it. Eyes in the back of your head, predicting trouble when it got too quiet, learning all those little signals that added up to a sixth sense.

Maybe Marlock was out in the parking lot? Getting breakfast? All those scars on him, and his black, black eyes.

We don't know what makes a Mark, or a potential. Reciting it, flat and even, as if he'd said it plenty of times before.

It was comfortable with her face in her hands. If she blocked out the world, maybe she could imagine Aggie's sleep sounds were covering up Essie's breathing, and Simon's. She could imagine them on a cot, maybe in front of the television, Sy's thumb securely in his mouth and Essie's arm thrown over her brother, their sleep-rosy cheeks and matted eyelashes. They both had such beautiful eyes.

Not anymore, Jude.

If she'd just stayed with Dave…maybe she could have moderated him. Maybe persuaded him to go to counseling, somehow. If she'd just done something different, not chosen Bath End that day. A pretty drive, she'd thought. It would help her calm down before she broke the layoff news to Aggie.

Christ. She didn't even whether it was a school day or a weekend.

Jude dropped her hands. Her hip twinged a little, the skin twitching over…it.

The Mark.

She probably would have checked herself into an institution if Aggie hadn't been there to see all the…insanity. It was the only word that applied.

You're glowing, Jude. This was completely crazy.

Where had Marlock gone? Maybe he'd come back. She should use the peace and quiet to think, and to form a few questions so she understood what the hell was—

Skreek.

It was the deadlock on the door, slowly turning. Jude's heart began to trip along quickly again. It had to be him. He'd probably gone to get breakfast. *Safer for you than for me.*

Still, her Mark kept twitching. A black ball of dread had settled in her guts. Was it just because she didn't like the idea of talking to anyone right now, or…

"Jude?" Aggie surfaced, blinking and yawning. "Oh, hey."

Jude tensed, watching the door. The lock was moving really, really slowly.

Maybe he just didn't want to wake them up? He was so weird, so cold one minute, and going out to get different food the next. Spiky on the outside, kind of weird and charming inside. What had his near-death experience been like? He hadn't said.

"Hey." Aggie stretched. "Is there any coffee in this joint?"

A terrible, terrifying certainty hatched from the dread-ball in Jude's guts. "Aggie," she whispered. "Aggie, I think there's someone—"

The knob turned, the door flew open, and Jude was off the bed in a heartbeat, spreading her arms, tripping on her jeans on the floor by the bed. Two hefty-shouldered men piled through, a third shadow looming in the doorway, and the last thing

Jude saw before the closest gorilla hit her a stunning blow across the face was that the shadow in the door had a gun, its strangely elongated barrel pointed straight at her, then tracking sideways with nightmare slowness.

Towards her sister.

A brief burst of light, a coughing sound, and Jude began, pointlessly, helplessly, to scream.

Chapter Forty-Four

A HAT-TRICK OR TWO

HIS PERSONAL CELL buzzed. For once, Marlock didn't feel like answering, even if it might be one of his little helper elves telling him there was another body to add to the rosary since he'd been dinking around so uselessly here. He fished it out, swearing as the pouch slipped against his fingertips, and had longing thoughts of chucking it out the window.

Dawn was rising rose and pearl, and it was going to be a beautiful spring day once the clouds burned off. He could just tell by the way it smelled. He had the window down despite the chill, and the Taurus had reached freeways speed easily enough.

He got the pouch undone and the phone slithered in his hand. Some days were like that. You just couldn't catch a break.

"What?" he snarled.

"Preston Marlock, what the *hell?*" a familiar, raspy bass snarled back.

He turned to ice, glancing at the rearview. "How the fuck did you get this number?"

"Oh, you think I just let you go off on your own for two years? After stealing that chunk of agency funding? I thought you were more of a realist. Listen, Press—"

"Did you pick her up?" He *was* going to throw the phone out the window, sure. As soon as he knew she was safe. If Phil had this number...Marlock's brain tried to freeze up, racing through alternatives. He forced himself to breathe, to watch traffic.

"Well, yeah, about that. There are contractors crawling all over, what the fuck gives? You trying to doublecross me, or—"

What? "You didn't pick her up?"

"Someone else got to the hotel before we did, Press. Your Marked is gone, and the sister—we think it's the sister, she's blonde—"

"Yeah, that's the sister." His lips were numb. *Shit. Shit, shit, shit.* "Who took her?"

"You tell me, you sonofabitch! The sister's in critical at Foss General."

He was cold all over. "*Fuck.* They took her. Do you have eyes?"

"Some security footage, a burner license plate. We think it's three of those goddamn crackerjack mercs Texas keeps spewing out."

He's got deep pockets, the bastard. "Trace them. Throw everything you've got at it. It's him."

"You think you can just bark fucking orders at—"

Things were about to get very simple. "You told me they wouldn't let me go after him, Phil. Two years ago." The next exit was creeping up fast, and Marlock started working over to the right lane. A horn blared, but he was past caring. "Now you—"

"Oh, yeah. Research wanted him brought in and fed candy until we got everything he knew. You know, and I fucking know, that's not fucking good enough. I *let* you go, and covered for you. Now you'd better have something to show for it, you freak-assed bastard, or things are going to get very fucking hot for *both* of us." Phil snorted, as if he couldn't quite believe Preston didn't already know this.

You goddamn... A sheet of red covered his vision. He just made the exit, snapping the brakes on, steering onto the shoulder and spewing up a sheet of gravel. "What. Did. You. Say?"

"I *said*, I let you go and I covered for you. Do you know what it was like, with Research breathing down my neck? They've tried to pin me for misappropriated funds *twice*, you bastard. Now, do you have a lock on this motherfucker or not?"

"I do," Marlock lied. "Chase down those mercenaries."

"What are you going to—"

Shut the fuck up. "Next time I see you, I'm going to punch you in the face."

"Likewise. You'd better have something to pull out of your ass, Press."

"Yeah. Get those mercs, and check their cashflow."

Phil hung up. Press sat for a moment, listening to the Taurus's engine, forcing himself to breathe. In, out. Easy, deep breaths. He had a car with no real pickup and was an hour and a half from the city. It hadn't been the agency Press had felt, that searchlight overhead. It had been the Skinner, and Preston Marlock had handed him Jude on a silver platter, sleeping trustfully.

The fact that it had been his original plan was just as bitterly amusing as anything else in his wasted, useless life.

"Fuck." His hands cramped. The steering column made a low noise of strain; he forced himself to loosen his grasp. *You son of a bitch. You managed to fuck up everything, once again.* It would do no good to hit something and cripple the car. Instead, the rage turned inward.

Just like usual.

He stared at the windshield, seeing nothing but the spatters of dead insects and the dust-marks left by drying fog droplets. Forced himself to go quiet, to go *cold*, and to think.

Agnes Altfall was in the hospital. If he could get to her while she was still alive, he might be able to pull a hat trick or two. It wouldn't be comfortable, and Aggie might not come away from the experience quite sane. If she was in critical condition, he'd need to draw the energy to look through Aggie's head from somewhere else, and Jude, that sunlight-source, was out of reach. So he'd have to decide, once again, who would live and who would die.

That was why he'd left Jude and her sister sleeping, really. Everyone, sooner or later, was expendable. He didn't want to expend either of them.

Well, he didn't want to expend *Jude*. Aggie he could live without, but still.

Get going, Marlock. You've got a couple hours to come up with a plan.

He eyed the gas gauge, checked his blind spot, and pulled out. In a few minutes he was on the freeway going the opposite direction, sliding his phone back into its pouch. After a couple miles he realized he was reciting them, the names of his rosary. An hour would just about get him to Erik's.

God damn it. I am not going to add hers to the list.

Chapter Forty-Five

A Treasure

The collector recognized the number, sighed, and turned the water off. Steam rose from the scalloped bathtub, and the tentacled markings on his ribs were raw. The collector dried his hands thoroughly, roughly, on a pale blue towel, and picked up the phone, blinking a little against the soft peach-tone lighting. Marble underfoot was dangerously slippery, but nothing was as nice as its chill against bath-warmed feet.

"Sir." It was Mr. Bell. "Half the package has arrived."

Well, wasn't that irritating. "Which half?"

"The more important one, sir."

That meant he had her. He had the woman who had stolen Sturmhalten's mark from him. The collector closed his eyes, savoring the moment. "Wonderful. Simply wonderful. Is there any damage?"

"Very slight. Very…enthusiastic delivery people."

Irritation boiled at the base of his spine; he throttled it. *I wanted her whole, not even bruised.* "Very well. I shall arrive soon. Please…unpack, and put the welcoming mat down."

"Yes, sir." For the first time, there was a shade of something in Mr. Bell's tone. Was it disgust, perhaps? The welcome the collector had planned for Jude Altfall was not pretty, true. Often, it was better to soften the prey before sinking one's claws in.

Yes, this employee of his was going to be sorely missed. Perhaps the collector's first test of the new item, with all its glorious glowing force, could do double duty in that area. Or perhaps not. It was altogether too precious to be squandered on an underling.

"Very well done, Mr. Bell. You deserve a reward." *And you shall receive one.*

"Just doing my job, sir. Anything else?"

"No, thank you. Oh—the champagne?"

"Already chilling in its bucket, sir."

"You are a treasure." He hit the disconnect button and eased himself down into the hot water full of expensive mineral salts, a slight hiss escaping his lips as his scraped ribs submerged.

Perhaps the collector would keep this particular employee for a little longer. It was time-consuming, selecting and training them. Still, safety demanded caution.

He did not have to decide until he peeled the item from a sobbing, possibly broken, but still breathing Altfall woman. Once he had that treasure in his grasp, much would be clearer to him.

The collector slid under the water, bubbles escaping his tight, bloodless mouth as he laughed for joy.

Chapter Forty-Six

PRETTY HORSES

HER FACE HURT. Jude huddled in a corner, her arms around her bare knees, shivering.

The room was a bare, white, padded rectangle with one open side. The only breaks in the padding on three walls were a small one-way observation slit in the door and a circular drain in the middle of the floor. Which meant they had to hose the vinyl pads down between visitors, right?

It was warm enough in here, even without her clothes. She wasn't shivering.

The fourth wall—the long one on the right—was not really a wall. Bars, with the same vinyl padding sealed on them somehow, marched down it in evenly spaced cadence, too close together for her to fit through. Not that she'd want to. Behind those bars was another room, concrete where this one was padded, and with no door. There was a drain in the floor over there, too.

The misshapen thing in the other room twitched. It smelled awful in here, and the heat made it worse. The tattoo-thing on her hip was going crazy, alternately burning and freezing. She could *feel* it moving, throbbing like a bruise.

The thing in the other corner exhaled a long fruity buzzing, and the stench got even more unbearable.

It's not there. You didn't see it. It's not there.

Except it was. Bloated and discolored, the light striping its face, her ex-husband's body lay. Even swollen and livid, she recognized him. He wasn't breathing. She recognized his hands, too, his blunt fingers, and the tuft of dark hair over his forehead that used to give him such trouble. He couldn't have a high-and-tight with that cowlick, it would just make him look like a cartoon. She'd teased him about it, long ago before they were married, back when he was sweet and funny and caring. When his possessiveness seemed like love, when he brought her long-stemmed roses and told her *you'll never need another man, sweetheart.*

Her hair, damp and tangled, couldn't cover much more than her shoulders and the upper slopes of her breasts. They'd jabbed her with a syringe in the hotel room, and though she ached all over, it didn't seem like she'd been…well, they hadn't…molested her.

Call it what it is, Jude.

They hadn't raped her.

No, they just shot Aggie and knocked you out. And put you here.

She squeezed her eyes shut. The smell was Dave's body decomposing. Who would do something like this? *Why* were there people who would do things like this? Shooting people, frying them with lightning, sticking them in a cell with their ex-husband's dead body, and the scars all over Marlock's torso. How could *anyone* do these things? What made them this way?

She remembered sitting in church on long drowsy Sunday midmornings, her mother straight-backed beside her and her father holding the hymnal, mouthing the responses to the priest's incantations, uncomfortable in her scratchy dress. Later, with Aggie squirming next to her, and their shared code of glances and eyerolls.

They'd both stopped going after Mom and Dad died. Father Dannon had called every once in a while, with gentle questions. *We miss you at Mass, Judith.*

The world grayed out again, but this time she heard faint singing. More a breath and a hum than actual words.

Hush-a-bye, don't you cry,
When you wake you shall have all the pretty horses...

Mom had sung that, usually when Jude or Aggie was sick. Later, they would sing it to each other. All the pretty horses, the dapples and grays, the blacks and bays. Dreaming of vast herds of them, surging motion and gentle, sad equine eyes.

Jude came back with a jolt. She was still naked, still too warm, sweating and shivering as if she had some sort of fever. Maybe she did.

He killed my friend, Marlock's voice whispered, swirling inside her head. God, why did things like this *happen*? Praying didn't help, it was simply begging. Maybe God was just a bigger version of

Dave, who could sometimes be placated if she abased herself enough.

Now, wasn't *that* an awful thought?

She pressed her face into her knees, hard. The smell was harder to block out that the glaring, faintly pink light.

Another long gassy sound from the cell next door. Something escaping the…body. The dead body.

Oh, God. Dave, you were an asshole, but I'm sorry. I'm sorry for everything.

Sorry even for *breathing*. Aggie's low disbelieving moan as the gun coughed, the starburst of pain when the man backhanded her. How did someone decide beating up women in hotel rooms and dragging them to cells like this was a good job to have? Were there benefits? Retirement? Health insurance?

Her face ached, ached. One of her eyes was swelling shut. It took a lot of force to break the cheekbone, she'd heard. A *lot* of force. Had they? No, if they had, splinters might be working into her brain right now.

The cold flashes through her hip began to fade. A steady heat-glow replaced them, but Jude kept her face buried in her knees. There were stealthy sounds from next door. Was it the processes of decay speeding up in the heat? How long had his body been there?

Jesus Christ, people are horrible. Everything is horrible. What kind of God could do this?

The lullaby came back, between bursts of static. A radio dial in her head, picking up a weird signal. Where had Marlock gone? Had he somehow…maybe just left them there, then went to make a phone call, or…

Or maybe he would come in that door. Maybe *he* was the Skinner, and he'd just been playing with her. Just like a cat playing with a half-dead, terrified mouse. Would he do something like that? She'd never thought Dave would hit her, so her judgment was seriously in question—

Who cares? You're here now, Jude. Look around. Find something to use.

There was nothing. Not a stick of furniture in the whole damn room. Nothing but that body over there, and the warmth on her hip, as the hateful thing that had made sure she wouldn't die with her children like a good mother should shifted, shifted.

More noise. Foul exhalations. A dragging sound.

Then, the impossible. A long, whispering moan from the other cell, whistling through a rotting throat.

"*Juuuuuude*," Dave's body whispered, as it began to twitch in sync with the mark on her hip.

Jude pressed her hot, wounded, throbbing face into her knees even harder. In a cracked, wavering voice, she began to sing.

Chapter Forty-Seven

WARM AND JUSTIFIED

PAPER-PALE, LOOKING oddly small in a jacked-up bed surrounded by wires and loops of tubing, her golden hair limp and dispirited, Aggie Altfall lay very, very still. She was intubated, the machine breathing for her, and it was probably only sheer cussedness that had kept her body alive this long. Maybe it was genetic, the sisters had plenty of stubbornness to go around. Marlock drifted past, taking his time to read the situation even though his entire body was shrieking with impatience.

There were two cops outside the ICU ward, and another two at the door to Aggie's room. Maybe that was due to the agency's interest in this whole clusterfuck, maybe it was because her family was old money, or maybe it was because the cops suspected something wasn't quite right with an heiress found shot in a cheap hotel. Who knew? Maybe they'd sent someone to the house and found the front door battered and the kitchen door nailed over with plywood.

Marlock slid through the hospital ward like a ghost, checking the exits, transmitting *don't see me* on every wavelength. His temples ached, throbbing in time to his footsteps, probably because he was gritting his teeth. This was what came from trying to be decent. He should have stuck to the goddamn plan, and if he had, he could probably have been throttling the Skinner at his leisure right now. As it was, right now he had to get both the door-cops into Aggie's room and get the blinds in there shut so he could work.

What was happening to Jude right now? Was the Skinner playing with her? The battered, broken bodies were all in Marlock's head, the rosary beating time to his footsteps as well. If he had to add Jude to that list…she already had enough to deal with, what was the bastard doing…

He hired mercenaries. They don't come cheap. Aggie must have seen something I can use to track them. She has to have. Then they'd have to transport Jude to somewhere the bastard can pick her up.

He'd been driving away, feeling all warm and justified because he'd been a good guy for once.

Well, never fucking again, that was for goddamn sure. If he got there too late, and Jude's body…the skin bearing her Mark peeled away, leaving a glaring patch of red muscle underneath and the white of tendon, or maybe a marbling because even skinny, women had a softness to their hips.

For fuck's sake, Marlock. Do your job.

Tucked in an alcove down the hall, he stripped his driving gloves off, closed his eyes, and tried to shut everything else out. First, get the meat into Aggie's room. Then—

Running footsteps. Something happening. He slid to the hallway and peered down it. Someone was coding.

Oh, fuck.

It was Aggie's room they were clustering.

Marlock sprinted down the hall, the smear making him noiseless. Slapped his bare palm on the back of a nurse's neck, under her ponytail, and *pulled*. Not enough to kill, just enough to put her down for a bit. He crowded among them, one of the cops reaching for his service piece with admirable speed, stopping when Marlock fixed him with a hot glare and slipped sideways into the smear, darkness taking over. The ECG at Aggie's side was flatline, and the machine was emitting a piercing noise that made it hard to think, for God's sake.

Inside the smear, time slowed down. He nudged the second cop behind the knee, knocking him sideways, and the flood of hot life pulsing into him was so good, so good. Dropped the doctor with a touch, and shoved aside one of the nurses, slapping a hand on hers and yanking at her maybe a little too hard, because she went down hard in a boneless heap. *Sorry, lady.* The cops were both barely holding on, he shoved the sleeve of Aggie's hospital johnny up and wrapped both hands around her slim arm.

The stolen life flowed from him, hot and juicy, his lips skinning back from his teeth. It was difficult to reverse the flow. For Jude it was probably easy as breathing, she just pumped all that energy out—

It wasn't enough. Aggie was slipping away. He could *see* the bullet now, lodged between her spine and the back of the abdominal aorta, lots of swelling around it. Lots of damage to the internals, and it was too deep for a scalpel to pick out. Anyone who did would risk nicking an artery and bleeding her out in seconds. Too goddamn deep to be fished out.

Not too deep for a miracle, he hoped.

This one's gonna cost you, Preston. He reached, blindly, for all the energy he could grab, his skin swiftly darkening. The lights fluttered overhead as he jacked into that current, but it still wasn't enough. The lump of metal was stubborn too, and everything around it so swollen and violated...

Goddamn you, do it.

Consciousness wavered. There were other struggling lives in this place as well. How much of an asshole did he want to be? How many names to add to the rosary, so Aggie would *live*? And it still might be no good, she might not have seen anything, or Jude might already be—

He bent over, his face turning to a mask of effort, the smear fraying around him. Then, in one blind lunge, he pulled on every life he could reach, every scrap of electricity he could touch, *everything*.

Sparks. Screams. Choking gasps and rattles as they sagged and fell, a whole ward going deadly silent after the soft, sudden exhales.

Almost there.

He *pulled* again, this time against the reserves in dying cells and the nerveglow left in suddenly-vacant bodies. More electrical current, too. The dark globe around him spread, sucking in every spark of light or life it could find, and his Mark was a pulsing, deeper-black star in the middle of it, funneling a point of bright white-hot light into a small, violated body.

Smoke. More screams. A siren somewhere, the energy of soundwaves falling dead into his sphere.

The distorted, flattened bullet smacked into his palm, searing metallic pain filling his arm, and Marlock coughed, blood spraying between his lips. On the hospital bed, a woman's body convulsed in complete darkness. It knew what to do and how to heal, he just had to give it enough power to do so. Enough time. Just another few seconds.

The ink-black sphere took another breath, and expanded a few feet, bleaching everything at its margins.

It shrank, receding, the walls it had sucked free of solidity began to crumble. Groaning and snapping, the entire hospital shuddered.

The bodies, shriveled papery husks, turned to greasy, gritty ash. Marlock's eyes rolled back in his head, one final awful grunt of effort falling lifeless to the thinning floor. If he pulled much more out of the structure, the whole goddamn building might collapse. He went down to his knees with a jolt, shaking his ringing head. The intubation whipped free, spraying blood, spit, and vomitus in a high arc.

Agnes Altfall sat up, and screamed.

Chapter Forty-Eight

RIPE, SIR

THE HELICOPTER BANKED, a glorious gliding motion. Every time he considered the expenditure to have such a vehicle prepped and ready at a moment's notice, he thought of situations like this. Convenience and quality were well worth the cost. He had wanted to pilot down himself, but it was much better this way. He could drive back at leisure with his new acquisition in its carrying case and that glorious feeling of serenity and satisfaction filling his every nerve.

The lakeside house, with its long pier and breathtaking scenery, sat on fifty acres of lovely forest and meadows. The familiar mountains in the distance were a somber reminder of the ultralight crash that had given him his own gifts, and sometimes he watched the sun go down from the pier, seeing the pile of rock thrust up from a planet's agony turn different shades as night rose. He could still see the exact spot where the craft went down, a trapezoidal patch just above the treeline.

It was the kind of sight that would force a man to think deep thoughts about mortality, even a non-evolved specimen. The vista presented itself from a different angle right now—it had taken too long to get here, really. Pleasures were sometimes best delayed, and his acquisition was safe. He could afford to dawdle a bit. Stretch out the fun, but not too long.

The landing pad, a grassy field, rippled under waves of disturbed air. There was Mr. Bell, a straight dark shadow in the gathering dusk, a powerful flashlight in one of his capable hands. The collector hopped down, nimbly, his travel bag bouncing against his knee. He bent as he scurried away from the whirring bird, and after a few moments, the heli lifted off again.

The collector's orders had been very clear.

A wide, dusty path led to the house, winding down a long, gentle hill. Normally, there would be an ATV to take him there, but tonight the collector wanted to walk. Mr. Bell greeted him quietly once the helicopter's noise had faded, and the flashlight's beam anticipated the collector's steps.

Finally, as they reached the bottom of the hill, the collector allowed himself a question. "How is the package?"

"Bruised a bit on the face. The sedation has worn off, she changed position."

One more question. "And her welcome present?"

"Ripe, sir."

Good. Maybe she would be catatonic. It would rob him of *some* enjoyment, but it would make the acquisition much smoother. He sometimes couldn't decide what he preferred, struggle or ease. This had been troublesome, but on the other hand, he was interested and engaged in a way he had not been for many a hunt. "Wonderful work, Mr. Bell. I commend you."

"Thank you, sir." Modest, almost to a fault.

He might have asked if the man would like to join him, as a special treat. But familiarity with employees could only go so far. "You may retire to the boathouse, once the security is checked."

"Yes, sir."

They reached the porch. It really was a very small affair, only four bedrooms, each kept ready for guests by employees who made the weekly trip from town. In the basement, behind dusty shelves in a partially-finished room, was a vault the architect had intended as a safe-room. The collector had made the further modifications himself, enjoying working with his hands.

Now, it was the playroom. There was the padded cell, the barred cell, and the anteroom with the operating table and its row of bright-shining instruments. He had checked the vault's security and equipment just a month ago, when he had begun planning to acquire Sturmen's artifact. He would have to review the footage from the security cameras, to make sure Mr. Bell hadn't been...tempted...by his prize.

The collector allowed himself a broad, genuine smile as he went up the steps and reached the screen door. A bird called across the lake, a long, distorted trill. It was good to be alive, and to have something to look forward to. "Good night, Mr. Bell."

"Goodnight, sir." Bell turned the flashlight towards his own feet, and struck off parallel to the house.

It was very sad, the collector decided. He really was going to have to train a new handyman. Not until after he had enjoyed himself, but still. Work never ended, there were always new peaks to conquer. Alexander the Great merely hadn't had the required altitude from mortality to see as much.

Humming faintly, the collector pressed his thumb onto the scan-lock next to the door. The small light on it flashed green, and he stepped into the warm cocoon of a house left unoccupied and smelling like it, even if the heat had been turned on in anticipation of his arrival. Nothing was ever quite perfect, really.

It was a shame.

Chapter Forty-Nine

CHOWDER TO CASHEWS

OF COURSE THE agency had been waiting for him to show at the hospital. Two teams, and if he'd been interested in getting out of here, he would have wasted them both to top up after expending everything on Aggie. Their orders were clearly to secure, not to engage, and only one of them gave a low whistle at the state of the whole ICU. They saw all sorts of shit, really, and got good bennies and fat pensions to make up for it.

If anything could make up for seeing the cracks in the world's sanity, that was.

Marlock's bare, callused hands lay empty in his lap. Aggie shivered, a hospital blanket over her shoulders. The cloth had been carried in from outside Marlock's reach, and it looked like it, fresh and new instead of bleached and frayed. The walls here were barely holding their load, and the lights flickered, buzzing. He'd probably blown out a few fuses.

More than a few.

Phil Grier, his hair much thinner and his potbelly much smaller than it had been two years ago, patted Aggie's shoulder, awkwardly. His suit jacket was rumpled, and under the hem of his trousers he was wearing a navy sock and a black one. For all that, his shoes were polished, and the chilly, calculating gleam in his eye was bright as ever. "Miranda here will get you some clothes. You're okay, Miss Altfall, we won't let anything happen to you." Beside Grier was a fresh-faced intern with a chestnut ponytail, hovering in her navy jumper and uniform pants, who kept glancing nervously at Marlock.

He didn't blame her. He just sat there, not even caring that his hands were bare and his Mark was digging its claws in.

It wanted feeding. He'd expended a lot of energy.

"Jude," Aggie husked. It hurt to hear her talk—the tube had done a number on her throat. "He was looking for her." Her arm twitched, as if she wanted to point at Marlock, but couldn't quite bring herself to do it. "My sister."

"That's what we're working on, Miss. Miranda will get you checked out, will get you some clothes, then we'll talk."

He didn't need to tell her again. Aggie slid off the bed, yanking at the needles in her arm. The intern stepped in, making soft noises, and hustled her out after a quick, professional detangling. Aggie would probably be in a nice room at one of the centers before she knew it, held gently in a velvet-covered iron fist. They would debrief her and give her a full battery of tests, and if she was a good little girl they might even let her go home eventually, after signatures on a few non-disclosure docs and explanations of just how fast the agency could ruin a civilian's life if said civilian opened their mouth without clearance.

Phil let out a long sigh. He was even wearing a sidearm, it showed as his tan jacket flapped a little. He tested the bed with a tentative shove, and it rocked. The sheets were friable, he could rip them with a fingernail if he wanted to.

He didn't look at Marlock just yet.

Finally, when the sound of Aggie's harsh breathing and hitching, gasping shudders had faded, he addressed the buckled, wilting IV pole next to the bed. "Tell me you've got something."

"Nope." Marlock didn't have the energy to lie. Aggie had been shot while she was still in mazy dreamland, lost consciousness quickly and hadn't even known Jude was gone until she woke up in a hospital bed with another nightmare looming over her.

Phil waited, but not for very long. His thin, bloodless fingers twitched slightly—he liked to fidget with a pen, when things got rough. "Seventeen casualties on this floor. Damage to the building. This is a *hospital*. So very *public*. We trained you better."

Marlock's own throat wasn't in good shape. There was something in it he didn't want to examine very closely. "Fuck. Off."

"Well, I'd like to. They'll throw you in a hole and throw away the hole, Press. You'll be in a real prison, not a turn-of-the-century sweetheart state pen."

Like they could stick him anywhere he couldn't escape. "Go ahead." *Two years. I blew it.*

"You would already be cuffed and stuffed if I was going to do that." Amazingly, the smirk of a satisfied vulture slid over the man's pallid face. His tie, a nice deep navy, was nylon, and Marlock felt a brief flare of interest as he considered strangling his former handler with it.

"Then what?" *If you're looking to re-recruit me, this is a shitty way to do it.* Marlock's shoulders hurt. So did his legs. His Mark dug its claws in some more. It was his chest that hurt the most, and he kept telling himself it was just the echoes of Aggie's injury.

"Cheer up. You might want to also *get* up, and get cleaned off. You look like shit."

"Thanks." *Why should I bother getting up?* He didn't move.

Phil executed a prissy little quarter-turn. He crouched, his knees popping, and peered at Marlock with bright, avid little eyes. "Oh, you'd better thank me, you suckass, and you'd better saddle the fuck up. Because I'm about to save your goddamn life *and* your goddamn day."

Then, very precisely, in that big voice that was so ridiculous coming from such a skinny, pasty little man, he began to lay it out, from chowder to cashews. They'd found the mercenaries.

Marlock, braced against a wobbling wall, just stared at him in disbelief.

Chapter Fifty

SEARCHLIGHT, SHADOW

IT SPLATTED AGAINST the bars again, and Jude flinched. She couldn't back through the wall, though sometimes she caught her feet working, her heels leaving bloody smears on the padding as she tried to force herself further into the corner. The corpse heaved itself up on its elbows—its left lower arm dangled drunkenly, something in the joint refusing to work quite right—and heaved itself in her direction. It kept making that *noise*, over and over, the long exhale that sounded like her name slurred in a drunken, tongue-swollen mouth.

The mark on her hip had started to throb in a different way now, a purposeful heartbeat. She tried desperately to think of something good, something *sane*, something that wasn't the rotting body trying to get through the bars or the horrible certainty that sooner or later the padded door would open and something even worse would show up.

All she could think of was Aggie's choked sound after the bullet plowed into her. Rain, drumming on a minivan's roof. Dave, when he was alive, screaming at her in the parking lot. The gun skittering away from his hand.

Even the lullaby didn't help. She'd sung it until her voice gave out, and it just seemed to madden the…the body. The corpse. The walking—no, the *crawling* dead. It thrust a dripping, filthy fist through the bars, flayed fingers spreading and grabbing empty air.

Maybe this was all a hallucination. But the *smell*, dear God, and no hallucination could be this *detailed*, the squirming little bits of tissue dropping off Dave's body, the scintillation on the surface of droplets of her own sweat, the fine hairs on her arms rising, the insistent prickle of stubble on her knees because she hadn't shaved her legs since…

The world threatened to fall away from underneath her, but she held on, grimly, the same way she'd held on that afternoon Dave came back to the house on Ash Lane while the kids were at school. He'd been so *quiet*, knowing every creak and squeak in the house, and he'd clapped his hand over her mouth and dragged her to the bedroom. *Don't make a fucking sound, or I'll kill you.*

Oh, she believed he was capable of it. Then *and* now.

Really, though, the theory that this was her own personal hell was starting to hold a lot more water.

She couldn't cry anymore. Her eyes were shriveled raisins. Her heart kept going, though, matching the pulsing on her hip. Her breath kept stuttering in and out, and each time she thought she'd lose consciousness she held on, trying to think of something, *anything* that would help.

No lullaby. Nothing but the sounds from the bars as the thing heaved itself, fishlike, towards her again. That arm thrust through the bars, fell, and scraped its rotting fingernails on the padding. Sooner or later it was going to shred itself to just a torso and legs. Would he be able to fit through then?

Oh, God.

There was no God. There was only this horrific, malodorous room—and a new series of soft sounds as the observation slit on the padded door glinted.

Someone was watching. She could *feel* it, the gaze creeping over her like sweating hands, leaving a slugtrail in their wake.

She glared at the door from under the damp, wildly curling strings of her hair. *See something you like, asshole?*

Was it Marlock? Had he been playing a game the whole time?

The door shuddered slightly. The thing next door redoubled its hissing moan, and she was suddenly very sure it wasn't Marlock peeking in at her. It was someone else, with soft grasping clammy tentacles where Marlock was all spikes and sharp edges.

The searchlight came back, popping into her head so hard and fast she gasped. It stood on a gantry made of black metal and flashes of old ivory, and as Jude's eyelids fluttered the image firmed. She realized the white bits were *bones*, fused with the metal, and that terrible bright sterile white light slicing the darkness behind her lids belonged to whoever was watching her. The not-tattoo on her hip warmed up even more, its pulsing taking on an edge as well. The image wouldn't go away, even when she opened her eyes and stared desperately at the white vinyl, now stained where Dave's body kept reaching through and grasping.

"*Jhoooooooooo,*" the body moaned. Even dead, Dave wouldn't leave her alone.

What had Marlock said? *You can work miracles.*

Well, she'd made Marlock's skull heal itself. What was she going to do? Cure the asshole behind the door of cancer? Bring Dave back to life? She shuddered, her torn heels slipping in blood.

It shows who you are. What you do makes it grow, and affects the shape.

It was a fine time to wish she'd asked him more questions. A fine time to wish she'd never thought driving down Bath End was a good idea.

Wait just a second.

Something occurred to her, a blooming realization that made her breath catch. Things slowed down, the door beginning to move slightly, and whoever was behind it was the owner of the searchlight that had been hunting her, sleeping and waking. It felt *familiar*, and she lifted her head, her hands turning to fists, short and broken nails digging into her palms with sweet piercing pain.

The searchlight, and the shadow. The shadow behind the lightning. Whoever was behind that door was the darkness behind the lightning-glowing man in the road. He'd—and she was sure it was a *he*, in some deep inexplicable way—killed Marlock's friend.

Had Marlock's friend, in his dying agony, been trying to shield the battered, rusting minivan that had the bad luck to show up at the beginning of this nightmare?

I shouldn't have taken Bath End. Well, that was true. But she couldn't have known there were guys with superpowers waging war on it, under the greening trees, next to the pretty creek.

It hit her, like thunder after lightning. The realization uncurled like a fiddlehead fern made of razors and liquid flame.

This shadow, whoever he was, had killed her children.

Jude's lips drew back from her teeth. She unfolded too, slowly, as the door opened. Her legs cramped, vicious claws sinking into the big muscles on front, and her ass cramped too. Her heels were raw-bleeding, and she could smell a sharp urine stink. Everything inside her narrowed to a still, small point. Not sideways, but fully, achingly present.

The door swung inward. Behind it was a glare, and Jude blinked furiously, her eyes watering. The shadowy figure—male, taller than her—stepped forward, into the cell, with a single nose-wrinkle.

He was blond, an expensively-styled haircut that flopped over his eyes. The boyish smile settling over his handsome face was sickening in its intensity, and his pale-blue eyes were dead as hard-boiled eggs. A red polo shirt stretched over his broad chest, and a Rolex glimmered on his wrist.

He looked *finished*, in that way only prep school boys could, and he looked familiar. Where had she seen him before?

The corpse in the next room made another hissing sound, and splatted against the bars. The newcomer glanced in its direction, his eyes widening for just a moment.

Chapter Fifty-One

EVERYTHING PERFECT

"WELL." THE COLLECTOR smiled—broadly, expansively. She was too thin for his taste, but that didn't matter. Under the dotting and daubing of blood and sweat, there was a rippling on her hip. It was small and powerful, the marking she'd stolen. "Hello, Judith."

A mop of dark hair hanging in lank, sweat-stiff stings. She glared at him from underneath, and he allowed it. In a few minutes, he'd begin the work. Until then, let her have her petty little defiance. She said nothing.

The body in the cell next door heaved against the bars. It was rank in here, and for a moment he almost regretted instructing Mr. Bell to acquire the body and place it here. As a tactic, it was undeniably effective, but it *stank*. What about the marking she'd stolen was infusing the meat in the barred half of the playroom—what he thought of as the naughty half—with a simulacrum of life?

"*Jhooooo,*" the body crooned, a horrid sound slipping past dead, stiffened lips.

The collector's smile faltered for just a moment. The marking moved on her hip, but she wasn't screaming, or crying, or desperately looking for an escape. She didn't erupt into wild motion, like some of them. She just stood here, and her chin rose. She *looked* at him, perhaps seeing his excitement pressing hard against the well-worn but sharply ironed chinos he'd chosen for this session. He'd thought to extend the pleasure, now that she was *finally* here and his property was returned.

Now, a faint thread of unease surfaced. The collector hesitated, shifting instinctively to reach for the door. Perhaps he should leave her in here a little longer, to take the edge off that defiant expression.

Except…it wasn't defiance.

She tipped her chin up, and her hair fell away from her face. Two patches of angry red shone high on her cheeks. What a washed-out little bitch, looking at him like that. There were even stretch marks on her tits—she didn't even have the respect for herself to get some work done, for God's sake. He couldn't see the marking clearly, just an edge of it, moving against pale, fine-grained skin.

"Turn." He made a dismissive little motion, pointing at her left hip. "Show me."

She just stared at him.

"*Jhoooooooo,*" the corpse moaned again. Good God, but it *stank* in here. He'd wanted a shivering, sobbing, pliable victim, not this. She'd stolen from him, and now she was…what? She didn't move, didn't say a word.

The collector's patience was wearing thin. "Turn," he demanded, pointing at her left hip. "Show me what you stole, Judith."

"*Jhoooooo!*" Something shifted in the corpse's throat, a crackling. "*Jhoooooooooooood!*" It heaved itself against the bars again, and the marking on the bitch sped up. She did turn a little, but not because he'd told her. No, she just glanced at the other side of the playroom, the long padded wall. The marking—what little he could see—was beautiful. His own marking responded, prickle-buzzing along his ribs, and the idea that perhaps what she'd stolen might be stronger than his was extremely unwelcome.

He took another step into the playroom, and held out his hand. His watch glinted richly in the fluorescent glare. "That's right, Judith. Just a little turn, and you can come out of the playroom." Maybe she was simply stunned, not recalcitrant. The bitterness of disappointment rose, but the collector manfully pushed it back.

Not everything could be perfect.

He took another step. His deck shoes slipped a bit—*damn* it. Spatter from the corpse, and she'd pissed on the floor, just like an ill-trained cocker spaniel. The meat of her ex-husband reached through the bars, and those almost-fleshless, liquefying fingers closed around the hem of the collector's chinos. He braced himself to kick it away, but just then, she spoke. A low, sweet voice, ringing with power.

"You."

The collector glanced down. He could see the marking on her now. It moved, pinwheeling like a galaxy, and its beauty took his breath away.

"You." Very softly. She sucked in a breath as if she would scream.

The collector reached out, disbelieving, as if he could touch that sun-shaped, star-shaped, beautiful harmony of proportions and power stamped into her flesh.

Chapter Fifty-Two

PROTECTING HER OWN

IT'S SO BRIGHT in here. Jude's eyes didn't water, but they stung a little. It was not fury that rose inside her, but something more.

The deepest, bloodiest corner of rage is not flame. It is so cold it burns, and only one thing unleashes it.

He killed my kids.

Something was happening. She'd felt it once before, a dilation in her core and a streak of pure white fury piercing her. It had given her the strength to simply endure Dave's fevered grunting and the accompanying beating, and wait for him to leave the house. It had driven her to Aggie's, both the kids sniffling with fright in the van, and driven her to the emergency room afterward. It was much, much deeper than the desperation of a woman who had nothing left to lose.

It was the pure, utter certainty of a mother protecting her own.

Dave's body moaned her name again, and the bastard who had killed her children spread out his hand. He wasn't even looking at her, just at the goddamn not-tattoo.

Jude Altfall raised her chin, and let the light take her. It sang between her cells, filled her nerves with sweet white-wine flame, and it burst from her eyes and mouth, swords of brilliant white.

The murderer began to scream.

Chapter Fifty-Three

FIRE

IT *BURNED*. ALL over him, but especially against his ribs, where the marking that made him special shriveled with the flesh that carried it. The collector writhed, his carefully styled hair catching fire. The sickening smell of roasting pork mixed with corpse-reek, filling the room behind him with steamsmoke and foulness. The greenstick crack of bones breaking echoed against padded walls and cement, against the bars and the operating table and the shining instruments laid carefully on an adjustable swivel. The television screens in his playroom showing closed-circuit footage turned to static before exploding, and a gigantic hand caught the rags of his body and threw him back.

The light shrank. It was golden at its edges, but its heart was a white flame, compressing on itself. The moving corpse behind the padded bars burst into flame, folding down with a grateful, weary sigh, and the vinyl-covered pads began to smoke.

"*You,*" her soft, throaty voice said in the middle of the chaos. "*You killed my babies.*"

Everything went black for a long breathless moment. The agony was all through him, every scorched nerve singing a chorus of violation, and his own fury was brushed aside, an inconsequential insect.

A small, white star, glimmering in the swirling dark. He saw it before his eyes burst, runneling butterfat streaks down his cheeks that had just bare minutes ago been patted with expensive aftershave.

It was beautiful. It was the power he wanted, the power he craved.

It exploded.

Chapter Fifty-Four

PRECIOUS CARGO

HELICOPTERS BUZZED, BLACK birds scenting prey. Searchlights stabbed the wooded property before settling on a massive, ugly stack of log housing on the lake's western shore. The ground arm, a long snake of headlights, was coming down the miles of bumping gravel driveway, and ATVs hummed in the woods to draw the net tight.

The house, a few windows lit with electric gold, was silent. Soon, they would reach it. A shadow detached itself from the smaller bulk of a boathouse, built with a studio apartment and security feeds over the slowly rotting rowboat heaped on the first floor. The owner, apparently, was not an avid boater, despite the house's lovely location.

Mr. Bell, in a black knitted cap, a sweater, and dark jeans instead of a suit, kept low. He moved with an ease that bespoke some training in running while bent double, taking advantage of every cover. He was almost discovered by a few roving helicopter lights, and they might have caught him when the flares lit up overhead, if the main house had not…

Well, *exploded*.

One moment, there was a pile of faux-cabin on the lakeshore. The next, it *disintegrated*, a globe of brilliant white expanding to swallow the whole structure. A shockwave boomed out, and the helicopters danced as a wall of heated air crashed into them. Cars slewed wildly, radio chatter lighting up like Christmas trees, popping zing of gunfire in the trees as two of the ATV troops thought they were under rocket attack and blundered into each other.

The light shrank, leaving ghostly shapes dancing on everyone's retinas. One of the helicopters slid majestically downward into the lake, but both pilot and gunner survived—and were docked later for incompetence.

Where the house had stood, there was a smoking crater twenty feet deep. The entire thing had been vaporized. At the very bottom of the charred bowl, a single pale spot. Water trickled over the thin edge separating the crater from the lake's edge.

The hide Mr. Bell had prepared high up in a stand of pines was still solid, even if the flooring was a little crooked because the trees had bent before the shockwave. He settled down with binoculars, peering down the wooded slope at the ruffled lake, the pier truncated between the shore and ten feet out pointing its lonely finger at the distant, silent mountains. He watched as the teams went into the fast-filling crater and a small form was lifted out on a stretcher. It was bundled into a waiting LifeFlight helicopter, probably bristling with medical equipment inside, and the heli rose slowly, bearing its precious cargo into the night.

Mr. Bell continued to watch. Later, when the hubbub died down, he would hike out. There was a new identity waiting for him, plenty of cash, and a report to make.

His real name was most decidedly *not* Mr. Bell. And, if pressed, he might have admitted he was rather relieved the foul sonofabitch was dead.

There was, however, nobody there to ask him what he thought. Which was probably all for the best.

Chapter Fifty-Five

MAKE ME THE OFFER

THREE DAYS LATER

"Dennis Rowland." Phil tucked his hands in his armpits instead of folding his arms. It was dim in this cubicle-sized room, because the one-way mirror worked better that way. There was no camera equipment in here, though. Not yet. "Fortune 500, one of those extreme sports types. Crashed an ultralight in the mountains, was *miraculously* unhurt."

"You're shitting me." Marlock slumped against the wall, staring at the open file folder in his thankfully-not-shaking hands. The picture clipped to the first page was a publicity still, a blond motherfucker with bright blue eyes and a smarmy smile. The man was worth a couple billion, and the file had a list of suspected and verified victims Marlock could add to. "Probably when his Mark triggered."

"Well, we'll never know. His body was vaporized, along with that fucking lakehouse. And probably his executive secretary too. *That* asshole could answer a few questions."

"Too bad." The only thing that mattered was on the other side of the mirror, and Marlock kept his eyes on the pages.

Phil rocked back on his heels a bit, came back to balance. Same old sports jackets, same old violently patterned ties. "Yeah, well. His holdings are nice and substantial, and they're ours now. Finders keepers; they cover the shortfall from Project Catch-The-Asshole-No-Matter-What-Research-Says nicely."

Oh, yeah. Let's talk about that for a second. "You should have told me." His own suit was familiar, and his hiking boots too. Everything he needed was in his pockets. He could stroll out of here and vanish for real, this time.

"And ruin your heroic moment? You work better when you think it's your idea." Phil bared his teeth, an approximation of a grin. "They're bumping you up a couple pay grades. For excellent service in deep operations. No back pay, though."

As if it mattered. Money was the easiest thing in the world for a Marked.

Marlock kept his head down, staring at the Skinner's face. He looked like a blow-dried turd, really, but that could have been because he knew what the man did. "I didn't really catch the fucker."

Phil snorted. "I'm not going to tell them that. We waited for him to make a mistake, and he did."

"Blind fucking luck." A potential on a long winding road. Sometimes Erik had *known* things, though. *I see them in the lightning, Press.* Was that what he'd been doing out there?

Who knew? Marlock could go back and tell Catalina the motherfucker that did for Erik was dead. He wouldn't have to say *how*. Let her draw her own fucking conclusions.

His handler shifted his weight again. Maybe it was stress that had shrunk his potbelly. "Well, it ended up with a Mark the research boys are creaming their shorts over and a nice chunk of change, so who cares? I still don't hear you thanking me."

His hands itched. Oh, he could thank the fucker but good, with just a few moments of attention. "Thanks for putting me down a hole like a fucking ferret, Phil."

"Dachshund, actually. They used to hunt rats. Your cute little wet nose."

"Rowland. Big philanthropist. I've read articles on him. Jesus." Marlock shook his head. His hair was still too long. No time for a trim. "He had other sites, didn't he." *He had to have.*

"Oh, yeah. Forensics is going to be pulling triple shifts. Get this, he had a penthouse in Manhattan, and a whole floor underneath it full of display cases. With Marks in them."

"Marks?"

"Still on the skin."

"That's…" He was about to say, *that's impossible*, but very little was impossible, when you had a Mark. There was just what you were *willing* to do, and what you had the will to accomplish.

"Forensics is saying there's footage of him peeling the skin off. While the victim was still breathing."

"Jesus Christ." Marlock went cold all over. To think of that, to think of your Mark, your *self*, being torn away while you were still conscious and able to feel... "Taking trophies?" It couldn't be just that. There was a method to the madness, and he bet Phil was doling out the information in small packets to make it manageable.

"Well, he had a Mark too. It's on some of the discs—he kept a Greatest Hits compilation, the bastard. He put them on."

"Put...them..." Marlock's skin turned cold all over, and his own Mark twinged a little. *That's why. He used them.*

"Put them on over his own. All the ones in the cases are decaying now. They're trying to get them all catalogued before they turn to goo."

"Jesus *Christ*." A ball of nausea settled high up under his breastbone. "That's why his methods kept changing." Now that the agency knew it was possible, they might start trying the same thing.

It was high time for Marlock to retire. Maybe to a tropical island somewhere. Lay on the beach and try to forget about this.

"Yeah." Phil took the file back, but kept his left hand tucked in his right armpit. "You really like her, don't you."

Fuck off. He decided to play it dumb. "Who?"

"You haven't looked at her once, dumbass. It's a dead giveaway."

So Marlock made himself look through the one-way mirror.

Sunlight streamed through a bulletproof window, and there was an antique rolltop desk in the room, as well as a high-end flatscreen that would serve any channel you wanted, televangelism to porn, sports to Lifetime. The carpeting was soft and thick, the dresser and wardrobe were cherrywood and worth a pretty penny. There wasn't a security camera in the attached bathroom, but there were nice, expensive hotel soaps and shampoos, a decent toothbrush, an assortment of dentifrices.

Jude Altfall sat cross-legged on a luxurious four-poster bed. She hadn't turned the television on, and she wore only a tank top and blue cotton panties. Bright bags and boxes full of new clothes in her sizes were stacked near the foot of the bed, but she made no move toward them. Her hair was a dark, tangled mass, and the bruise on her face was visibly shrinking as she breathed.

She just sat there, staring, and it did something funny to Marlock's chest. Her expression was slack, unconcerned. She looked like a blank-faced, breathing doll.

"She asked about you," Phil said. "*Mister* Marlock. Seemed pretty concerned."

They would swab and poke and prod her, put her through a battery of psych and other tests to find out what her Mark was capable of. In the back of Rowland's file was a high-quality still taken from the air, showing the crater where the Skinner's lakeside playhouse once stood, rapidly filling with foaming water.

Preston cleared his throat. "What about the sister?"

"Asked about you too. Guess you made an impression." Phil sounded like he was grinning, the fucker. "She's clearing security, should be along any moment."

Marlock studied Jude's profile. Could she feel it? His Mark was awake, sensing that bright, warm clarity. He was even picking her up through the *wall*, for God's sake. Did she know it was him? Did she wonder where he'd gone? "What did you tell her?"

"That you were still alive."

"That's it?" He knew very well that wasn't it. He could tell what was coming up, and the only thing more miserable than the knowledge was the squirming sense that he was luckier than he had any fucking right to be.

She was still alive. Lucky, lucky, lucky.

Aggrieved, Phil shifted his weight again. He stared through the glass like he was at the zoo. "What the fuck else did you want me to say?"

"Go ahead."

"What?" His eyebrows up, now. The picture of innocence.

"Make me the fucking offer." Press let himself look through the glass again. She just *sat* there. It wasn't right. He didn't even want to begin thinking about all the goddamn trauma she was going to have to sort through. At least they had trained therapists here.

"You're optimistic." Maybe he'd been expecting Press to make trouble.

"Why the fuck else would you brief me *here*, Phil?" This tiny room was filling up with the smell of them, two males with bad diets and high stress. Or maybe Marlock was just projecting. Whatever way you sliced it, they were both fucking voyeurs.

Phil sighed. He freed his left hand, let it drop. "She'll need training."

For the love of God, you can't do this to her. "You're going to agent her?"

"She's a resource now, Press. Property of the US Government."

You bastards. "Just like me."

"Yeah, well, let's hope not. Besides, they want to know what that Mark of hers can do, and you've had contact with her. So, really, the question is, are you going to take another powder, or are you going to play big brother with this new toy the agency's all excited about? I told them it was a stretch for you to be anything other than a cantankerous old bastard, but they want to know. You take off again, I can't cover it."

Two years. Marlock pretended to think it over. He was going to need a good stiff drink soon, he could just tell. Maybe he'd even barricade his own door, sit in the dark, and really think about how much he'd fucked everything up. How he'd *still* come out with something he wanted.

The world wasn't built for nice guys. It was built for real dickheads, and you had to be one to get anywhere. "You officious little prick." There was no heat to it. Really, Phil deserved a fucking medal. It was a shame he was such an oil-oozing little worm.

"Your vocabulary's getting better."

"Fine. You play nice with her, and I'll be a good little sheep in the fold."

"Just wear the wool costume, Press. We need the wolf in it."

Jude finally moved. Raised her head slightly, looking at the door. She must have heard footsteps, or something else, and a dull, pained expression floated over her pretty face. The bruise on her cheek was only a yellowgreen shadow.

The door slid aside, and Jude's sweet mouth opened slightly. Some life came back into her big dark eyes.

Marlock's chest hurt. Like a spike through it, cracking the ribs apart.

A blonde blur ran into the room, colliding with the bed. Jude rocked forward, settling on her knees, and flung her arms around her sister. Aggie looked a little wan, and her blue eyes had deep circles under them, but she clasped Jude close and began to stroke her tangled hair.

Marlock looked away. "Come on. Let's give them some space."

"You don't want to watch the reunion?"

One day, motherfucker, I am going to strangle you with your own tie. "No. I need full debrief and check-outs at the range. There's probably a fuckton of paperwork, isn't there."

"Another reason you should be grateful to me. If you're a good boy, you can have dinner with them."

Marlock's pierced and aching heart, for some reason, sank like a stone. *Great.*

Chapter Fifty-Six

PARTNER

TALBOT WAS ALREADY out the door, but Louie Vantarello had to wait for his computer to shut down. While he did, he turned the Sturmen case over in his head, one more time. It was signed, sealed, and delivered, closed like a nun's legs, and it bothered him. He scratched at the side of his potbelly, a meditative movement, as he watched the screen go dark. The fuckers in Vice had nicer equipment. Probably because of all the confiscations.

Homicide was warming up for the early-night glut. Spring fever, everyone getting antsy, and a full moon riding high and cheese-pale over the city. He was glad to be going home.

His phone rang. Louie let out a *sotto voce* curse and smoothed his balding head before picking it up. Rick called it a compulsion—*you'd even pick up in a phone booth if it was ringing, you bastard.*

Rick was good folk. Fighting the good fight. Every time Louie woke up on his couch in the dead of night, the bottles clinking on the floor and his service weapon looking like a better way out than staying to put up with this shit, it was Rick's mournful, golden retriever face that stopped him. The man would have to have a whole new partner, and his wife didn't need the grief. Louie might be a slob, but he was a generous one, or so he liked to tell himself.

The desk phone rang again, insistent, demanding. Louie hitched a sigh, winced internally, and hooked up the receiver. "Homicide, Vantarello speaking."

His body knew before the rest of him, before the man on the other side said a word. A click, and a funny underwater gargling—calls from *there* were always run through a filter or two. They believed in privacy. "Louis." The following sound might have been a pleased chuckle or a gasp of pain. "*In hoc.*"

"*Signo vinces*," Louie responded, automatically, a pale, thin murmur. Sweat sprang out on his lower back, under his arms, and in the creases of his neck. "Yes, Father?"

"You're a good son."

"Thank you." *Oh shit oh shit. I didn't do anything. Maybe it's a case. I swear I didn't do anything.*

"You are needed."

Oh, fuck me. No. No. He wished, suddenly, frantically, that he'd joined the Freemasons instead. It would have been better, even if those arthritic fuckers couldn't find their peens with both hands and a map. Or the Elks, they were good fellas and knew how to drink. "How may I serve?" His voice had gone up an octave, as if he was a teenager again, and scared shitless.

Father was nobody you wanted to mess with.

"Put your ring back on. And keep watch."

Louie's left hand turned into a fist. How did he know? He'd stopped wearing the gold band with the crest years ago. It was technically against the rules, but—

"Yes, sir," he mumbled. "Will do."

"Thank you. We will call again soon."

"Looking forward to it," Louie lied.

"The Oracle will return," Father whispered.

"Yes." Louie licked his dry lips. His heart pounded. "Oracle. Yes. Will return." He waited for the click of disconnection before hanging up, the handset slipping greasily against his sweating fingers.

The ring. The crest was a lamp, and the motto snaked around it.

Oraculum auter convertentur. For a moment he was in the Priory again, firm handshakes all around after the ceremony, and the first intimation that this wasn't a club like the Fraternal Order of Police. No, these guys were serious, and they'd helped when the bottom dropped out of the market and the house was almost foreclosed.

Father's dark, burning eyes. *You've made the right choice, Louis.*

Louie got up, shoving his much-abused chair back into stacks of paperwork and the back of Callahan's desk. Thank God neither him nor Ramirez were in, or Rick. Rick would take one look at Louie and begin digging, and what could he say?

The detective grabbed his coat and hurried for the door. He knew, miserably, that he would drink himself to sleep again tonight, and wake up in the dark, thinking about crazy things.

Chapter Fifty-Seven

NOT OKAY

THE ROOM WAS close, and stale, and it smelled of new clothes and old dust. She couldn't even open the window, and she knew the big mirror over the dresser was a spy-hole. There wasn't any padding, or any bars, but it was a prison all the same.

"Shhh." Aggie whispered into her dirty, reeking hair. "Shh, Jujube, it's all right."

As if Jude was the one crying, and not Aggie. Really, there were no tears left. The mark on Jude's hip was warm, and the bruise on her face was healing too rapidly to be real.

"Aggie," she whispered back, her throat dry and raw. "*Aggie*. I saw them...I saw you..."

"It's okay. It was—oh, goddammit, Jude, cut it out, what happened to *you*?"

I don't want to talk about it. "Bad," was all she could say. "It was bad."

A great gulf had opened inside her, where the white light came through. There was nobody to talk to, nobody who could possibly understand what it was like. She had nothing left, not even her body, because she knew they were eager to start testing. Experimenting. Seeing what she could do. Simon and Essie were gone, Dave was dead, Aggie…

Her arms crept around her sister, and she hugged as hard as she could.

"Okay." Aggie, true to form, was about to shift into fussbudget mode. "You need a shower, and they…yeah, they bought clothes for me too. They say we can go home in a little while, as long as you come back for tests. They want to make sure there's no…oh, for fucksake, these guys are *assholes*, but at least they're polite, right?"

For now. Jude nodded. "I thought you were dead." Five small words, impossible for them to carry the full weight of terror and shame. She hadn't *quite* believed the little man with the funny deep voice telling her Aggie and Marlock were both fine.

"I'm fine. I have a sort of…well, there's a scar where the bullet went in."

"Nothing else?" *You have a bullet wound? A scar? How long was I in there?*

"Nope." Aggie shook her head. Her arms tightened some more. "Nothing else. I'm right as rain, Jujube. What about you?"

Jude's body began to relax. A great wave of shudders went through her, and Aggie held on. She sagged, and ended up full-length on the bed, her sister hugging her as if it was childhood all over again, one of them sneaking into the other's room to be comforted by nearness. "I'm not okay," Jude whispered. "I am not okay."

Aggie swallowed, hard. "You will be."

Nothing will make this okay. "Aggie?"

"Yeah?"

"Can you...can you sing to me?" *Like when we were little?*

"Sure." Something in Aggie's throat. It had to be strange for her, to be the strong one. Or maybe she always had been, and Jude hadn't noticed.

Aggie patted Jude's head, smoothing her hair, and began to hum the old familiar tune.

Jude couldn't cry. She just shook, and shook, and the Mark on her hip was a soft warmth she hated, hated, *hated*.

So let them do their tests. See if they can reverse it.

If they couldn't, she was going to have to take matters into her own hands. The thought spun away, and the shaking intensified.

And *still*, Jude Altfall couldn't cry.

Chapter Fifty-Eight

THE ORACLE

He retrieved the briefcase from the train station's lockers and hurried for the safehouse. It had taken him much longer than he liked, because he could not quite shake the feeling of, well…

Being watched.

It could have been nerves, because of the strain. Being in the same room with Rowland and knowing what the man was capable of would put *anyone* off their feed, really. Those bright blue eyes, and the way his skin would ripple over his cheeks every once in a while when he got excited. And the expensive cologne, but the line of grime under his thumbnails.

None of the fingernails, no. Just the thumbs. The suits were expensive, but they clothed a goddamn monster, and each time the call light showed up, the man called Mr. Bell had thought, *well, that's it, I'm dead.*

Knowing the other male secretaries had all disappeared hadn't helped. Oh, there was a cover story in each case, a suicide here, someone moving to Bolivia there, a car accident over the hill. He'd known going in that he would be risking a lot.

His superiors were going to be annoyed that he hadn't fully achieved the mission, but he had other news for them that might lessen the sting.

He approached the safehouse with caution, circling a few times before choosing his approach. The derelict building on Martell Street looked like a hazard from the outside, and it certainly was. Still, there was a blank metal door on its highest floor, and a keypad that accepted his code, grudgingly but efficiently.

Once inside, he looked over the single cot, the dust-obscured window choking off the sunlight of a beautiful early-summer day, and the sink. Nothing else, but he'd had worse, and it was a distinct and welcome change from the stifling luxuriousness of Denny Rowland's penthouses and nouveau riche hideaways.

There was a flimsy table bolted to the floor near the window. He opened the briefcase, and the handset inside, nestled next to a stack of cash and two fresh passports, was a *distinct* relief.

A few moments of fiddling with it got a live line, and he tapped in his code.

It beeped a few times, went dead. His back crawled, but when he glanced back, the room was still the same.

It was just nerves, of course. All he had to do now was wait, and get his message out clearly.

"Gary." A dry, leathery voice. "You're early."

"Sir. Objective seventy-five percent complete—"

"We've seen the newspapers. The Board is most displeased."

"There was a complication, sir." It was like talking to Rowland, for God's sake. Psychopaths with power everywhere, and he had to go and get involved with them. "The Oracle has returned. The Oracle is alive."

Ten long ticks of silence passed. The sweat was all over him, greasy and rancid, and he could still smell the last body he'd dragged into Rowland's underground playroom. If Rowland had killed *him*, the brothers would just insert another one in his place until they got everything they wanted.

It was the way of the world, as one of his instructors had been in the habit of dryly remarking.

"You are sure?" No hint of surprise in the leathery voice. Just checking off boxes. But that pause—it had to be a surprise. *Had* to be. He'd be commended for bringing the news, right? He damn well *should* be.

"I saw it, sir." *It was beautiful.* But that was something he couldn't say, even if it was true.

Another few moments of silence. His back kept crawling. He turned again, saw nothing but the dust, the cot, the sink, the door slightly ajar—

"Good work, Gary," the leathery voice said. "Goodbye."

The bullet entered Mr-No-Longer-Bell's skull, mushroomed, and blew out half his face, painting the window with a bright crimson stain and gray-splatter brainmatter. Shards of skull plinked against the glass, which shivered on the edge of breaking.

The man holding the gun picked up the handset, raised it to his ear, and listened carefully to his next set of directions. "Yes sir," he said, a colorless mumble, and the dim light played over a scarred, twitching cheek and heavy beetle brows.

When the leather-voiced man was done speaking, the scarred man replaced the handset in the briefcase and took the cash and the fresh passports.

Waste not, want not, the same instructor had always said.

He paused, looking down at the vacant meat that had once held one of the brotherhood. "*Requiescat in pace*," he whispered, and made an ancient sign over the fallen warrior. "The Oracle will return."

With the formalities observed, the scarred man left the room and its meat to the rats, and headed for his next assignment.

TO BE CONTINUED...

About the Author

LILI LIVES IN VANCOUVER, WASHINGTON, with two dogs, two cats, two children, and a metric ton of books holding her house together. However, referring to her as "Noah" will likely get you a lecture. You can visit her online at www.lilithsaintcrow.com.

Also By
Lilith Saintcrow

The Dante Valentine Series

The Jill Kismet Series

The Bannon and Clare Series

The Strange Angels Series

Tales of Beauty and Madness

Romances of Arquitaine

Selene: A Saint City Novel

SquirrelTerror

The Gallow & Ragged Trilogy

Rose & Thunder

...and many more.

CPSIA information can be obtained
at www.ICGtesting.com
Printed in the USA
LVOW12s2348211016
509811LV00001B/33/P

9 780989 975360